Also by Adam Gaffen

Godsfall
The Book of One
The Book of Two
The Book of Three
Godsfall: Books 1-3
A Roman Holiday

Tales from the Cassidyverse
Into the Black
The Heart of Space
Midnight Relics

The Artemis War
The Road to the Stars
The Measure of Humanity
A Quiet Revolution
Triumph's Ashes

The Cassidy Chronicles
Run Like Hell
The Cassidy Chronicles
Terran Federation Technical Manual
Quantum Quirks: A Science Fiction Childhood
Embers of Eternity

The Missions of the TFS Pike
The Ghosts of Tantor
Tracking Tantor

Standalone
The Kildaran
Roots of Love
Refuge
The Artemis Wars Omnibus
The Vault & The Vixen

Watch for more at www.cassidychronicles.com.

Embers of Eternity: A Cassidy Chronicles Novel
Published by Ad Astra
Copyright © 2024 by Adam Gaffen
Cover Art © Ad Astra

All rights reserved. Except as permitted under the U.S. Copyright Act of 1976, no part of this publication may be reproduced, distributed, or transmitted in any form or by any means, or stored in a database or retrieval system, without the prior written permission of the author.

All Rights Reserved.

The characters and events portrayed in this book are fictitious. Any similarity to persons, living or dead, is purely coincidental and not intended by the author.

For more about the author, future works, and events, please visit:
https://www.cassidychronicles.com

Trigger and Content Warnings

Graphic Violence: Multiple scenes involve intense combat, injuries, and descriptions of blood and physical harm.

Death and Mortality: Character deaths, including significant, emotional scenes involving near-death experiences and the use of celestial power to attempt healing.

Supernatural and Demonic Themes: Includes interactions with demons, angels, and other supernatural beings, as well as descriptions of hellish realms, demonic characters, and infernal hierarchies.

Physical Assault and Injury: Detailed descriptions of characters suffering wounds, including near-fatal injuries, impalement, and depictions of physical trauma.

Mild Torture and Pain Infliction: Some scenes describe supernatural forms of torture or punishment (e.g., characters receiving burns or cold-induced wounds from celestial beings).

Emotional Manipulation: Characters experience and use psychological tactics and manipulation, particularly during interrogations and intense confrontations.

Existential and Spiritual Themes: Themes of immortality, celestial/demonic justice, and afterlife-related topics may be unsettling for readers sensitive to religious or existential subject matter.

Power Dynamics and Authority: Strong themes of domination, power struggle, and authority within a supernatural hierarchy, which could be sensitive for those triggered by authoritarian or controlling dynamics.

Blood and Gore: Frequent, graphic descriptions of bleeding wounds, the aftermath of violent encounters, and other gore-related elements.

Romantic and Familial Bonding in High-Stress Scenarios: Depictions of intimate relationships tested under extreme, life-threatening situations, which could affect readers sensitive to relationship trauma.

Weapons and Combat: Numerous scenes depicting the use of weapons (guns, swords, etc.) in combat situations, with some passages including detailed descriptions of the injuries inflicted.

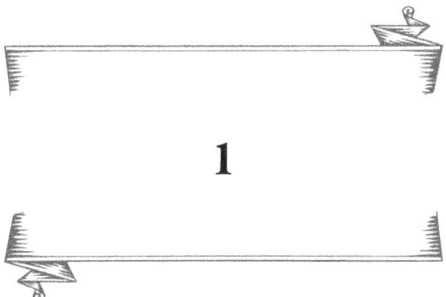

1

"I hate this."

"Shut up and pack."

Faith didn't like the snarl in my voice, but she didn't argue. Truth be told, the snarl wasn't directed at her, but at the situation around us, and we'd been together long enough that she understood. I apologized anyway.

"Sorry, love," I said, brushing my hand against hers so our *taaqats* mingled, balancing.

"For once, it's not even our war," Faith added, though I could tell she was somewhat mollified by my apology.

It was true. We'd survived the Schism with our apartment in New York intact. The fighting that sundered the United States into squabbling nations had never touched the City.

Was that the influence of a pair of semi-retired Immortals? Maybe. Neither of us was above wielding our powers to prevent the deaths of the humans around us, and if it had the side benefit of preserving our comfort? Two birds, one stone, right?

But this was different.

The grumblings had been building for months, if not years. The New England Collective was collapsing on itself, unable to bear the pressures of creating a humanist utopia while maintaining ties to traditional capitalism. With the withdrawal of General Electric, the largest single employer in the nation, to more business-friendly climes? The grumblings grew to a roar.

Here in the Empire of New York, we looked on with concern, but it wasn't our problem. The banks and other financial institutions that provided the lifeblood of our little nation were cheering for reform—but quietly. The three dozen that Faith or I sat on the boards of, at least, had consistently urged restraint and tolerance, and given our ownership stakes, we were listened to.

Even now, the Empire was officially at peace.

That didn't change the fighting going on in the streets around us as elements from our southern neighbor, the United States, tried to pass through to support the rebellious factions to the north. The Collective, though it might be borderline incompetent as a practical nation-state, didn't lack in military resolve. The Schism was barely a generation past, and many of the teenagers and twentysomethings who successfully snapped the grip of the United States were running the military. They knew if they could stop the rebels from gaining reinforcements from the south, they could hold their jobs.

And their heads.

I looked around the penthouse. It was painfully bare. Well, no, not bare. Not empty. Most of the furniture was still here, and appliances, but everything that made a space a home? Gone. Ninety-two years of accumulation, plus the various trinkets and gotta-have-its from the previous ten centuries, packed up and shipped away.

I felt a hand on my shoulder, followed by a gentle voice.

"It's only things, love."

I rested my hand on hers. "Avy, you have a literal palace filled with items from the dawn of humanity, and you're lecturing me about things?"

Our other lover laughed and came around to face me. "When you put it that way, I suppose not."

A nagging question bubbled up. "Did you take care of the talisman?"

Avareth was instantly serious. "I did. It's—"

I shook my head. "Don't tell us, don't think it, nothing! What I don't know, I can't tell, and I want that dammed thing forgotten for the rest of time."

Surprised by my vehemence, Avy acquiesced and unearthed a smile. "That reminds me. I found room for your treasures."

"I should hope so!" Faith mixed humor and indignation as she entered the room, suitcase in hand, messenger bag over one shoulder. "Hi, Avareth." She bent enough to kiss Avy, then took my hand. "Ready?"

"Honestly? No."

Faith smiled at my reaction. "I've warded the building as best I can."

"And I have two of Czaibrir's most trusted warriors on guard. Your building, and the people who refused to move out, will be as safe as they can make it." Avareth frowned, her lilac eyes darkening. "Why aren't you just jumping out of here? Why go through all this human role-play?"

"Because our friends might be freaked out if we pop out of existence in one place and appear in another," I said, hefting another bag. "Sierra and Alex moved to the West Coast a decade ago, and Chelsea's, well, I don't know where she is. Somewhere on the road, but which road is a good question. Dakota and McKenna, though. They refused to leave as long as we were here, and I'm not going to see them die. Not on my watch."

A look of subtle sadness stole over Avy's face. "They're mortal, Kal."

"Yeah, I know, and they're not young, either, but that doesn't mean I won't move Heaven and Hell to give them all the minutes they deserve."

Faith pressed her shoulder to mine. She'd known of Dakota for as long as I had, going on forty years, and had become good friends as well. Avy, since she spent most of her time running Hell as Lilith's

Chief of Staff, hadn't spent as much time Earthside and didn't quite get our connection. Oh, she *felt* it, through the bond we all shared from a millennium of togetherness, but she'd never *gotten* it.

She also knew better than to question it.

"The truck you ordered is downstairs. I'll take care of the Jag personally."

I rolled my eyes at her. My silver 1952 Jaguar convertible was one of my favorite possessions. I'd owned it since it came off the boat from the UK and had babied it. I wouldn't say losing it would be like losing a piece of myself, but it was a close thing. "It's only taken you a century to get your hands on it. Do you even know how to drive?"

Our lilac-haired love laughed. "How hard can it be? Humans do it every day."

Faith's eyes widened in horror. "Avareth ca'Thalinn! You wouldn't!"

"Faith—are you still going by Burroughs?" Faith nodded. Avy was born a demon, and so had a full demonic name. Faith and I, being the last Thirteens, had only our first names. Living in the human realm most of the time required us to have surnames to blend in, so Faith picked up her current one in the 20s. 1920s, that is. Mine was newer, dating only to the 40s.

"Faith Burroughs, *of course* I would." She cupped Faith's face and kissed her. I knew those kisses, slow and lingering while over far too soon. When she separated, she looked at me. "Don't worry. I won't scratch your baby. I've known how to drive for decades. Who do you think taught Karl Benz? But I couldn't resist teasing you just a little."

With the important things settled, I took a final look around. "I love this view," I whispered.

"Avy will take care of it. It will be here when we return." Faith rested her head against my shoulder, and I pulled strength from her touch.

"I know." I straightened, summoning my resolve. "Come on. We've got to get to Brooklyn."

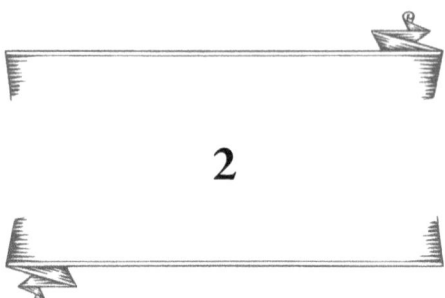

2

Driving a heavily modified, bright red Jeep Conqueror through the streets of Manhattan was surreal. Despite the constant low-level guerrilla fighting between factions, on the surface everything seemed to be normal. It was one of the traits which attracted us to New York over a century earlier, when we first took residence in the suburbs.

New Yorkers had a sense of certainty about them which was refreshing, compared to other humans. They were just as prone to their faults and foibles as any of the other ten billion people on the planet, but they didn't display it. At any moment, they knew what they were doing, where they were going, and by damn they weren't going to let anyone interfere. Traffic? Rats? Crime? War? Nothing fazed a New Yorker.

The Conqueror was a giant, compared to my beloved Jag, and that was before the modifications I'd had done. We'd had it modified as the war news heated up. Little things, like mounting an additional set of the most advanced batteries. A second fuel tank for the engine which did nothing but recharge the batteries. Discreet carbon fiber armor over every vulnerable spot, especially the undercarriage. Military-grade run-flat tires. Bulletproof glass, which was transparent aluminum rated up to twenty thousand joules, enough to stop a fifty caliber.

Then there was the power. Oh, yes, the power. She mounted six wheels on three axles, one in front and two in back, all with their own 276kW electric motor. It was a New Yorker's kind of car. Once it got moving, nothing was stopping it. Despite the abundance of power, all this extra weight meant the handling was nothing like my Jag, and I growled every time I had to accelerate or stop.

"Sweetheart, you're going to have a stroke if you don't calm down."

"I'm immortal," I grunted as I wrestled the beast around a corner, mashing my foot against the accelerator to beat a taxi, earning me a blat from the cabbie's horn and a single-digit salute as he returned the favor and sped past. "I can't have a stroke."

"Then you'll give a human a stroke. Or a heart attack."

"Then they should've stayed off the road," I growled.

"Kalili. Slow down."

That was cheap. She was using The Voice, the one she only pulled out when I was being particularly stupid or obstinate. But it had its desired effect, and I relaxed enough to take a deep breath. The traffic around me caught up as I eased off.

"Sorry, love." I took another breath. "I've just got a feeling that this could all go south, fast. Remember Dunkirk?"

She winced. Dunkirk was an absolute clusterfuck, and we'd been stuck in the middle of it, playing the role of volunteer nurses while trying to miracle away as many threats to the humans around us as possible. We didn't often involve ourselves directly in the affairs of humans, not on a macro scale, but that was an exception. Without us, and the other Immortals we recruited, it would have been infinitely worse.

"You think it's going to get that bad here?"

I shrugged without allowing the car to waver from our course. "I don't know. We've never figured out how to see the future, though those damn scrolls say we can."

"It would be useful," she agreed. "But no, we haven't. Then why?"

"A feeling. That's as much as I can say. Maybe you can track it down?" I invited her into my mind.

After nearly 1100 years bonded, we were as comfortable in the other's mind as our own. What we'd learned, fairly early into our bonding, was it was less disruptive to our selves to stay on the fringes of the other's consciousness. We'd experimented, a little overzealously, at how merged we could be. It turned out, it was quite a lot, and withdrawing from that conscious union was agonizing. It was vastly different from the merger we shared when we took on our full inheritance as Thirteens and became a god.

I felt Faith's presence now, poking around, feeling for the vague unsettledness I'd described. After a moment, she withdrew to her usual place.

"I see what you mean," she said. "Drive faster."

I gleefully mashed my foot to the floor.

The Brooklyn Bridge was the only good choice to get over the river. The Manhattan Bridge, which I would have preferred, had been dropped two weeks earlier by—well, nobody knew. Neither the US nor the Collective took responsibility, and the Empire was claiming catastrophic material failure. That didn't explain the source of the explosions surviving witnesses reported, but it was accurate enough.

The Tunnel? I did not trust the Tunnel.

We made our way across and down into the borough. Much like Manhattan, Brooklynites were going about their business, but they were less impacted by the war tensions than the island. The major arteries that connected the US to the Collective went through Manhattan, and points north. Yes, there were bypass routes that went through Brooklyn and Queens, but they were bypasses, not direct. Should the fighting ever heat up to the point they were vital, the war would be far too hot for our liking.

I aimed to be long gone well before then.

I pulled up in front of Dakota's bar, the Vault & Vixen. She had bought the joint shortly after one of our little adventures went sideways in a spectacular manner. When McKenna returned to town a few months later, they'd picked up where they left off. Three-plus decades later, they were still there. Dakota planned the occasional job, and McKenna's safecracking was as in demand as ever, but the bar was their home; to be precise, the apartment that took up the entire floor above the bar. It was a testament to their relationship, and an oasis in the desert of Brooklyn, but it wasn't a place for them to stay.

Not now.

It had taken many arguments before I convinced McKenna they needed to cut and run. Once I'd done that, we'd tag-teamed Dakota until she gave in, gracelessly.

I tapped the horn to let them know we'd arrived.

McKenna came out first with a single duffel. Her short blonde hair was cut the same as ever, but if I looked closely I could see the white intermingled with the blonde strands. Her body was still toned, and if she wasn't quite as nimble as she'd been, time had been kind to her. She jerked open the back and tossed the bag on our cases.

"Hey. Dakota's coming, she's just locking up." McKenna returned to the door and went inside.

"Faith?"

"On it."

Neither of us were magik users, not the way Lilith was, or a human could be. That didn't mean we hadn't picked up some tricks along the way. Faith was more skilled than I, so she climbed out of the car to do her thing.

We'd decided on two-fold protection for their place. First was a simple warding spell, to turn back the worst depredations of war. The second, more complex spell would render the building unnoticeable to anyone who wasn't supposed to find it. It was up to us to determine who that included, and we'd narrowed it down to the four of us.

Yes, we. Dakota and McKenna didn't know we were Immortals, but several years earlier we'd admitted we were more than we appeared. After all, we could hardly claim to be the twenty-somethings we'd been presenting as, not with the length of our friendships. We'd settled on calling ourselves wiccan, being a good catch-all term for beliefs most people didn't want to examine too closely, and often joked about making deals for eternal youth.

Dakota had given me a look that suggested our admission had created more questions than it answered. I'd returned her gaze with as much bland innocence as I could manage, which is to say not much. After a muttered, "I wonder how much Mort got right," she'd dropped the issue and never mentioned it again. I suspected she'd done some digging, or perhaps had Sierra do it, but how she treated us didn't change. That was all I cared about.

Faith disappeared around the corner of the building, moving clockwise, something about walking the circle closed. I didn't know the details. I let my thoughts drift to the best routes out of the City before being yanked back by the sound of bickering.

"...don't care! She's never steered us wrong." A most unladylike snort was the reply before McKenna continued. "I trust her. So do you. And we agreed, so suck it up."

A plaintive yowl interrupted the nascent argument. I turned in time to see Dakota lifting a cat carrier to her eyes, then saying, "See? Bandit disagrees, too."

McKenna opened the back, dropped in another duffel, then pivoted. "Bandit would disagree if we gave her sushi-grade tuna for dinner every night."

Dakota's lips quirked in a grin before she forced them back to present the stern look she wanted. I decided it was time to intervene.

"Hey, Dakota." I climbed from my seat and around the car to where she stood. "Hi Bandit." I waggled a finger through the bars. "Ow!" I stuck my clawed finger in my mouth. Dakota laughed.

"Serves you right, dragging us from our home for a big fat nothingburger. Hi, Kal." She set the cat down and gave me a quick hug.

Being in a near-constant state of semi-retirement from crime had done wonders for Dakota, too. Running a bar wasn't an easy job in any century; we'd done it ourselves, running the Green Dragon Tavern back during the 1700s. We'd done it of necessity. Avy told us it was a focal point of dissent, and wanted to encourage the Sons of Liberty. It was enough to convince us to steer clear ever since. Revolutionaries could drink, but they were crap at paying bar tabs. No thank you.

Dakota started bartending from necessity that had long morphed into satisfaction and contentment. She was part of the fabric of her community, loved by her neighbors and companions, and it suited her well. She wasn't as athletic as her wife, and her long brown hair, tucked back into her usual ponytail, was liberally streaked with white. But the fire I'd always known her to possess was still bright in her eyes, and her voice as firm as ever.

"Hi, Dakota," I said, returning the hug. I held her at arm's length. "If you're right, and this is a waste of time? Not only will I cook you a gourmet meal, I'll personally cover all your lost business."

She burst out laughing, the reaction I'd aimed for. "You? Cook?"

"Well, by cook, I mean order in the best chef I can hire and have them do it," I admitted. Seven thousand-plus years hadn't granted me any supernatural abilities to prepare food.

"That, I believe. You're on." The cat carrier was positioned on the floor between the two rear seats. "We're almost set."

I quirked an eyebrow. "Oh?" But she was already heading back into the building.

"Kal, level with me." McKenna's tone was more serious than usual, so I bit back my usual jibe.

"Of course."

"This isn't a waste of time, right? You wouldn't make us leave our home if we weren't in danger?"

I might lie to just about anyone—six thousand years believing I was a demon would do that to a person—but not Faith, not Avareth, and not my friends.

"No. Shit's about to get real, McKenna, and anyone who doesn't get while the getting is good is a fool." I fixed her with my most convincing look. "I'm no fool, and neither are you or Dakota."

She nodded. "Good enough for me."

We waited a moment, the usual street sounds of Brooklyn accentuated by the protests of Bandit, until Dakota re-emerged. She set down a box, locked the door, punched in a security code, then hefted the box again and made for the car. I could hear muffled clanks.

"Liquor? Really, Dakota?"

"Really, Kal. Full bottles of Zacapa XO, Beluga Gold Line, Booker's 60th Anniversary, Clase Azul Reposado, as well as two Macallan Sherry Oaks and three of McKenna's Johnny Blue. And for you wine snobs, I brought the Penfolds Grange and the Domaine de la Romanee-Conti Montrachet Grand Cru. Now, I can put them back...?" She stopped about five feet from the car and waited. I could see now it was a wooden crate, not a box, which made sense considering there was probably fifty thousand dollars' worth of liquor in it.

"No way!" McKenna and I reacted as one. "We have more room," I suggested, helpfully, and Dakota laughed.

"Nothing like this, Kal." McKenna opened the back for her wife, moving the duffels to make space on the floor, and Dakota carefully set the crate in place. The duffels went on top, concealing it from view.

"We're ready. Is Faith...?"

"I'm here," Faith said, coming around the last corner. "Give me a moment."

Dakota and McKenna climbed in the back, the volume of protests increasing from Bandit.

"You can let her out once we're all in," I said. "If she won't piss on my foot in irritation."

"No promises," laughed McKenna.

I settled in and closed my door, watching Faith. She made a gesture I recognized but couldn't identify, nodded once in satisfaction, then headed for the car.

As she opened the door, her thought came to me. *All set, love. Nobody less than an archdemon's getting in there.* Aloud, she said, "I've done what I can. Aww, Bandit sounds upset."

"She doesn't like her crate. She associates it with the v-e-t," McKenna said.

"Everyone ready?" My anxiety about being in the city had jumped a dozen notches, and I didn't know why.

Faith picked up on it and answered for everyone. "Let's go."

I pulled out into the street, heading back to Manhattan, then south.

I just hoped we were ahead of whatever I felt was coming.

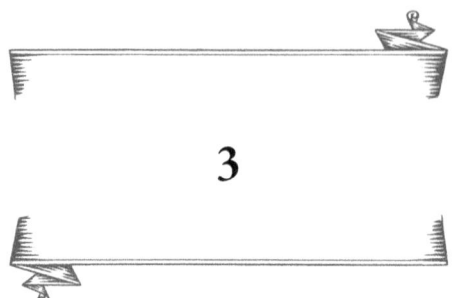

3

I headed right for Canal when I got off the bridge. Hitting a tunnel was a risk, but the Holland Tunnel was the shortest route off the island. Going uptown to the George Washington would take at least an hour, and I didn't think the marginal safety a bridge gave was worth the extra time. Too many things could go wrong on the streets of Manhattan.

Why would I take the Holland and not the Brooklyn tunnel? Because the time for the bridge or tunnel was about the same, heading to Brooklyn. The same wasn't true heading out of Manhattan. I'd trade risk for time; if it all went to shit, Faith and I could miracle our way out of the worst trouble, but we couldn't bend time.

At least, we'd never figured out how, and Ariel didn't know.

Dakota broke my concentration as I was navigating the surface roads. "Kalili, where are we going?"

"Denver." I dropped the name casually, hoping nobody would argue.

I was disappointed.

"Denver? Seriously?"

"Yes, Dakota, Denver."

"Why the fuck are we going to Denver? I get it, there's a war brewing, you convinced me of that," she said, voice rising, "but I thought it was something local, the Collective having its head up its ass. Denver's way the hell and gone from Brooklyn!"

"Because there's an opportunity out there, and I need to check it out." I was being cryptic, and hated it, but until we were out of the war zone, the less they knew the better. "Shit!"

It seemed the war zone came to us. Ahead was a rolling blockade, with massive signs blinking the message that drew my curse.

"All Westbound Traffic—No Access To Holland Tunnel—United States Border Closed—No Entry"

"Dammit. Faith?"

She was already on her tablet, searching for alternatives.

"It's all over the news," she said. "Two hours ago. The United States officially shut down the border with the Empire to prevent infiltration from the Collective. We're not at war with them, diplomatic relations are still good, blah, blah, blah." She looked over at me. "We're not getting through the US."

I was refiguring the route. If the US border was closed, we had to head north, which I didn't want to do. The Canucks were having issues of their own. Still, it was the only choice left.

"Uptown it is." I took the next right, aiming for the FDR and muttering darkly about the fools who designed New York streets. "Hon, I'll need you to guide me around the traffic."

That drew hearty laughs from the back seat and an acerbic, "Get off the island," from Faith.

"Yeah, yeah. Fine. Whatever." I dodged past an old sedan with an out-of-country plate. "Damn tourist."

"We're on 14th?"

I looked at the sign at the cross street. "Yes. Just crossed 8th Ave." I leaned on the horn and swerved around another idiot who decided to double-park.

"Okay, get in the left lane, turn onto 6th Ave, we can run that up to 34th St. At least, we can now. If it changes, I'll let you know."

The less said about the next forty minutes, the better. Eventually, despite the vagaries of traffic, we were across the RFK and negotiating the snarl that was the I-278 and I-87 confluence.

"Tell me again how this is better than fighting off looters? At least then I'd be in my home," Dakota groused as we sat. Again.

All around us, military vehicles flashed lights and blared horns, bulling their way through the stalled traffic.

"I can't. Hold on." I edged as close to the side as I could. "Faith, how far up are we?"

"From what?"

"The surface road."

"Oh, Kal, that's not—"

I saw a gap in the fencing and headed for it, earning blats from horns and envious stares from drivers who didn't have as capable a vehicle. The Conqueror flattened the remaining fence, and we bumped down the incline. I yanked the wheel hard to the left, lining up with the street, and gunned it.

"Shit!" We were headed the wrong way into one-way traffic. I swerved onto the sidewalk, then cranked the wheel around, still barreling ahead, this time with the traffic. Any cop who saw me decided I was too insane to arrest, and soon we were far enough from the highway that I started to relax. A few more horns sounded, but we were down and moving.

"Where are we?"

"Hell," McKenna offered.

"Been there. It's nicer than this," Faith answered absently, tapping at the tablet. "I think we're on East 139th. Tell me the next cross street."

"Cypress," I said as the sign whizzed past, weaving through the traffic. "Learn to drive!" I shouted.

"Third cross, turn right. That's Willis, and it'll take us to 3rd Ave, then we can get 149th St. Do we want 87 or one of the Parkways?"

"How do you stay so calm?" marveled Dakota.

"I've flown with her," Faith said. "This is nothing."

I knew the incident she referred to but bit my tongue since it was a hundred years earlier. "Any difference in the traffic?"

"No, but the Parkways are prettier."

I let her guide me through the surface roads, out of the Bronx on the Saw Mill Parkway. She was right; she usually was. It was much prettier.

4

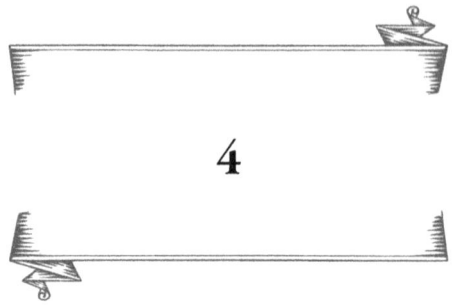

NOTICE
THE NEW YORK THRUWAY
IS A PRIVATELY HELD ROAD

ENTER AT YOUR OWN RISK

POLICE ASSISTANCE UNAVAILABLE

HAVE A NICE DAY!

"FRIENDLY," REMARKED Dakota.

"Typical," added McKenna.

"Are you sure about this?" asked Faith.

"Do you have a better idea? Canada's that way." I waved westish.

"Or we could keep heading north."

We'd stayed on the Saw Mill to 684, then onto 84 dangerously close to the border. How close? I thought I could hear artillery impacts. From there we'd headed west again, putting miles between us and the fighting, heading over the Hudson at Newburgh before getting onto 87, much farther north than I'd intended.

We'd seen several of these signs along the way, but it hadn't been bad yet. Then again, it wasn't this stretch of the Thruway which had the reputation.

"North brings us to Montreal, then we head southwest, and it's about an extra ten hours. If we head west on the Thruway, we cut out all of that. How good is your Quebecois?" I finished.

Quebec had broken away from the Canadian Confederacy in the Forties; I didn't remember the precise date. We had better things to worry about than the slow-motion acceptance of the truth north of the border. One of the first things the new government did was to make the use of any language other than Canadian French—Quebecois—illegal. How illegal? If you couldn't pass a literacy test at the border, you weren't allowed in.

Faith and I knew almost every language humans spoke, including Quebecois, but we refused to use it. We spoke French fluently, and slipped into it at times because of its beauty. But Quebecois?

No. Just no.

"I speak two languages: American and bad English," Dakota joked.

"Then north is out. Ontario is much more relaxed. Besides, have you ever seen the Falls?" McKenna and Dakota shared a look. "What?"

"We did a job there. When was it?"

"December of '32," McKenna said immediately. "The Seneca Casino."

I almost pivoted in my seat, remembering at the last instant I was driving. "That was *you*? And you didn't tell me?" That casino job netted someone eighteen million bucks. Now I knew who it was, and why... "That's when you redid the apartment!"

Dakota grinned, pleased. "I can't believe you didn't figure it out in twenty years. Yeah, we wanted you, but you were busy. At least, every time I messaged, that's what you said."

I tried to think back. What was I doing that would have kept me away from a caper? They were the highlights of my year, any year.

The assassination of King William, Faith reminded me.

Right. That mess.

"Yeah, okay. You got me, I was busy." I couldn't tell them what we were busy with, but that wasn't anything new. "Still, I'll bet you didn't visit the Falls, did you?"

Another look. "No," Dakota admitted. "We didn't have much time, you know?"

"Fine. Well, we'll spend a day there, on the Canadian side. Don't want anyone with long memories picking you up. What's the statute for grand larceny?"

"Five years." Dakota's answer was instantaneous. "For all of the potential charges, and since it was before the Empire was founded, we're clear. New York State doesn't exist any longer. But we weren't caught, obviously. We brought Sierra in on it."

We made our way along the road, heading west at Albany, while Dakota and McKenna entertained us with their stories. Traffic was light, and we made good time. In a few hours we were blasting through Buffalo, approaching Niagara. Faith had secured accommodations on the Canadian side, and I was ready for a break. Driving the Conqueror wasn't terrible, but it wasn't my Jag.

"Border crossing ahead," Faith said as I wrestled through the traffic. The change in plans had thrown off my timing, which meant we were in the city just in time for rush hour. Traffic wasn't unbearable, and most of it was heading out, not in, but there were still idiot humans on the road.

Watch out!

I swerved in time to miss the fool striding into the road in the middle of the block without a single screech of the tires.

"Thanks," I said to Faith. "I'm gonna hit the Q-L bridge instead of this. I've run out of patience to deal with more idiots."

"You had some? Not since I've known you, Kal," Dakota's tone didn't hide her amusement.

"Funny." I let the easy banter roll over me as I backtracked and headed north. It was only a couple of miles, but the Queensland-Lewiston border crossing was more efficient than the touristy one in the city. It was busier but made up for the increased volume with additional lanes.

I pulled up to the exit point, expecting to speed through.

"Passports." The Empire's border officer sounded bored, as well he should be. When the Empire won its independence, they'd added exit checks to the borders, a step I thought wholly unnecessary. But then, I hated bureaucracy on general principles, going back to my days as one of Hell's good little demons, so maybe I was biased.

I handed over the passports, and he started scanning them. I knew something was wrong when he hesitated.

Shit. There's a problem.

What? Faith asked.

Don't know.

"Pull over to the side, please." He gestured which way I should go.

"Is there a problem?"

"Please pull to the side." He side-stepped my question, and I got a sinking feeling.

"Passports?"

"They'll be returned to you after a few more questions." I could tell he was done with patience. "Pull over."

There wasn't anything to gain, so I said, "Thank you," and did what he said.

"What's going on?" McKenna asked as I parked, maybe twenty yards away from the control booths.

"I don't know. Some questions? You two haven't done anything I need to know about, do you?"

Both Dakota and McKenna's answers were emphatic no's, with Dakota adding, "I haven't pulled a job in at least a half-dozen years, not counting the one a few months back we did for you."

Right. And we'd gotten away clean, so that wasn't it. We sat and stewed for a good twenty minutes before another pair of customs agents approached. I lowered the window.

"Hello, Officer Anderson," I said, as politely as I could, taking the name from her badge.

"Please turn off the vehicle."

Her tone told me I'd better not argue, so I pressed the button that disengaged the drives.

She handed back the passports, saying, "License, insurance, registration."

I found my license while Faith dug for the other documents. I asked, "Is there an issue with the car?"

"Registration and insurance."

Faith handed them across. "Here you go."

The other agent was behind the car, hand resting on the butt of a pistol, as if they expected me to try to back out of the spot and flee. Not likely, not with my friends with me, but it ratcheted up my nerves another notch.

Anderson handed back my papers. "Dakota Chase. Identify yourself."

"Me."

"Please step out of the vehicle."

Now I really didn't like this. "Officer, she's my friend and hasn't done anything!"

Dakota replied before Anderson could. "It's fine, Kal. My mom always taught me not to try to change the weather." She opened the door and stepped out, moving slowly and raising her hands.

The other agent grabbed her and spun her against the side of the car with a thud, pulling her arms back and slapping cuffs on her. Anderson came around and announced, "Dakota Chase, you are under arrest." She continued with the legal warnings, but I didn't hear them. Dakota? Arrested?

The nameless agent dragged an unresisting Dakota away, a bruise already forming on one cheek, and I couldn't hold my tongue any longer.

"Officer Anderson. Officer Anderson!" She turned, halfway back to their office. "What's the charge?"

"Who are you?"

"Her friend." I wasn't stupid. Not always.

"Parole violation. Attempting to leave the country without permission." Anderson resumed walking, adding, "You'll want a good lawyer," over her shoulder.

Parole violation?

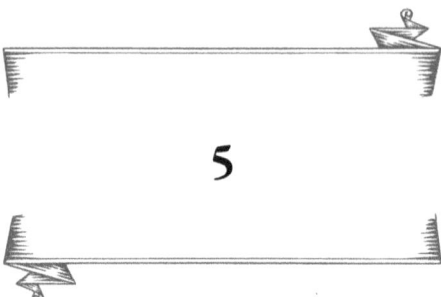

5

Parole violation.

While I calmed enough so I wasn't about to tear limbs from agents, Faith dug into her bag of tricks and followed the threads. Every half-century or so, she'd find a law school, go through the rigamarole of classes, and pass the Bar or its equivalent in whatever place we called home on Earth. Most recently, she'd attended Fordham's, having already done NYU and Columbia, in the Thirties.

"When the Empire took over, they also took over the penal system," she explained when we were safely away from the border, holed up in a hotel a few minutes away.

"Right, I remember that," McKenna said, giving Bandit an idle scratch. "Different name on the door, but nothing much changed."

"Pretty much," Faith agreed.

"But what's this bullshit about a parole violation? Dakota's been off parole for over twenty years!"

"See, that's where I think it went wrong. In theory, all the penalties and sentences in place remained the same from one administration to the other. But you remember the border issues?"

I thought back. Borders didn't particularly concern us, since we could use Hell's portals to appear anywhere on Earth any time we wanted if we didn't jump there directly. "No."

"It's the reason for the exit checkpoints. The Empire agreed, in treaties, to prevent any convicted felons from leaving the country. They called it being a good neighbor, but it was more of a bribe to allow their independence to stick. What it meant was the restriction on leaving the state most felons had as part of their parole or release was made permanent."

"That's fucking stupid!" I exclaimed, followed by McKenna's groan.

"We've been such homebodies we never ran into it," she said, and Faith agreed.

"You two have focused on that bar, yes. When Dakota tried to leave, it flagged her last conviction, and boom."

"But what about McKenna?" I turned to her, questioning. "You've done time."

McKenna nodded, but Faith answered first. "You never served time for a felony."

McKenna's eyes widened, and I realized Faith's mistake at the same time she did. When we got involved with humans for any significant length of time, we learned all we could about them, quietly. Knowing which team our friends batted for didn't change how we saw them, but it clued us into their likely acquaintances and paths.

McKenna's gaze turned inquisitive. "No, I always pled down to misdemeanors. How did you...?"

Faith rallied. "Because they didn't flag you. Misdemeanors don't carry the same penalty, so it was only logical."

Nice save.

You love me for my mind.

"So, what now?" I asked. "I don't feel like trying to break Dakota out, not if we want to bring you back to Brooklyn one day."

Faith and McKenna said, "Sierra!" at the same time, and I slapped my forehead. Of course. Sierra might be old, as hackers went, but she was still one of the best. Better still, she had expanded her network of contacts, legal and less so. If anyone could fix this, it was her.

"I'm gonna go down there and keep my wife company," McKenna said, holding up her hand expectantly. I tossed her the keys.

"Don't get arrested for jaywalking," I joked.

"Not a chance." She slipped out, and Faith pulled out her phone. A few taps and we had Sierra.

"You want me to get Dakota released and scrub her records," she greeted us.

"Uh. Yeah. How did you…?"

Sierra laughed, and her hair—still blue after all these years—shook with her mirth. "I keep tabs on all of my friends, just in case. Dakota's name came up today, so I've been waiting for someone to call." Sierra sipped from a glass of dark liquid I suspected was rum. Some things never changed, and how she wasn't an alcoholic was beyond even an Immortal.

Faith joined in the laughter. She'd been on the outside of most of my extralegal activities but had gotten to know Dakota and her crew. She held a soft spot for Sierra and her first spouse, Alex. "I should have guessed. Hi, Sierra."

"Hey, Faith. Alex finished that piece for you. Where do you want it shipped?"

This was news to me, but Faith said, "Hold onto it for a bit, would you, dear? And tell Alex they're magnificent. I can't wait to display it."

Sierra smiled. "Of course. So, what did Dakota do to get the Empire's attention?"

"Nothing. We're on a road trip, and heading out of the country," I growled.

"Okay, that makes it simpler." I heard computer noises but had no idea what she was doing. "That ought to take care of it. I've purged her records from her legit persona and attached them to a fictitious Dakota Chase. She'll be released as a case of mistaken identity."

"You're an angel," Faith said.

"Don't you dare!" But Sierra's voice was light, with no heat. "Safe journeys."

"Thank you!" I managed before Sierra hung up. "What did you commission from Alex?" I asked.

"You'll see," Faith answered, walling off the portion of her memories with the information. "It's a surprise."

I had a complex relationship with surprises. "Fucking wonderful."

"You'll like it, *arima bikia*." She dimpled, and my sourness evaporated.

"What next?"

"Get Bandit and we'll jump over to the office, meet McKenna, collect Dakota, and get into Canada. I can't wait for you to see the rooms I have reserved for us."

This sounded like an excellent plan to me. Over the years, we'd learned the trick Archangels used in jumping to a place they didn't know. Instead of relying on perfect memories, as angels did, archangels made a series of jumps. First they covered the bulk of the space, getting close to their destination. While still in the unreality of the jump, they would peer out at reality, choose a target, and make that their focus. They'd repeat this process over and over until they arrived at their chosen point. And since it all took place in jump space, it didn't take any time in reality. A clever trick, once Ariel taught it to us.

"We should wait a few minutes," Faith continued. "Otherwise, we'll get there before McKenna does."

She made no attempt to hide her thoughts this time, and I grinned. This was the wicked side of Faith, one I appreciated more and more every year.

"I wonder what we'll do?"

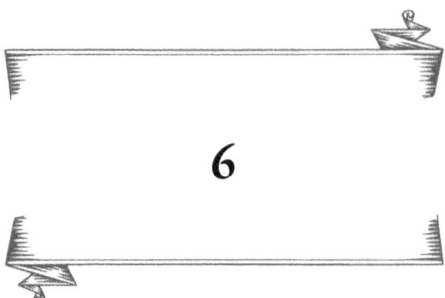

6

An hour later, we popped into existence around the corner from the Customs and Border Security office, Bandit in Faith's arms. The cat hadn't reacted at all to the jump. Whether that was from Faith's influence, or because cat, I couldn't say.

Of course, now that we were here, she was ready to scratch someone's eyes out.

The Conqueror was in front, so I took a moment to put a protesting Bandit back in her travel crate. I didn't think we'd be here long.

Faith had all the necessary documents on her tablet, ready to print if needed, and was fully into her lawyer mode. She wore a suit that screamed high-priced lawyer, which she'd popped back to our NYC apartment to retrieve. I was amazed by her transformation, from passionate lover to cold defender of justice in minutes. But that was my Faith.

"Are you holding my client?" she demanded as soon as she walked in the door. The agent behind the desk tried to look officious but only succeeded in appearing constipated.

"Who are you, and who is your client?" they managed.

Faith dropped a business card on the desk between them. "Faith Burroughs, attorney at law. My client is Dakota Chase, and she's being unlawfully detained."

The agent looked puzzled, then their expression cleared. "Chase? The parole violator?"

"My client has no parole to violate." She pushed her pad across, leveling her sternest glare at the unwary agent. "Please release her."

The agent didn't look down. "You'll have to talk to the Agent In Charge." We could hear the capitals.

Faith folded her arms across her chest. "Fine. Get her."

"Him."

"Whoever. Every minute my client is here is another minute I'll be bringing suit for damages."

The mention of a lawsuit got the uniform scurrying off with Faith's card, and I hid my smile.

You're not playing fair.

Who taught me to never give a sucker an even break, hmm?

We didn't wait more than thirty seconds before an older man came in, looking appropriately bureaucratic in a suit which maybe cost a quarter of Faith's. His hair was mostly black, flecked with gray, and his once-handsome face was sagging and creased from too many years of sedentary life. His body, what I could tell under the suit, was along the same lines.

I wasn't impressed.

"Ms. Burroughs?"

Faith nodded, once.

"I'm Frank Chillura, Agent In Charge of the Lewiston CBS office. How can I help you?"

"You can release my client, Dakota Chase, and then inform your superiors that you will be sued for wrongful detainment and violation of my client's civil rights."

Chillura raised his hands in a gesture I'm sure he meant to be placating. "Ms. Burroughs, please, there's no need to toss around words like lawsuit and violation. Come back to my office and we'll talk." He gestured, and Faith glowered briefly before heading in the direction he indicated. I followed, but the desk agent intercepted me.

"Not you."

"She's my assistant," Faith called over her shoulder, and Chillura said, "Let her pass."

I smiled my winningest smile and hurried after them.

Chillura's office was standard bureaucratic blandness, without even a photograph of his family to break up the boring. I stood behind Faith, who claimed the one visitor's chair and sat before Chillura could offer.

"What do you want, Ms. Burroughs?"

"Are you—no, scratch that. I told you what I want. My client, released. Immediately."

Chillura made a show of considering her demand. "Dakota Chase?"

"Yes."

He typed the name into his terminal, then turned the monitor so we could see. "I'm afraid I can't do that. Dakota Chase is on parole, and the conditions of her parole clearly state she is not to leave the country. Attempting to do so is a violation, punishable by the automatic revocation of her parole." He raised his hands. "I'm sorry, Ms. Burroughs, but it's out of our hands. The Imperial Law Enforcement Bureau has been notified, and they'll be taking her into custody shortly."

Faith tapped the screen with a perfectly manicured nail. "That's not my client."

Chillura laughed, then choked it off when he saw Faith's expression. "I assure you, Ms. Burroughs, the person we detained is Dakota Chase."

"Yes, I know she is," Faith persisted, "but my Dakota Chase and *that* Dakota Chase aren't the same person. See?" She tapped the screen again. "Look at the birthdate."

Chillura smiled and turned to the screen. "March 4, 2026. So?"

I don't know how, but Faith resisted rolling her eyes. "Do you have Ms. Chase's passport?"

"All of Ms. Chase's personal effects are in secure storage."

"I suggest you retrieve her passport and examine it. Closely."

"Really, Ms. Burroughs, I think—"

"Agent Chillura, I am a member of the Bar. I insist on positive identification of the accused in front of the accused's counsel, that is, myself, per Empire Legal Code Section 4, Subsection R, paragraph 12. This serves as your official notice under the Code. Failure to comply will result in civil and criminal penalties of up to five thousand Cuomos and sixty days in jail."

All color disappeared from his face, replaced instantly with the red of fury. Without a word, he slammed back his chair and stomped from the office. I heard him yelling for Dakota's goddamn belongings before it faded.

"Are you making that up?" I asked.

"No. I might have done a little refresher," she admitted.

We kept quiet, waiting. It wasn't long.

Chillura stomped back in, burdened by a steel box which he dropped onto his desk.

"Her belongings," he growled, all of his good-naturedness lost.

"Very good. Have you verified her identity?"

"No, I have to do that in front of you."

Faith dimpled. "Very good, Agent Chillura. Proceed."

He unlocked the box and rummaged. In a moment, he pulled out the green booklet and flipped it open. "Dakota Chase. That's the person we have in our holding cell."

"What is her birthdate, please?"

"March—"

"Agent Chillura, not the one you pulled up. The one printed on her biometrics page."

This time he did roll his eyes, but he looked. "September 29, 1976." His eyes came up, and he said, "That's impossible!"

"I assure you, Mr. Chillura, that Ms. Chase is seventy-six years old, as indicated on her passport, and will turn seventy-seven later this year. If you doubt the authenticity of the passport, you can check her driver's license. I assure you, it has the same information."

He paled again. "I—I don't know what to say."

"Say that this was an error and you'll release my client immediately, for a start."

His head bobbed frantically. "Yes, of course." He nearly ran from the office.

"Nicely done, Ms. Burroughs."

"Thank you, Ms. Keoka. I hope you were taking notes."

"Always, Ms. Burroughs."

In a few minutes, Dakota entered the office, followed by McKenna and then Chillura, who hurried to retrieve Dakota's belongings. I winked at our friends, hoping they'd keep their mouths shut.

"Ah, Ms. Chase. I see they've released you. You have released her?" Faith turned back to Chillura. "She's free to go?"

He was searching through files. "As soon as I get a signature—"

"Mr. Chillura." Faith made it sound like a disease. "My client will sign nothing, as she's done nothing wrong. Indeed, your attempt to get her to sign any sort of statement is foolish and will be remembered during any legal action my client chooses to take." She leaned in and said, in a whisper that couldn't be heard more than ten feet away, "You shouldn't try to cover your ass in front of witnesses. It never ends well."

Knowing he was backed into a corner, Chillura stilled. "Yes, she's free to go."

"Very good. Ms. Chase, will you confirm that all of your personal property is accounted for?" Faith pushed the box toward Dakota, who made a show of pulling every item out and examining it.

"It's all here," she said at length, the last item disappearing into her bag.

"I'll be escorting Ms. Chase across the border, Mr. Chillura, just to ensure that nothing untoward happens. You know about unfortunate accidents, and we don't want any of those, do we?" She beamed sunnily. "We're done here. Good day, Mr. Chillura. Ms. Keoka, if you'll lead?"

I moved past, McKenna slipping the keys to me in as smooth a move as I'd ever seen. With Faith in the rear, we left the office, climbing into the Conqueror.

"Say nothing at the checkpoint," Faith whispered. "We can relax once we're in Canada."

McKenna and Dakota nodded and I motored us to the booth. After the trouble on the Empire side, I was ready for the Canadians to give us a hard time, but I was wrong. We were waved through with only the barest interest in the passports, and no awkward questions about why we were carrying several thousand Cuomo's of liquor.

Don't ask, don't tell.

Fifteen minutes after leaving Chillura's office, we were on the 405 and heading for the Canadian side of Niagara Falls.

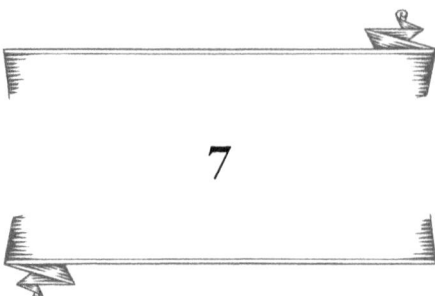

7

Driving through Niagara Falls on the Canadian side wasn't substantially different than the Empire side, and we found ourselves at the hotel soon enough. It was a towering casino, a stone's throw from the Falls, and across the road from the Tower.

"That looks like fun," Dakota said, noting one of the elevators crawling up the side. McKenna took her hand.

"Want to?"

"Let's get checked in first?" suggested Faith, always practical.

Someone has to be with you bunch of dreamers.

We left the luggage in the Jeep; I hated dragging it around before I knew where I was going. Faith led the way through the ornate lobby, past casino tables and holographic slot machines, to the registration desk, the three of us lagging behind.

"Stop scoping it out," I warned Dakota.

She had the decency to look sheepish. "Habit."

I grinned. "Yeah, just don't act on it. We need to stay clean, at least until we're back across the border."

Dakota fixed me with a glare. "Tell me again why we're not hiding out in the Empire? We could stay on the other side of the river and not have to worry about any of this crap."

She had a point. The problem was, I *knew* the Empire was going to get dragged into this war. Avareth had quietly informed me of what her spies on Earth had reported months ago, and we'd been working toward this end ever since. But how could I tell my friends this? "Oh, well, our lover, who's Chief of Staff to Lilith and a demon, warned us," wouldn't go over well.

"A business opportunity," I said, knowing how lame it sounded. "In Denver."

"You want to tell us a little more?"

I was saved from answering by Faith's raised voice. "What do you mean, canceled?"

I knew that tone. Faith might be the more angelic one, but *that* note in her voice meant her patience was at an end. I hurried to her side.

"What's wrong?"

She whirled, fury on her face. "According to James, the reservation I made was canceled."

"Didn't you use the Centurion?"

She nodded. "I did. Since it was last minute, I pre-paid in full. Two nights, Executive Suite, southeast corner."

I turned to the luckless clerk, who'd stood his ground. I slipped into my sweetest, most persuasive voice.

"Hi, James. There seems to be a problem with our reservation, but I'm sure you can fix it."

So maybe I leveled some of the succubus tricks I'd learned along the way at him too. Sue me.

He sputtered. "I'm sorry, no, it's—"

I waved him off. "No matter. If the reservation isn't there, it's not there. We'll just get a different room. Which of those suites do you have available? We want a view of the Falls, of course."

"None of the suites are available for rental."

"That's bullshit. An hour ago, I had my pick, and now none are open?" Faith's tone could have flayed a human to the bone. I was forced into the unlikely role of peacekeeper.

"Can you get a manager, James? I'm sure it's a simple misunderstanding."

He scurried away, and I pulled Faith into a hug.

"It's bullshit, Kal!" she repeated.

"I'm sure it is. Do you have the confirmation?"

"Of course." She opened her phone and the document. "See?"

I took it from her. "Yup. Okay, we'll handle this."

A woman dressed in a sleek, navy blue power suit approached. I took a moment to appreciate her, the suit tailored to perfection, with sharp lines and subtle metallic accents that gave it a modern look. Integrated high-tech features were discreetly incorporated into the design of the suit. For her youth—I guessed she was in her mid-thirties—her authoritative presence exuded confidence and control, making her stand out in the bustling, high-stakes environment of the casino.

"I'm Ms. Lake, the hotel's manager. How can I help you, Ms. Burroughs?"

I smiled at her error, natural though it was. "Ms. Keoka. Kalili Keoka. Burroughs is my wife's name." I slipped into a British accent without thinking too deeply about it.

She didn't so much as twitch. "My apologies."

I looked at her more closely. She had a sharp, angular face with high cheekbones, giving her a striking and commanding appearance. Her eyes were intense and focused, a shade of piercing blue, reflecting her determination and control. Her neatly styled, shoulder-length hair, was tucked into a sleek bob. Altogether, she didn't seem like someone who would rattle.

Time to shake.

"No problem. My wife made a reservation, and now your clerk says it's canceled." I slid the phone across to her. "And yet here's our confirmation, with the full amount paid."

She didn't glance at the screen for more than a second. "Yes, I canceled it." She pushed the phone back. "I thought it likely a fraudulent charge, and was attempting to protect Ms. Burroughs."

Damn, she was slick. "I appreciate your courtesy, but we're here and we need our suite." I smiled as winningly as I knew. "I presume you can arrange that?"

"Of course. I'll need Ms. Burroughs' card again."

Before Faith could fire off, I intervened. "Why? Simply reinstate the prior reservation, which has been fully paid." I tapped the phone, still displaying the receipt. "See?"

"That was canceled and refunded."

"Faith?" I wanted Ms. Lake to know I didn't trust her word. After all, canceling a reservation was one thing. Blocking us from renting while on site? Not cricket.

"I'll check. No, no refund. Still shows a full charge."

Now, our Centurion cards had no limits, no cap on our spending. They based that on our payment patterns. A long, *long* time on Earth had convinced me of the benefits of credit cards. Carrying cash was dangerous, especially if you confused denominations. A little piece of plastic? Much safer. Since we spent thousands, and sometimes millions, every month, and paid it off immediately, we had a virtually unlimited line of credit to draw on.

The short version was we could afford to pay for another room while we waited for the original charge to be reversed.

But there was a principle at play here, and I had an idea.

Faith, find out who owns this place.

She started the search, and I returned to Lake.

"Ms. Lake, I'm afraid that's not acceptable. We paid for a suite for two nights, and we intend to have that suite for two nights. We don't intend to pay twice."

Her lips set in a stubborn line. "Ms. Keoka, that's simply banking. If you want a room tonight, you'll have to pay for it."

TransGlobal Enterprises.

TransGlobal? Why is that familiar?

Walt Moore owns it.

Ah. Walt was a friend of ours and an occasional visitor to our irregular, high-stakes poker games. The last one, a few weeks ago, he should have skipped. His holding company was having a shitty quarter, and it affected his game.

How much does he owe me again?

About fifty million.

"No. We've paid. We won't pay again." I leaned over the counter. She was taller than me, but I summoned my entire seven thousand-plus years of experience into my posture. "So, Ms. Lake, you have three choices. Deny us our room which we paid for, resulting in us finding a room elsewhere before taking you and your company to court. Now, that's lengthy and expensive, as well as hugely irritating, and doesn't solve the problem. We want to stay here, not somewhere else."

She held her ground, so I laid out my next point.

"You can give us our keys and do whatever you need to do in your system to reinstate the reservation with the original payment."

She didn't show any sign of budging, though I could feel the tension rising.

"Or third, I could buy this hotel and replace you with a potted plant." I held up the Centurion card. To my surprise, Lake relaxed.

"I'm sorry, Ms. Keoka, but your threat to have me replaced is pointless. You seem to be unaware that this property is owned by a conglomerate, and they are unlikely to sell a single location. Now, please leave before I call security." I could see from the gleam in her eyes that she thought she had the upper hand.

Never bluff a demon.

"Yes, Ms. Lake, it is owned by a conglomerate. TransGlobal Enterprises, which is a plaything for Walter Moore. He stashes all sorts of things in his company, including your lovely resort." She didn't react, so I continued. "Unfortunately, Walt is having a rough quarter, and his investors aren't happy with their returns. Having some ready cash would probably go a long way toward easing their grumblings, and give him more time for his long-term investments to pay off. I'm sure if I called him and made a reasonable offer, he'd be happy to entertain it. And then I'd replace you."

Lake paled. "Are you threatening me?"

"No," I said with an evil grin. "That wasn't a threat. Now, if I said that I'd buy this hotel, fire you, blackball you in the hospitality industry throughout North America, persuade the Canada Revenue Agency to take a close look at your records, convince the RCMP to examine all the financial records of the casino under your management, and have the government freeze your passport so you can't leave the country, then that would be a threat. Do you see the difference?"

She nodded, jerkily.

"Excellent. So, Ms. Lake, what shall it be?"

"I'll open up the reservation."

"Quite good." I slid the card across. "I know you'll need this for incidentals."

You're evil.

No, just determined.

In a few minutes, the suite was sorted, and we left the desk. I fell in next to Dakota.

"Remember what I said earlier about not casing the joint?"

She nodded.

"Forget it. Just be subtle."

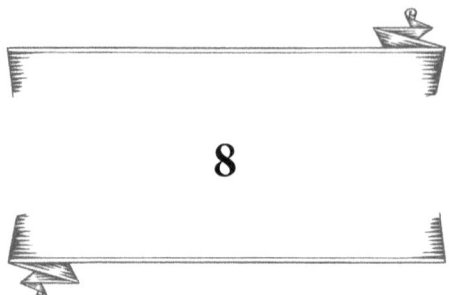

8

The suite was everything we'd hoped. Unfortunately, I didn't have time to explore before the questions began.

"What was that all about? And why did you sound all British?"

I winced. That was a question I'd been asking myself.

"Canadians have a thing about hearing a British accent. Makes them feel all subservient."

McKenna snorted. "As if. She didn't look subservient until you threatened to get her ass fired."

"Could you have done that?" Dakota asked.

I shrugged. "If I wanted to buy this place, yeah. But I hate being too involved."

Faith laid a hand on my shoulder. "She does. You'd be amazed at the lengths she goes to stay out of things."

Dakota shook her head and laughed. "No, I really wouldn't. But damn, Kal. I knew you were loaded, with your apartment building and all. This? It's next-level rich."

"And I still want to know why we're going to Denver," McKenna added. I jumped on it, being the less-dangerous topic.

"A business opportunity."

"You said that, and it tells us nothing," Dakota griped. "Explain."

"I talk better with a drink." She took the hint and found the bar, appraising it with a critical eye. A few moments later, Dakota had served us all.

"Talk."

I'd run out of excuses, so I talked.

"You both know what we used to do." I'd stuck to my cover story for many years, that Faith and I used to work for people who solved problems, sort of professional troubleshooters. This also explained why I kept my hand in on occasion. It was the truth, too, if you stretched the definition of employer and troubleshooting.

"The problem with my contacts is they're not reliable. Oh, they tell me the truth when there's something they need, but if it's not important to them? I don't hear about it. This whole bullshit with the Collective, for example? Everything we knew came from the street, not my contacts."

Jaws dropped in disbelief. McKenna found her voice first.

"That's not important to your employers?"

"Former employers," Faith corrected. "And no. Kalili's told you about their interests being limited to end-of-the-world events, right?" McKenna nodded. "This doesn't qualify."

"They're awful confident it won't go NBC," Dakota said.

How was I gonna get around this? Ariel could visit the future; it was a perk of being the de facto ruler of Heaven. While Lilith might not care about nuclear, biological, or chemical warfare, Ariel did, and she'd ask us to intervene. Or do it herself, but that was problematic.

"Good analysts." Okay, it sounded lame, but it was just about true. "The point is, they didn't tell me, so I was almost as blindsided as you were. Oh, I knew there were issues, but anyone with eyes could see what was happening and take basic precautions. The point is, I hate not knowing shit's going down."

Dakota grimaced. "Yeah, like not knowing about the fifth guard when you plan for four."

I tried to repress my chuckle and mostly succeeded. "That was a mess, but you're exactly right. This opportunity in Denver? It's a company that gathers information and then resells it. They're very, *very* good at what they do, and I want them working for me."

Faith beamed, while Dakota goggled and McKenna examined me as if I'd told her that cats gave chocolate milk.

"You want your own CIA?" Dakota finally managed.

"More or less. Yes. I expect to turn a profit, but that's less important than knowledge and not being obligated to someone else for it."

"Wouldn't it be easier to read the news?"

I waved my hand. "And fill my mind with that shit? Not a chance."

"What's the company called?" McKenna asked.

"OutLook. Stupid name, but whatever. I can always change it if it bothers me too much."

After a few more questions, they seemed satisfied and wandered off to find their bedroom. Faith dropped into my lap.

"Sweetheart, don't you think it's risky, telling humans so much about our business?"

I winced. "Maybe, but I'm tired of hiding, hon. It's been a long time since I could be me, completely and honestly, with anyone but you and Avareth. Dakota and McKenna are as close to family as I have, and..." I didn't have to finish the sentence. They were mortal, and we weren't. If everything broke right for them, they might have another two or three decades. "It's a risk, but I trust them."

She kissed me and smiled. "So do I, *arima bikia*. Now, for the important question."

I waited, keeping my mind out of hers.

"Are you going to tell them what we are? Or is that just a fantasy I see in here?" She tapped my forehead, gently, with her forefinger.

"I want to," I began, but Faith interrupted.

"Then do it."

"...What?"

"Do it. Like you said, they're our friends, the closest friends we've ever had on this world. They deserve to know."

"..."

"Close your mouth, dear. Your imitation of a goldfish leaves much to be desired."

I clopped my teeth together, trying to gather my wits. "Uh, Faith? Do you think that's smart?"

"Smart? No, but it's the right thing. I'll leave the timing to you."

Holy shit. I didn't think Faith would agree, which is one reason I hadn't brought it up since it first popped into my head twenty years earlier. "You...what?"

"Of course. Sweetheart, you're closer to them than anyone else we've known in eleven hundred years. If we could have children, well, they couldn't mean more to you than Dakota and McKenna." She cocked her head, arms still encircling me. "Why is that, love? I've always wondered."

"I'm not sure. Maybe because they were like us?"

Faith frowned. "How so?"

"They're basically good people who had to do shitty things to survive?" I shrugged. "I don't really know. They vibe with us, or maybe we vibe with them. But I think I'll wait until we're safer to blow their minds."

Faith giggled. "I remember what happened to Dionisio."

"As long as you don't pop out your wings, I think they'll do better than he did."

"Better than who did?"

Shit. McKenna.

Faith answered first. "Oh, just someone we knew a long time ago. We gave him advice, but he didn't take it." She shrugged. "His loss."

McKenna nodded, accepting it. It was truth, or close enough, and Faith's voice resonated with it.

"What's next?" Dakota asked. She'd taken time to change out of her traveling clothes into something less rumpled.

"How about dinner with a view of the Falls?" Faith said. She shared the location through our link, the revolving restaurant at the top of the neighboring tower.

I peered at our friends. "Do you have nicer clothes?"

Dakota groaned. "Kal, we own a bar. This *is* nice."

I grinned. "Then I guess I get to take you shopping again."

"Oh, crap."

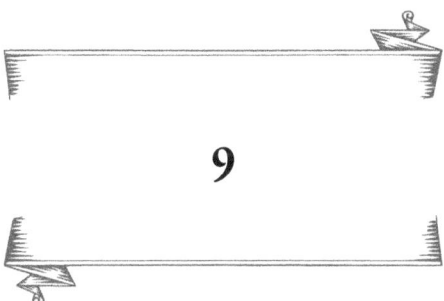

9

"You've learned restraint."

I chuckled. "I always knew restraint, Dakota, but I don't always need to exercise it."

We were back in the suite with our purchases. We hadn't even needed to leave the building to find them, which I appreciated. Even better, the clothiers in the shopping concourse were all high-end, which suited me fine. I'd worn everything in my long life, from skins to silk, and much preferred the silk end of the spectrum. I didn't mind paying for quality, either. Of course, that sometimes led to problems, as I'd occasionally pull an outfit from my closet which was in fashion four or six decades earlier. Faith usually rescued me before I headed out, but not always.

That wouldn't be a problem tonight.

"Meet back in an hour. Sunset's in two hours, and I think seeing the Falls will be spectacular." With that, we separated to clean and change. Technically, Faith and I didn't need to bathe or dress. As Immortals, we had the power to shapeshift, which meant we could make the dirt disappear and bring clothes into reality with an effort of will and spending *taaqat*, celestial energy. But there was something sybaritic about bathing and changing into well-fitted clothes, so why not indulge?

The evening sun cast its fading light over the suite as I buttoned my suitcoat. The deep charcoal gray fabric felt luxurious, fitting my frame perfectly. I wasn't wearing a blouse or bra beneath it, appreciating the style that had been going in and out of fashion for the past ninety years. I glanced in the mirror, my long red hair cascading wildly over my shoulders. I ran a hand through it, attempting to tame the unruly waves, but ultimately gave up. Some battles weren't worth fighting.

Faith's voice echoed from the sitting room. "Kalili, are you ready? We don't want to miss the sunset."

I took a deep breath and adjusted the hang of the coat. "Always waiting on you, Faith," I teased, stepping out of the bedroom. As I entered the living area, my eyes landed on her, and I couldn't help but smile.

Faith stood by the window, her long blonde hair catching the fading sunlight. She wore a halter neckline dress in a soft, muted gold that complemented her skin tones beautifully. The fabric shimmered subtly in the light, flowing gracefully around her figure. The dress accentuated her elegance, the halter neckline drawing attention to her shoulders and neck.

"You look stunning," I said, my voice amazed, again, at the love I'd found.

Faith turned, a smile playing on her lips. "Thank you, Kalili. You clean up pretty well yourself." She stepped closer, her eyes briefly scanning my suit. "Ready to go?"

I nodded. "Let's do this."

Just then, Dakota and McKenna joined us in the shared space of our luxurious rental. McKenna wore a tailored suit I'd picked out, the dark fabric highlighting her strong frame and giving her a distinguished, yet rugged look. Dakota, standing beside her wife, wore a sleek, elegant dress in a deep, rich burgundy, which contrasted beautifully with her hair and brought out the intensity in her gaze.

Faith greeted them with a warm smile. "You both look amazing."

"Thank Kalili for that," McKenna said, her voice tinged with appreciation. "She's got a good eye for these things."

I shrugged modestly. "I want us all to look our best."

We made our way to the top of the casino and the edge of the revolving restaurant, where a clear view of the Falls awaited us. The sun was setting behind the building, casting a warm, golden light over the water. The restaurant revolved slowly, giving us a panoramic view of the breathtaking scenery.

Faith had done her magic and secured us a table at the edge, with a clear view of the Falls and the Empire side of the river. "Will we see the sunset from here?" I asked, my gaze fixed on the horizon.

"That's the idea," Faith answered. Dakota, who was already admiring the view, smiled appreciatively. "The restaurant revolves once an hour, but I don't know when that is."

"What time is sunset?" I asked the AI on my wrist. Sabrina answered, "Sunset at your location will be at six fourteen p.m."

"Perfect. We'll be coming around at the right time."

We dove into the menus, after a brief argument over who would pay. I was all for us picking up the tab since the four-course prix fixe was over $400 per person, not including wines. Faith convinced me to give in gracefully, which I nearly managed, insisting that I'd pay for the wines.

The dinner and accompanying wine pairings were fantastic. That might have been a function of the food, or the company, or the sun shining behind us and turning the Falls into a shimmering curtain of gold. The sight was mesmerizing, the light dancing on the water, turning it into a cascade of beauty rarely seen on Earth. The mist caught the sunlight, creating an ethereal glow that added to the magic of the evening.

As we enjoyed our meal, I couldn't help but feel a sense of peace. Despite everything, moments like this made it all worth it. I glanced at Faith, her eyes reflecting the light, the beauty outside outshone by her radiance, and smiled. Tonight was perfect.

Or it would have been perfect.

As we enjoyed the dessert wine, I was startled by a presence in my mind.

Avy?

Where are you?

I let her see through my eyes. Before I could warn Faith, there was a *pop* and Avareth appeared between the table and the window. Neither Dakota nor McKenna screamed, to their credit, though McKenna's hand dropped to the holster I knew she had hidden.

"It's okay." I hastened to reassure her. The caliber she carried wouldn't kill Avy, but would piss her off and ruin the rest of the evening. "She's—"

"Our wife," Faith finished, brave as always.

McKenna's hand retreated a few inches, but she didn't take her eyes from Avy. Understandable, since she was dressed in her usual, preferred form, and I tried to see her as our friends might.

Avareth stood, petite yet commanding, her long, flowing lavender hair cascading down her shoulders. Her features were both delicate and intense, a calm expression masking the formidable power she held within. She wore a form-fitting, metallic purple top that clung to her athletic frame, the sheen of the fabric like twilight captured in cloth. Gold armor adorned her shoulders and forearms, exquisitely wrought and impossible to ignore. A wide, ornate belt cinched her waist, adding to her majestic presence.

The lower part of her outfit flowed with layers of black and purple fabric, each movement creating a ripple. Black leggings hugged her legs, highlighting her toned physique and readiness for whatever might come. Her tall, golden boots, adorned with delicate filigree, completed the ensemble. She dressed entirely befitting her position as Chief of Staff to the ruler of Hell, Lilith, and a Prince of Hell in her own right.

And her timing sucked.

What the fuck, Avy?!

Sorry, sorry. I wouldn't if it wasn't important.

Dakota recovered first. "Wife?" Her eyes tracked from Faith, to Avy, to me, and back again. "You're a throuple?"

I shuddered at that word. "Triad. Yes."

"Why haven't we met her in the past forty years?"

"It's complicated." How complicated, I didn't want to say.

"Where did she come from, Kalili?" That was the question I desperately wanted to avoid, so of course McKenna would growl it. How could I answer her? I needed time, so... stall.

"Let's talk about it in the suite."

I'm out of here.

Not so fast, Avy, Faith sent. *You have to help us!*

I can erase their memories.

Not like that!

Well, what do you suggest?

How about talking to them?

Avy's mental voice was aghast at my suggestion. *That's against the rules!*

Fuck 'em. You're the second most powerful demon in Hell, and best friends with the de facto ruler of Heaven. Who's anyone gonna complain to? I thought it was an excellent argument.

Fine, but I think it's stupid. Avy didn't agree with my argument, but I'd take what I could get.

"Sounds good." *Where is it?* Avy added in my mind. I sent back a memory. "I'll see you there." With another *pop*, she vanished. Well, in for a penny...

"Where did she go?"

Oh, Avy. "She went back. I'll explain it all somewhere more private, okay?"

We settled the bill and made our way across the street to our suite. It was a silent walk, filled with awkwardness and uncomfortable glances. Faith and I shared our thoughts, but didn't plan or prepare. Rather, we used the time to rebalance each other and find a calm place. Now, in addition to the little issue of our immortality, we were figuring out how to explain to our very human friends why we had a spouse we'd kept hidden our entire friendship. We needed every second of the walk and then some.

It wasn't long enough. Seven minutes later, we were in the suite, in the living room that separated our spaces. Avareth, of course, was already there, lounging on a sofa.

"Time to answer questions," Dakota said, dropping next to Avareth, ignoring the anachronism of her clothes. "Who are you?"

"Faith told you. I'm their wife."

"Who nobody's seen in decades? Who they've never mentioned once? And how did you do that trick at the restaurant?"

Avy sounded desperate. *Ideas?*

The truth, Avareth.

I was afraid you'd say that.

"My name is Avareth, and you haven't seen me in the City because I don't spend much time there. Maybe one night a fortnight?" She looked at us for confirmation. "They don't talk about me because we've run into issues about our relationship before, and it's easier to avoid them this way."

That was the right note to hit, and it was the quintessential Avareth: tell the truth, but not all of it, and tell it in a way that appeals to the listener. Both Dakota and McKenna had grown up when homophobia was a force to be reckoned with, lived through the occasionally violent process of acceptance and equality, and enjoyed the liberalization of civil rights.

"And you disappearing?" McKenna pressed.

"That's a little more difficult to explain."

"And you look like you're about twenty. How long have you been married to them?"

Avy didn't speak, but her eyes pled for help.

"Dakota, McKenna." Both turned to face Faith. "Do you trust me?"

"Yes," Dakota answered instantly. "You've never given me a reason not to."

"McKenna?"

"What my wife said."

I'm going to tell them.

I clutched her hand and let her feel my support.

"We're not human."

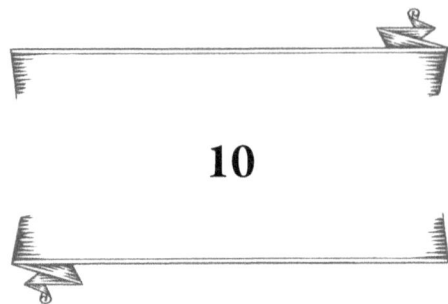

10

"What?"

"We're not human," Faith repeated.

What the fuck are you doing? Avy screamed in our minds.

Trusting them. Faith's voice was calm, but her anxiety lurked below the surface.

You know the two of you are nuts, right? But Avy didn't try stopping her.

"Bullshit. You're as human as we are," Dakota insisted.

"If you're not human, what are you? Androids? Aliens?" McKenna asked.

"We're Immortals. Specifically, Kalili and I are Thirteens, and Avareth is a Prince of Hell."

"Hell's real? Damn, I guess I should've gone to church more," Dakota scoffed.

"Hell's real, but it's nothing like what the churches teach."

Our friends both looked skeptical, and I realized we couldn't prove anything by talking.

I'll demonstrate.

Before Faith could argue, I stood, shed the suitcoat, and concentrated. *Stand back*, I advised my loves. With an effort of will, I pulled my wings from my *taaqat* and summoned them into reality.

"Fuck me." It was as near to a prayer as I'd ever heard from McKenna, with all the reverence usually reserved for meeting a holy person.

I didn't have to look to see my wings; I knew how they appeared. Folded, like they were now, they were about seven feet long, rising a couple feet from my shoulders before dropping down. Extended, they were fifteen feet across, and covered with brilliant white feathers. I didn't think I needed to spread them, judging by my friends' reactions.

"What did you say you are?"

"I'm a Thirteen, and so's Faith."

"Is that—is that like an angel? Because those look like angel wings."

"Sort of. Avy?" I tossed the question to her because she'd spent most of the past seven thousand-plus years learning all she could about what Faith and I were. *Keep it simple, Avy. Don't blow their minds.*

Like your wing trick didn't. "I could go on for hours, but I'll give you the short version, because I really need to talk to my wives. The Thirteens were the original combatants in the battle between Lucifer and the Maker in this universe, and they're the last two. All the others have been destroyed, because when they're together and bonded, they're more powerful than the gods. They have abilities that other Immortals have problems understanding, so I'm not going to waste your time with them all. Essentially, if you think of something, they can probably do it."

See? I can do short. She sounded smug.

McKenna waved a hand. "Are you on the side of good or evil? I mean, she says she's a Prince of Hell, and you've been pretty open about your illegal activities, so I'm guessing evil?"

I shook my head. "No. We're free agents, not bound to either side. Like Avy said, Hell isn't what you think it is." I sighed and sat down on the arm of the chair Faith was in. "Look, it's complicated, okay? The larger point is, we're not human, but we're still your friends."

Dakota and McKenna shared a look. I knew that look; I'd seen it often enough between the three of us. We were telepathic, and humans weren't supposed to be, but I'd been around long enough to know that close pairs, like Dakota and McKenna, could almost read each other's thoughts.

"Do you have wings too?" was Dakota's question to Faith.

"I do, and they're exactly like hers."

"And you? Avareth, right?"

Avy nodded.

"What do your wings look like? You're not a Thirteen, because you said they're the last two of them. You're from Hell, so are you a demon? Bat wings?"

Avy laughed, that low, growly chuckle which meant she was in good humor. "Bat wings on demons is a popular myth. Yes, some demons manifest them, but demons and angels derive from the same stock. They have the same wings. My wings are just like theirs." She pointed at me. "If smaller. And I am a demon."

"Cool."

McKenna grinned. "I've got questions."

Now it was my turn to laugh. "I'm sure you do, but Avy wouldn't have come here if it wasn't important." I tried redirecting her, but McKenna shook her head.

"Just one."

"Fine. But I'm putting my wings away." I pulled them back into my *taaqat* and slipped back into my coat. I wasn't shy about my body, but it was getting chilly.

"Okay, now I have more, but one for now. How long have you been together?"

Faith spoke first. "Kalili, Avy, and I have been together for one thousand one hundred and one years. Kalili and Avy were together before I met them, though."

"Six thousand, two hundred and twelve years, on and off."

Both of their jaws dropped. Dakota recovered first. "I guess the whole 'til death do you part' thing doesn't apply to Immortals. Bet divorce is a bitch and running into your ex at a party. Do you do divorces? Or what?"

"We're not officially married, but our bond is more permanent than any legalism, so yes, we're together pretty much forever." I grabbed the opportunity and pivoted to Avy. "Not that we're not happy to see you, but why are you here?"

Avy looked at me with horror that was reflected in the thought she sent me. *Are you sure you want to talk about this here? Now? In front of them?*

Yes, now. All our cards on the table, Avy.

She sent a mental shrug. *On your head be it.*

Her tone was level, businesslike, as if the words were no more than routine. "An Archangel and Duke of Hell have joined forces. They're coming after you and Faith to eliminate you and restore the Maker and Lucifer to their rightful places."

"Oh, shit."

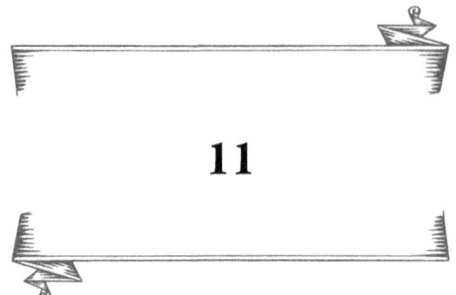

11

"Archangels are real, too?" Dakota didn't squeak; her register didn't go that high any longer. But she was not as calm as she imagined she was.

"They are," Faith agreed absently. "Which Duke?"

"I don't think you know him. Valaferion?"

I searched my memories, but the name didn't connect. "No. Where did he come from?"

"He's been around for ten, maybe twelve thousand years. Created as a demon, he's fought his way upward. Killed Molochar to take the Dukedom. Nasty character, but we thought he was onboard with Lilith's program."

"Molochar? That name's familiar."

"He was one of Mammon's. Old school, ruthless and cunning. He swore allegiance to Lilith when Mammon had his little accident—"

"Time out!" McKenna didn't shout, but her voice cut through our conversation. "It sounds like you've dragged us out of one war into another. That one, I understood, but I'm lost. Lilith?"

I'll explain, Faith volunteered.

Good. I'm still bleeding from writing out the whole story.

"You have to keep an open mind," she began. "Almost everything you think you understand about the gods is wrong."

"Gods? Like, Roman? Norse?"

Never mind, someone else can do it.

Nope, you volunteered.
Fuck.

"Hold on. I'll explain, but you have to give me a chance, okay?" Faith waited until both nodded, then said, "First off, the universe we live in was created by Na'le Vesmiru, and this world was given to her younger brothers, Lucifer and the Maker, so they had a place to play a game. The point of the game is to see who's better, not whether good or evil rules the universe. Human souls are the markers that they use to keep score." Faith paused, looking from McKenna to Dakota and back. "With me so far?"

"I'm wrapping my mind around a trinity of siblings," McKenna admitted.

"Lucifer and God are brothers?"

Faith smiled. "They are. To play the game, they first created the Thirteens."

"Why are you called Thirteens?"

"Nothing clever. Each god had thirteen on their side, and they were supposed to engage in single combat. Whichever side prevailed meant a win for that brother. Unfortunately, the first two Thirteens destroyed each other—"

"Or were destroyed. We still don't know, and nobody's talking," Avy interrupted.

"Right. Think of them like a super-supernova. They destroyed a cluster of galaxies when they went, so Na'le got pissed and told her brothers to break all the pairs."

"Pairs?"

"Yes. See, each pair of Thirteens—call them good and evil, for convenience—were bonded to each other. It was part of the contest, whether their obedience to their side would overcome their natural attraction. A test of free will. If they obeyed, they'd fight to the death. If they disobeyed, they could have overthrown the gods."

McKenna winced. "The gods didn't think this through very well, did they?"

Faith chuckled. "They're not all-wise, no matter what they want you to think. Anyway, Na'le is the oldest, so she got her way. Six from each side were supposed to be killed, breaking all the remaining pairs, but they screwed up. We were a pair, but they didn't kill us. Kalili was hidden by Lucifer, and I was overlooked, somehow. They probably assumed that with my bondmate gone, I was harmless. The Maker created the Archangels to continue the contest, and Lucifer responded with Princes, and it escalated from there. Meanwhile, Kal slept, and I was in a timeless place. I had one job, millions of years ago. You hear of Chicxulub?"

"I think so, back in school. Dinosaur-killer?"

Faith nodded. "That's it. I rode the asteroid that created it. I didn't know that was what I was doing, but I learned." She took my hand, and I squeezed. All these years later she still felt the pain of the lives she had helped wipe out. "Kalili was awakened in 5212 BCE, and that was an accident. Lucifer hid her because he wanted to use her in the final war, but he couldn't tell anyone. All the bureaucrats knew was she was a demon who could be sent to Earth to corrupt humans."

"And that's where I enter the story. Lucifer told Beelzebub, who summoned me and assigned me as Kal's minder. Nobody planned on her falling in love with me, and vice versa," Avy added. "Threw a monkey wrench into everything, eventually."

"Kalili and I nearly met at the Council of Nicaea but missed. In 952, I was sent to Rome with a mission to kill her. I didn't, couldn't, because our bond asserted itself. We spent the next days, weeks, months, running all over Heaven and Hell, trying to learn who we were to each other and what that meant. Along the way, we learned that the Maker is basically sulking and the Archangels were running things. And we helped Lilith overthrow Lucifer, though he's still the official face of Hell. What am I missing?"

"Other religions?" I reminded her.

"Oh! Yes, all the other religions are simply angels and demons playing roles. Neither Lucifer or the Maker were going to give up an advantage in gaining souls, so pretty much everything you've learned is bullshit. Evolution is real, the Big Bang happened, and God *does* play dice with the universe." She dimpled. "We broke free of our obligations, and we've been living on Earth ever since."

"That's what you meant by former employers?" Dakota asked, aghast. "Heaven and Hell?"

"Yes, and that's why I want OutLook, so I have ears on Earth. Makes more sense now, doesn't it?"

McKenna nodded, and Dakota went to the bar. She found a bottle of rum and examined the label. It passed because she opened it and took a healthy drink from the neck.

"And where does Lilith fit into all this?" McKenna hadn't forgotten the original thread.

"Lilith rules Hell."

"I thought that was Lucifer?" Dakota said, sitting next to McKenna and passing her the bottle.

"Officially, yes, but he and I made a deal—"

"A literal deal with the devil?" said McKenna, taking the bottle from her lips. I shrugged.

"It was a busy year. Anyway, Lilith had taken over Hell, and the only way I could fulfill my oath to her was to work out a contract with Lucifer. I had help," I nodded to Avareth, "but we stitched him up good. Lilith runs it, and Faith gave up her Princedom to Avy—"

"I thought she was an angel?"

"I was never an angel, though I was told I was."

"How did you become a Prince, then?"

Faith groaned. "Very long story. To give you the short version, I was in the wrong place at the wrong time and killed Beelzebub before he could kill Kalili. By the rules of Hell, that made me Prince."

"Fuck, that's confusing."

Faith laughed at Dakota's comment. "You think so? Imagine what I felt! There I was, discovering that most of my life was a lie, falling in love with a demon, allying myself with Lilith, and then becoming a ruler of Hell. It was a rough few weeks."

"If we're done with the trip down memory lane?" Avy's acerbic tone snapped me right back to the moment.

"Yeah, we can talk about this later," I agreed.

"Why are they coming after us?" Faith asked Avy. "Valaferion and who else? An Archangel?"

"Seraphina."

Faith winced, and I groaned.

"What?" McKenna looked between us, head swiveling like she was at a tennis match.

"We know her. She didn't take kindly to Ariel's takeover, and wants to go back to the bad old days. Shit." I ran through our handful of encounters with her, cataloging her preferred abilities. Archangels could do almost anything, but like people, they had skills they used more than others. "Why now?"

"They got word you left the City and your warded home. You're vulnerable, or so they think."

"Well, we'll jump to Denver, then jump home." I thought it was an easy solution, but guessing by Avy's reaction, I was wrong. "No?"

"No. This is an opportunity to eliminate them and their followers."

I knew I wasn't the smartest Immortal in the room. I wasn't even the smartest person. But seven thousand years gave me plenty of time to recognize patterns, and I was suitably outraged. "We're *bait*?"

Avy shrugged. "Not bait. Bait implies you're helpless, and I know you're anything but."

"Avareth!" I bellowed. "Two thousand years ago, I would have expected this, but I thought you'd changed!" She'd been the epitome of selfishness for much of the time we were together; only later did I learn it was a defense mechanism, an attempt to hide her growing feelings for me. "This is cold, even for you."

Faith gripped my hand. "Kalili, will you open your mind and shut up?"

I stilled my mouth and listened through our link. Avareth had her thoughts open to us, as we usually did, and I saw her plan. It was nothing like what I assumed.

"Shit. Sorry."

"You've always jumped first, Kal. I expected it."

Dakota's eyes looked like they were about to pop out of her skull.

"Telepathy?"

I nodded. "I mentioned it before. It's a link, a bond between the three of us. I can't read your mind from here, but I can communicate with Avy and Faith across a few miles and feel their presence no matter where they are." I mixed truth with a few omissions, but my friends didn't need to know I was touch-telepathic with them. "No jumping, and we have to lure them out."

Avy nodded. "If I'd known this was happening, I would have told you. As it is, you might want to leave them here." She tilted her head toward Dakota and McKenna.

"What? No!" Dakota's response was vehement.

"No," agreed McKenna. "Faith asked if we trusted her. We did. We still do. Besides, from what you're saying, it sounds like a few demons won't bother you too much."

"Immortal doesn't mean invincible. We can be hurt, even killed. It just takes more than normal efforts."

"Think about it," Faith added. "Overnight. Avy, can you mask our presence?"

Avy thought about it. "If you two damp your auras, I can obscure them."

"All night?"

"I don't have to be in Hell until tomorrow. Yes."

"It's settled." Faith stood, pulling me with her and addressing our friends. "I know you have lots of questions, and this has come at you fast. Think about it tonight, and then we'll answer what we can in the morning. If you choose to come with us, we'll do everything we can to keep you safe. And if you choose to stay, we'll figure out how to get you home."

Dakota and McKenna rose, too, the rum having taken major damage during the discussion. "Sounds fair. Goodnight."

They went to their side of the suite, and we linked hands with Avareth and headed for ours. There was plenty of time to work over details of Avy's plan. For now, a night with our love was an unexpected, and welcome, bonus.

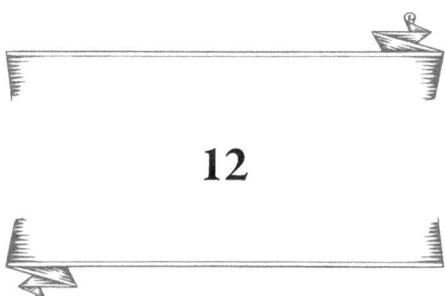

12

As soon as the door closed, I asked the obvious question. "Why isn't Lilith taking care of this? Or Ariel? Or you?"

"Thank you for waiting," Avy said, releasing my hand. "And you could have seen the answer if you'd looked."

"I like talking," I answered. "So?"

Avy started pulling her leathers off. I took that as a sign and undressed as well. "We know who the ringleaders are. Valaferion hasn't been quiet about his displeasure with Lilith's rule, and he's gotten louder since he acceded to the Dukedom. Seraphina, we didn't know about until Valaferion was seen meeting with her in Copenhagen—"

"Wait, Copenhagen?"

"Neutral ground."

"Copenhagen??"

"Not Heaven, not Hell. Yes. You want to hear this?"

"Sorry." I hung up my suit—I might be Immortal, but I appreciated fine clothes—and stretched. It had been a day. "Go on."

"An angel spotted them. He reported to his Principality, who reported to her Archangel, who brought it to Ariel. She rewound time to see for herself, then dragged Lilith upstairs and did it again. Lilith was all for blasting them both into oblivion, but Ariel was more thoughtful and realized they had to have supporters. I agreed, and between us we convinced Lil."

"Unzip me?" asked Faith. While I did that, and she extracted herself from the dress, I asked, "How long has this been going on?"

"A while." It wasn't like Avy to answer vaguely, unless she was trying to evade a tough question.

"How long, Avareth?"

"When was Hitler in power?"

Faith dropped the dress. "Avareth, are you seriously telling us this has been going on for over a hundred years? And you didn't tell us?"

She shrugged. "For a thousand years, you've been adamant you want nothing to do with running either celestial realm, and I've backed you up. Now you complain that we didn't involve you?"

Faith fumed, but I nodded. "Fair point. What have you been doing for the past hundred years, then?"

"Watching them. Tracking their movements, as best we can. Logging who they meet with, especially angels and demons who wouldn't fall under their normal purview. Unfortunately, they're both smart. They've met with thousands of Immortals, and we can't interrogate them all, certainly not without putting the ringleaders wise."

"You waited until they made their move."

Avy nodded, relieved that I was being reasonable. "We think they wanted to try something when you took your trip to Rome, but when Onnirrech's spirit returned and nearly fucked things up, you did the smart thing and yelled for help. Since then, you haven't gone much of anywhere, at least not on Earth, and not without protection."

"No," Faith agreed. "Running into his vengeful spirit was enough excitement for one century. It didn't seem wise to risk a similar encounter."

I shivered. We still didn't know what happened to the soul of the Archangel Gabriel. If he found a way back to this plane, he'd be as motivated as Onnirrech, if not more so, and Onni was only an archdemon. It had taken both of us to cast Onni out for good. Gabriel? Who knew if we could manage it?

"Then what's the plan, Avy?" We were all undressed now and Faith pulled out our nightwear. I pulled on the loose shorts and dropped the cami over my head, while she shimmied into a satin slip. Avy never wore clothes to bed.

"As you observed, you're bait with a serious sting. We'll be watching you the entire time. Czaibrir's got a quire of demons lined up, and Zophiel's arranged for the same number of angels. They'll be here tomorrow, and they'll accompany you, their forces a quick summoning away."

I pondered this as we prepared for bed—human bodies, human needs. Teeth had to be brushed, and so forth.

When we were settled, Faith on my right and Avy on my left, I said, "Avy, how many is a quire?"

"Twenty-five."

"Why didn't you say that?"

"Why use two words when I could use one?"

I rolled my eyes. "You always had to be the smartest one in the room."

"I usually am."

"Quit it, you two," Faith said, but there was no heat in her words. "Let's get some sleep."

"One last question." I felt both heads turn to me. "How are Czaibrir and Zophiel getting around?"

I swear, I felt Avy's grin. "They're driving."

"Oh, shit," Faith muttered.

"Tell me they're not in my Jag."

Silence.

"Avareth?"

More silence.

"This isn't funny, Avareth!"

She finally answered. "What other option did I have? It's not like they can walk into an agency and rent a car. The lack of ID would be the first issue, don't you think?"

I groaned. "Tell me one of them knows how to drive."

Faith answered. "Zophiel does. Remember? When she visited us back in the Thirties? She was taking a vacation and driving around the continent."

I felt a little better. It might have been nearly twenty years ago, but at least it was something. I wasn't sure Czaibrir had ever moved past chariots.

Faith and Avy leaned in from both sides, our lips meeting in the middle, before Avy settled in on one shoulder and Faith on the other. Okay. This made up for a lot of the bullshit.

Bait?

Go to sleep, Kalili.

13

The next morning started well, with unhurried lovemaking before the sun rose. After, cleaned and dressed, we went out into the shared space. I made coffee, and together we sipped and savored the spectacular sight of the Falls coming to life under the long rays of the sun. Reds and oranges danced in the mist before taking on a brilliant rainbow-hued aspect. An hour later, we were still talking, relaxed in our familiarity, when McKenna stumbled out of their side.

"Good morning," Faith said. "There's coffee ready."

"You're an angel," she muttered, then stopped. "I mean, former angel?"

Faith laughed. I felt the source of her amusement and agreed. It was good to be open with them.

"Angel is fine. I identify more with angels, having thought I was one for most of my life."

McKenna yawned and continued to the kitchen. "What's the plan?"

Avy?

"I'm taking the threat seriously—"

"Hey! So are we, but we just learned about it!" I protested.

She ignored me. "I reached out to our allies for support, and two of our friends are on the way here. They won't arrive until later, so you won't have to rush off. There's time to relax. I understand you were going to see the sights?"

McKenna raised a hand. "Back up. When you say friends, you mean…?"

"Immortals," Avy confirmed. "An angel and a demon."

"Like you two?" She waggled a finger between us.

"No," I answered. "Regular angel, regular demon. We're neutral, neither good nor evil, neither angel nor demon. Czaibrir and Zophiel are our friends, and we've trusted them for a thousand years."

I noticed she didn't mention the fifty assorted angelic and demonic warriors who would be riding shotgun. Then I idly wondered how they'd travel, but decided it wasn't my problem and put it aside.

"This is too much before coffee," McKenna muttered, and poured two mugs. "Short version is nothing's happening until later."

"Right," Faith said.

"That's a start. I'll get Dakota out of bed."

"Breakfast in an hour soon enough?"

She grunted, nodded, and kept moving to the other rooms.

"You're cooking?" I asked Faith. She chuckled.

"At home, sure. Here? No way. But there are restaurants."

It was a surreal breakfast. On the surface, everything was normal, a quintet of women out for a meal. Underneath? We danced around our origins and the prospect of our friends being caught in a celestial crossfire, masking our worry behind chatter about the Falls and what we could do this morning.

My nerves were screaming. Then again, I'd never been good with hiding my feelings.

We returned to the suite, and I broke down.

"Are you coming with us or going home?" I demanded, a touch shrill.

"Where? Denver? Of course we are." Dakota sipped her water. "You've always backed our plays, even when they were your idiotic ideas—"

"Hey, my idea brought you two together!"

McKenna took Dakota's hand with a fond smile. "She has a point."

"Which is why we're doing this." She leaned forward and fixed me with as serious a stare as I'd ever received from her. "Kalili, whatever species you are, you're a good person who's been there for us. We're going to be there for you. End of story."

Avareth jumped in. "You know these aren't common criminals and hoods, right?"

I shot her a shocked look. "Hoods? Avy, it's not the 1950s any longer." She waved me off.

"They know what I mean. You can't point a gun at these people and expect them to react."

"She won't let me carry." McKenna jerked a thumb at Dakota. "Got out of the habit."

"Good. When trouble starts, stay out of it. Odds are they won't pay any attention to you, since you're just human. No offense," Avy added quickly. "There are ten billion of you on this world, but individually? You're not much of a threat to an Immortal."

"Duck and cover. I can do that," Dakota said, and McKenna agreed. "But we're coming with you, if for no other reason than I want to hear your stories. No, no, lemme change that; I've heard your stories. I want to hear your truths, Kal."

I winced. "I never lied to you."

With surprising mirth, Dakota laughed. "No, but you didn't tell us the whole truth, did you?"

"No."

I knew that whole 'Tell the truth to my friends' policy would bite your ass, Avy's smugness coming through her thoughts.

Bite me.

Later.

"I had my reasons," I continued, desperate to explain my reasoning. "We're Immortals. That's a pretty big leap for friends, you know."

"And it explains so much," Dakota mused. "Like your building, and why you have a hundred-year-old Jag that looks like it rolled out of the showroom yesterday."

I shook my head. "No magik involved there, just lots of elbow grease and more money for parts than I want to think about."

Faith concurred. "Every week, she washes that car. Sometimes I think she appreciates it more than me," she added with a mock pout.

"Not a chance! But you're much less fragile." I squeezed her shoulders in a side-hug to emphasize my point.

"We're getting off-topic."

I knew that tone. That was Avy's Prince Avareth, Chief of Staff to Lilith tone, the 'Don't fuck with me right now' tone, and it meant her patience was utterly exhausted.

"Sorry, Avy," I said, hoping to deflect most of her pique. "When will Czaibrir and Zophiel arrive?"

"Mid-afternoon. Zophiel's being careful."

I didn't tell her how relieved I was, but she knew.

"Great. Who's up for the Falls?"

McKenna waggled a finger at us. "We're not done talking about this."

"No," Faith agreed. "But it would be a shame to be here and not see them."

Things still unsettled, we got ready to head out and said our farewells to Avy, who was due back in Hell.

"I have a trial today at noon," she said, wrapping me in a hug. "Should be open-and-shut, but the funniest things can happen."

"At least your trials are honest and fair." Faith put her arms around the both of us and we stood, reveling in the contact for a moment. Yes, it had been over a thousand years, but I treasured every touch like it was our first.

"I blame you," Avy said, and Faith giggled.

"I'll accept that." Faith dropped a kiss on Avy's cheek before releasing us. "But I have to book our excursions. Again." She gave Avy an arch look, then turned it on me.

"What? I didn't tell you to cancel!"

"Not in so many words, no. 'Gee, Faith, do you think we ought to be ready to head out first thing?' Sound familiar?"

"And I'm leaving," Avy announced. "I'm not refereeing another one of your arguments."

Before I could protest, she jumped, leaving only the *pop* of inrushing air and a faint trace of her perfume.

I yelled anyway. "Coward!"

It didn't take long to re-do the reservations, despite Faith's grumbles, and we were on our way down to Niagara City Cruises, barely five minutes' walk away.

"Kal."

I turned at Dakota's unusually serious tone. "Yeah?"

"Level with me."

"Always."

She quirked an eyebrow but didn't argue. "How much danger are these—gods, I have a hard time believing I'm saying this! These Immortals. How much of a problem are they?"

I thought hard before answering. Scaring Dakota would be easy; all I had to do was tell her some of the nastier things I'd seen Archangels do in the past. I didn't want to do that, though. Wary, yes. Underestimating an Immortal was never wise. What I needed was the Dakota I'd known for almost forty years: calm, collected, and thinking eight steps ahead of everyone else.

"Individually? Annoying to us, but not a threat, not unless they have some sort of artifact."

"Is that likely?" The penny dropped. "Or that thing we lifted with you! Shit, Kal, that's some sort of magical thing, isn't it?"

I shrugged, thinking of Thakumis' Blade. "They turn up occasionally, and yes, it is, but it's safe in Hell."

Dakota gave me a strangled laugh. "I suppose that's supposed to make me feel better. And Avareth – I know Faith called her your wife, but that's not right, is it? Would partner be better?"

"Partner works. What about Avy?"

Dakota nodded. "She said they were working together, and there are other angels and demons involved, too, so would that make them a threat?"

"Definitely, and that's why we have help coming. If they're smart, well, if they were smart they wouldn't be trying." That pulled a grin from her. "Given that? Their only option is to divide us, get Faith and me separated." How much was too much? In for a penny, I guessed. "We're powerful apart, but when we're together—"

"You're more powerful than the gods. I remember that bit. I know what Avareth said, but I think I'll relax a bit on McKenna carrying. I might even borrow a piece." My shocked look rolled over her. "Most of all, we don't do the horror movie cliché and split up."

I laughed, appreciating her reference. "Exactly. At night, Czaibrir and Zophiel will keep an eye out, so we don't have to sleep in the same room."

Dakota winced. "No, that's not something on my plans. I'm sure you don't want to see two old ladies, either."

I heard the plea beneath her words. "Dakota, I'm seven thousand years old. I don't want to show this body to *you* youngsters!"

"Touche," she said. "Though I hope I look as good as you at that age."

I looped an arm over her shoulders. "If I have anything to say about it, you will." It was an empty promise, but a harmless one. "Come on, they're leaving us behind."

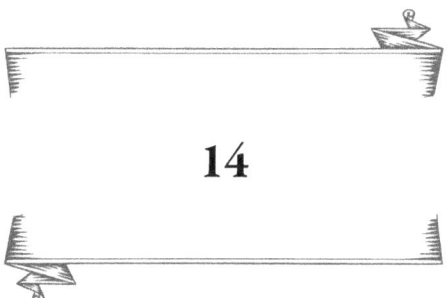

14

We did the behind-the-Falls tour, and the caverns, and the tunnels, before we found the boat that would cruise to the waterfall. In high spirits, possibly inflated by the danger looming over us, we boarded the *Niagara Thunder II*, a sleek catamaran with a glass canopy and open decks below.

There wasn't any hesitation as we headed for the enclosed upper deck. Seeing the Falls was one thing; I wouldn't pass up the opportunity. Getting soaked by the millions of gallons of water that pounded into spray at the base? If I wanted a cold shower, I'd take one, thank you very much.

The upper deck was quiet, which surprised me. I expected the humans to cluster around the best sight without the chance of getting wet.

"It's funny," Faith said, leaning in to kiss my cheek. "I agree, seeing the Falls without getting soaked is preferable. But people are strange. They want the whole experience, and that means water and mist and soaking. I don't understand."

"I think they're trying to take in all of the experience, like Faith said," Dakota added. "Get it from all their senses—touch, taste, smell, sight, sound. Immerse themselves in it. This thing ain't cheap, y'know. Most people won't be able to do it more than once in their lives."

McKenna shook her head. "No, you're wrong. They want to act like they're three again and splash in puddles."

Dakota laughed, and we joined it, even though I felt Faith's confusion.

I don't get it either. Humans are weird.

We separated, with Dakota and McKenna surprising us by joining the throng on the open deck, while Faith and I stayed behind – and dry. There were probably another two dozen people milling about, waiting for the boat to position itself for the best view, so we found a quiet corner to relax, and I went in search of coffee. It had been a long, stressful couple of days, and I needed the caffeine. Faith stuck to a caramel latte, having had a sweet tooth for centuries. I brought them to the table she'd secured and passed hers over. She gestured to mine.

"What's that?"

"An Amy's Jet Fuel."

"A what?"

I sniffed the steam rising from the cup and grinned. "Remember a few years ago, when we went to Carlsbad for a visit?"

"We visit so many places," Faith said, her face adorably scrunched in concentration.

"The coffee shop with the cute name and the gorgeous owner?"

"Maybe?"

"Taste this." I passed it over. Faith wrinkled her nose but sipped. Her face transformed from mild curiosity to disgust as the hot, bitter liquid filled her mouth.

"What the fuck?"

I took the cup back before she could fling it. "That, love, is four shots of espresso added to a tall black." Pleased, I drained half of it. "Just what I need."

"Kalili Keoka, you're absolutely insane." She took a pull of her own to rinse the taste of mine away.

"You love me anyway."

"Sometimes I wonder why."

As I opened my mouth to answer, a meaty hand gripped my shoulder and squeezed.

"Ow! What the—" I was out of my chair, gripping the offending wrist, before I finished my exclamation. He didn't release me, and we stood there for a frozen second.

"So. You're a Thirteen. Not as tough as I thought you'd be."

A chill tingled through every nerve. Two humans knew what a Thirteen was, and even though I wasn't getting an aura...

"And you're an idiot," I hissed, furious. "Hell doesn't look kindly on demons making a scene in front of humans."

He squeezed harder. "Demon? I think not."

"Then you're doubly a fool," Faith said, a quiet edge to her voice that screamed danger to me but meekness to others. "Heaven is even less forgiving."

"Quiet. Others will deal with you."

It was time to refocus his attention. "You don't want to make this harder than it has to be." I still couldn't see his aura or read his thoughts, so he'd come prepared to conceal his identity. I could break through, given time, but I didn't need to. This wasn't a random encounter with a disgruntled Immortal. This was an ambush.

"You want to let go. Don't hurt my demon."

My grin returned. That was Faith's edge-of-mayhem voice.

"Really, I'd listen to her," I advised. "Leave now, and you get to keep your hand."

He laughed evilly, then moved, faster than I expected. A blade appeared in his free hand and I had a flash of silver before he slammed it into my chest, scraping my ribs as he sought my body's heart. His aim sucked, but it still hurt. Except for one mishap a few months back, I hadn't been in hand-to-hand combat in years, but I'd fought with blades for millennia. The old, familiar steps came back quickly.

"You missed." He'd nicked a lung and my words came out in a rasp. I dropped his wrist and backed off, the knife pulled from my chest with another burst of agony. Closing with a blade-wielder was never wise, not when I couldn't use my flashier abilities.

I didn't need them.

"I won't this time." He slashed at me, and despite his bravado, missed badly.

Watch my back!

I'm cloaking us. No need for humans to see this.

Good. I'd forgotten about the people; getting stabbed will do that to a girl.

"Last chance," I gasped, with a burble. I'd have to fix that, but first? Dealing with this asshole. "I'm not known for my mercy, but I'm on vacation. Fuck off, and I'll forget this until we meet again. Then I'll take it out of your skin."

He slashed again and scored, catching my collarbone. I think he was aiming for my neck, but he was out of practice. Angels didn't go in for personal combat.

I did, or had. And I fought dirty.

Thakumis' Blade, one of the wing feathers of a fallen Prince of Hell transmuted into metal, was in its usual place on my belt. I drew it, hearing the echo of Thakumis' personality whisper of blood and pain in my mind. After so many centuries I was used to it. I snarled a mental "Shut up" at it and fell into a fighting stance.

The angel smirked. "You think to threaten me with a feather?"

"Run away, little angel, and tell your boss to send someone competent next time." Why wouldn't this asshole listen? Goddess, these holier-than-thou morons really had their heads screwed on too tight!

He lunged, nearly catching me off-guard. Nearly. I lurched to the side. As I wobbled, my hand flashed out, the Blade barely scraping the skin of his wrist.

"I'm sorry," I said after I'd recovered my balance.

"This won't stop—" His voice cut off with a strangled gurgle, which morphed into a wail that ended abruptly. A hand clamped over the injured wrist. "What—did you—do?" he grated.

"Killed you. Who were you?"

He dropped to his knees. Under his palm, I saw the telltale red and gold fissures spread up his wrist. It was a small injury so it would take longer, but Thakumis would claim another victim.

"S-Sariel."

Faith turned away from the people and repeated the words I'd first heard in our first weeks. "Sariel, *eithe iii psyche sas nha anapauthei.*" *May your soul rest in peace.*

"Stop fighting it and it will be over faster," I advised him. I didn't know if it was true, but I hoped it was, and that he could find his peace sooner. I sheathed the dammed Blade and staggered to Faith's side. She wrapped an arm around my waist, holding me up, as we watched.

It was a horrible process, but Sariel endured it with surprising grace. We'd seen it many times, and each time I was fascinated by the beauty that emerged from the pain. It was a paradox I'd never wanted to explore, but the reddish chasms, rimmed in gold, that opened along an angel's flesh as they were consumed? Spectacular, and a sight I sincerely wished I'd never see again, every fucking time.

The process sped up as Sariel listened to me, releasing his hold on this world, and allowed the dark magik to consume him. There was a final blast of red-gold light, and when it faded, he was gone, as if he'd never existed.

"Stupid fucker," I muttered, doubly miserable from the waste of his life and the pain in my side. "Are we still covered?"

I thought we were—no humans were gawking—but it didn't hurt to ask.

"We are." Faith guided me back to the seat. Conversationally, she added, "Your top's ruined."

I groaned. "And I liked this one, too. Got it back in '31." I turned my attention inward, directing my *taaqat* to heal my injuries.

"I'll get you a sweatshirt," Faith said when I opened my eyes again, and I couldn't miss the dimple. She was pleased with herself, despite the situation.

"I'll never hear the end of it." My grousing was staged. Mostly.

Faith walked off, not hurrying but not dallying, leaving me with a bigger challenge: getting out of this and letting Avy know. Fortunately, Avy had joined the 21st Century and had a mobile. Don't ask me how it worked in Hell; there may have been Immortal intervention to allow the signal to pass through Realms.

She picked up on the third ring. "Kal? What's wrong?"

"Why do you assume something's wrong?"

"Because if it wasn't, you'd message me."

She had me there. "Fine. I was just attacked by an angel. Sariel."

I heard her sigh. "Where are you?"

"On the Falls boat. *Niagara Thunder II*. Somewhere in the river."

I heard a muffled conversation. Obviously, Avy had covered the mic with her hand, but I could hear another voice raised in, what? Anger? Frustration?

"Hold on." Avy's voice, but still muffled. I huffed out an irritated breath, then winced. Right. Injury healing, not healed yet.

"Kalili, what's going on?"

I'd been free of my celestial masters for eleven hundred years, but I still reacted to Lilith's voice like I had for thousands of years. That she ran Hell now reinforced my reaction, even if I was a free agent, bound to her only by mutual agreement.

"Nothing we can't handle, Lil." I used her nickname when I wanted to irritate her. Childish, maybe, but her hissed breath told me I scored.

"Then why is Avy about to—no, she's gone."

There was a soft *bamf* as Avareth appeared a few feet away.

"Sorry, Lil, gotta run. Someone's just dropped in." I hung up and turned. Avy was scowling.

"Where's Faith?"

"Getting me a sweatshirt." I gestured at my ruined top, bloodstained and torn. "Asshole deserved to die for his crime against classic fashion."

Avy relaxed, but I could read the tension in her body. "How did he get close enough to do this?"

I was immediately defensive. "I wasn't expecting an attack out here, and not in front of human witnesses." I softened my tone. "I got sloppy."

She sighed. "Same old Kal, relying on luck instead of planning ahead."

I bristled. "Hey, I got us out of the City before it went to hell, didn't I?" The news reports over the past twenty-four hours told me we left in the nick of time. The Bronx was more of a war zone than usual, and the current front line was centered around New Rochelle. The Empire was squawking, but neither the States nor the Collective were listening. I wondered how long it would be before the moneymen tired of the loss of profit?

"That's different. They're just humans, with human weapons. You could have withstood them far better than a celestial death squad."

I snorted. "You weren't this concerned yesterday."

"Yesterday, you hadn't been stabbed by an angel."

She had a point. "What do we do?"

"I'd like you to wait for our friends and their troops, but I don't think we have time. You have to leave, as soon as you can."

A scowl crossed my face. "Won't be easy, but once we dock—"

She shook her head. "Now."

"Now?" I waved at the scenery. "We're in the middle of the fucking Niagara River, Avy!"

"Keep your voice down," she hissed.

"River, Avy. The Jeep's on shore, and—oh." The penny dropped. "Jump with humans? Can they survive it?"

"Can they survive another assassination attempt? Next time, they might be closer."

I hadn't thought of that, but Avy wasn't done.

"Where are they?" she added, scanning the crowd.

"On the deck, getting the full experience."

"Getting wet, you mean," Faith commented, resting her hand on Avy's shoulder. "Avy."

"Faith." Avy laid her hand atop Faith's and squeezed.

"Your sweatshirt." She tossed a bright pink bundle of cloth at me.

"You're shitting me."

The grin told me she wasn't.

"It was this or a purple hoodie that said, 'I got wet at Niagara Falls.'"

I shuddered. "This is fine. Are we still masked?" Without waiting for her answer, I stripped off my ruined shirt. "Damn. I have to clean up." Blood covered my front, drying against my skin. I shrugged back into the shirt, since it was already trash.

The washroom was mercifully vacant. Faith stood guard outside while I cleaned, Avy inspecting my work when I finished. Faith went in search of our friends while Avy and I headed back to the table. I downed the last mouthful of coffee. I suspected I'd need it.

"You'll do," she said, dabbing at a spot I'd missed. "You'd feel better after a shower, but you don't have time."

"Listen, Avy, you can't be serious. Jump Dakota and McKenna? We can't wait to dock?" I checked the time. "We should be tied up in forty minutes or so."

"Then everyone has to queue up to get off, then through the gift shop, up the hill to the exit, across to the hotel, pack, and down to the Jeep." She shook her head. "First, we don't know if the angel—"

"Sariel," I supplied.

"Sariel. We don't know if he was the only one here. Crowds are a great place for an ambush, Kalili. Second, if he was the only one, how long until one of the rebels notices he hasn't come back? They're not stupid; they've kept themselves out of our eye for decades. Whether that means they're smart about their tactics is something else, but I'm not willing to bet your safety. Are you?"

When she put it like that? "No."

"Good. We'll find a quiet corner where Faith can meet us—"

I'm already on my way. Dakota was complaining about the wet.

I grinned despite it all, imagining her expression.

"—and we'll get off this tub."

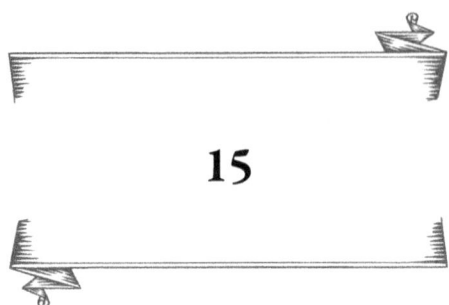

15

"We're gonna what?"

I played my trump card. "You trust us."

"Of course."

"Then shut up and take my hand."

We'd found a room, or compartment as McKenna had informed me, which was available. Well, maybe not technically *available*; the sign with 'Do Not Enter' in unfriendly red letters was a hint, as was the locked handle. But I'd never cared about signage, McKenna dealt with the lock in short order, and we were in. Guessing from the décor, it was a VIP excursion room. All that mattered was it was empty.

"I—fine."

I clamped down on my misgivings. Jumping—instantaneous translation from one point in space-time to another and across Realms—was as natural to us now as flying. Jumping with another Immortal was commonplace. But Jumping a human?

Unprecedented.

Avy had advice for me. Of course. *Keep your barriers up. Don't let them in your mind.*

Why not?

You want them roaming around in there?

Point. Won't I need to keep them calm?

They'll be fine, Avy's mental whisper assured me.

You don't know that! Faith shot back.

I felt Avy's hackles rise and stepped in. Our triad had survived countless trials, but there were still spots of contention.

We'll make it work, I thought with more conviction than I felt. *Game faces.*

In the instant it took to quash the argument, McKenna's hand slid into mine. "I never thought you'd come between me and Dakota," she joked. It was weak, but I chuckled.

"I'm honored to be the woman who could."

Dakota punched my shoulder on the other side before taking that hand. "You know, Kal, you've always been a brat."

"Hey!" I kept my barriers well-erected, resisting the impulse to peer into either human mind.

"I like you, Dakota," Avy said with a wicked grin. She held Dakota's left hand, Faith held McKenna's right, and they closed the circle with their clasped hands across from me.

"Thank you?"

"Knock it off. I need to concentrate." I closed my eyes, visualizing our suite.

You're cute when you try to be commanding. Ooh, now your face matches your sweatshirt! Faith teased.

"Do we have to do anything?"

"Don't panic and don't let go." Without looking, I knew Dakota was fixing me with a look of extreme dissatisfaction, so I added, "We do this all the time, but it's scary if you're unprepared." I grimaced. "Scared the shit out of me the first time I jumped solo. Here we go."

Before anyone could react to my little bombshell, I reached into nothingness and twisted.

Tandem jumping was more challenging than a regular jump, but Faith and I had done it often enough that we'd learned how to deal with it. We'd jumped with Avy a few times; more important, they both knew what to expect.

In the void between, time passes differently—an instant outside can be minutes, or years, to the mind within. The senses don't work, because your body isn't any more than your memories of it. It's terrifying and perfectly safe, while you're within. Exiting has its own risks, but as long as you knew your destination, you'd be fine. I knew this as surely as I know anything.

Dakota and McKenna didn't. I heard their screams in my mind despite the barriers I'd erected. Dropping my defenses, I extended my mind to theirs, calming their fears as best I could.

We're safe, I promise.

Kalili?

It's me. Hold on. We're getting there.

Where are we? Oh my God, McKenna? I can—

Right, I know!

Panic turned to amazement as their personalities, separated by flesh all their existence, flowed and merged. Their joy was almost physical as they experienced what my triad knew.

There's going to be repercussions, Avy said.

It was that or let them panic and drag us into nothingness, I returned. *I'll deal with repercussions.*

I felt Avy mentally wash her hands of the situation, but then we were approaching the exit and I turned my attention outward. I sensed the suite. In the instant we were closest, I twisted again and wrenched us out of the between. Our minds remembered what our bodies were, and reconstructed them.

"That was fucked up," McKenna wheezed when she'd filled her lungs. "Okay, yeah, and fun, like the world's worst rollercoaster." She spun and stared at Dakota. "Hold on. Did you say that?"

"I thought it, but I don't think I said it." Dakota's tone was full of uncertainty.

"I didn't hear anything," Faith added helpfully.

"Then how did she know what I thought? I don't think it's because we've been married so long."

I told you not to open your mind to them!

What the fuck was I going to do, Avy? Let them panic between and drag us into oblivion? This was your idea, remember?

She didn't have a good answer for that.

"Can we pack and get out of here?" Trust Faith to defuse everything and get us back on track. "Avy, help us. Get a luggage rack."

The next fifteen minutes were hectic. Bandit resented being stuffed back in her travel crate, but Dakota soothed her with a pinch of catnip and we were all forgiven.

"Do you want me to drop off the keys?" I asked, but Avy shook her head.

"No. Don't even check out. Just leave. I don't know how much these Immortals know about Earthly ways, but the demons probably use human agents, and they'll check the hotel registries to see where you are. If they waste time doing that, they may think you've holed up in the suite and wait for you to come out."

"Smart," agreed Dakota. "Gives us a head start. We're ready." She dropped a bag on the cart.

With a little help from McKenna, bypassing security on the service elevator, we got to the parking garage and the Jeep without difficulty. Avy gave us each a kiss, then said, "I'll watch your back while you hit the road. Once Zophiel gets here, I'll pop out, catch up with things in Hell, and reunite with you tonight." She popped out.

"That's still damn odd."

"You'll get used to it," I assured Dakota. "Now that you know what we are, we don't have to hide things from you two."

"That's a good question. Wait—Mac, I heard you in my head again!"

I ignored the amazed byplay and concentrated on getting us on the road. "Faith, where am I going?"

She checked her phone. "Get on the 430 to Queen Elizabeth Way. That leads to the 406, and we'll take that to Hamilton. Ought to be pretty easy, then we have to decide if we cross back into the US in Detroit, Port Huron, or somewhere between."

I groaned. "Anywhere but Detroit. Remember '67?"

"I hope you mean 1967." Dakota shook her head. "I'm still wrapping my mind around the thought that you're thousands of years old. You look like you're twenty-five!"

"And what did you do to us?" McKenna added.

"What do you mean?" Faith asked, but I had a sneaking suspicion I knew.

McKenna waggled a finger between herself and her wife. "She's in my head, and I'm in hers. We're good at figuring out what the other is thinking, but now? I *know*, and so does she. Explain."

Shit.

This is what Avy was warning us about.

You think?

At least they can't read our minds, Faith added in consolation.

So not what I needed!

Time for as much truth as I had. "I don't have an explanation. Avareth told me not to open your minds to mine without telling me why. When you panicked—"

"I was not panicking!"

"Dakota, you kind of were," McKenna said, gently.

I ignored the interruption and spoke over my shoulder. "—I had to do something to calm things, or we could have lost our destination. That would have been bad."

"Can't you just go back?"

Faith stepped in, having studied jumps more than me. "No. It's not like a highway, where you can get off at the next exit. You enter between with a singular destination, and your mind carries you there. If your focus wavers, if the destination is unclear, you don't emerge."

"Oh."

I took over again. "Like I said: bad. So I did what Avy told me not to do, which was connect with your minds."

"I think, sorry, unintentional." We all groaned at Faith's terrible pun. "When Kalili made the connection, she awakened an ability in you. What I don't understand is why it didn't fade when we left the between."

"Maybe it will fade in time?"

"Mac, I don't want it to!"

I tuned out the good-natured bickering as Dakota and McKenna debated the pros and cons of their limited telepathy, concentrating on the road. It wasn't as challenging as City traffic, and the Canadian drivers tended to avoid me when they caught sight of my Empire plates, but it was unfamiliar territory.

Faith clasped my hand, her fingers intertwining with mine, and our thoughts merged.

Clever angel.

What do we do?

Get to Denver and hope this war ends soon.

I mean about our friends! Faith didn't hide her exasperation.

Do we need to do anything? Before she could form her objection, I rolled on. *I don't know how long either of them have, but they're so in love, why shouldn't they have this kind of connection?*

Because...

I waited.

I was going to say, 'Because it's not the way the Maker designed them,' but that doesn't matter, does it?

When have I paid attention to what the Maker wanted?

True. Faith's voice fell silent, and I concentrated on navigating traffic. *I guess there's no reason, except it will hurt more when one of them finally dies.*

Compared to the joy they have now? A price I think they'd pay. I hinted at Faith, and she turned enough to see Dakota and McKenna. They were like two teenagers, eyes agleam and faces beaming.

You always did know people better than me.

We drove down the road in silence.

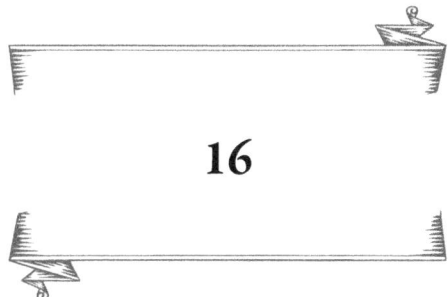

16

"Where are we?"

"Canada. Ouch!" I exclaimed as Dakota smacked the back of my head. "Faith?"

"London, or nearly."

"We didn't cross an ocean," I said, adding a plaintive note of confusion to my voice. "Ouch!"

Faith withdrew her hand. "Idiot."

"Your idiot."

"London, Ontario. We've made good time."

We'd been on the highway for two hours, and I'd pushed our Jeep as hard as I dared, ignoring the speed limits.

"Need a break?"

"I don't know if it matters to you immortal beings, but us humans need to eat occasionally."

I opened my mouth to explain that we ate when in human bodies, but Faith clapped a hand over my mouth.

"Food is a good idea. I could stretch my legs."

I took the hint and found a restaurant off the highway that didn't look like it would cause immediate food poisoning. The meal was full of chatter, but it was the gossipy stuff I was used to with them. Nothing about vengeful angels and demons, nothing about interdimensional jumping, nothing about our true identities.

It worried me.

Finally, I couldn't take another second of it.

"How are you coping with this so well?" I demanded.

Dakota and McKenna shared a look, and probably some thoughts, before McKenna answered.

"Kal, I've known you forty years. You've done some stupid shit, some crazy shit, and some brilliant shit, often at the same time. Telling us—no, proving to us you're some sort of immortal being? At this point, nothing surprises me."

"Yeah, I'll bet you'll tell us that you're friends with Lucifer next," added Dakota.

"I wouldn't say we're friends. Guarded respect, maybe. It helps that I killed him once."

"You what?"

Whoops. I stalled. "Let's get where we can't be overheard."

Back on the road, I gave them the story of my moment of insanity with Lucifer. I'd intended to give them bare bones, but they knew me too well and kept at me. Dakota would ask a question, which I'd answer as briefly as I could, but that gave McKenna an opening. She'd jump in, wanting me to clarify a detail, and then Dakota would follow up.

You're not as good at lying as you used to be.

Bad habit picked up from an angel, I snarled back at Faith, and immediately regretted it.

You could tell the truth. For better or worse, they're here, and they're not letting go. Just tell them.

"Let me start over."

I ran through the tale from the beginning, this time leaving in all the details—including Avy and Faith's body switch, which led to a discussion on shapeshifting. Faith led that part of the discussion, as I navigated the traffic and got us back on the right road after missing the turn north.

North?

Damn right. No way was I driving through Chatham-Kent, let alone the hellhole known as Detroit. No, I'd take our chances crossing into the Northern Imperium at Port Huron. That meant rolling on the 402, not the 401 as I'd put us on. Navigating the cross-roads to get us heading in the proper direction was a pain in the ass, complicated by my passengers' utter faith in my abilities.

Which might be why the car that rammed us came as a surprise.

The window on my side shattered, Faith screamed, Dakota cursed, and I wrestled with the steering, bringing the Jeep back under control and swerving into the attacker.

Yes, into.

Six thousand years as a demon taught me to hit back harder. A thousand-plus years as a Thirteen hadn't washed away those instincts.

The screech of tortured metal and the shaking of the wheel told me I'd hit them hard. My knuckles went white as I locked my arms in place, keeping us on the road, while I scanned for whoever hit us. A dirty brown pickup was wobbling to my left, front quarter smashed and the passenger door crumpled.

"I can't get a bead on them!" shouted McKenna.

Guns. I'd forgotten that McKenna regularly went around armed. It made sense she wouldn't drop the habit just because she was in another country.

"Keep an eye on them," I yelled over the din, mashing the accelerator. "I'd rather not fight them on the road."

We were on 11, between the Oneida and Chippewa territories, passing through fields. Whoever ambushed us planned it well, or maybe they took advantage of the isolation. Either way, it was four kilometers to 2 and the next turnoff. I glanced at the nav screen to confirm my location.

Unless...

This was either genius or idiocy. I slapped the control that activated the all-wheel drive and jerked the wheel to the right. The tires protested but grabbed, and we rattled in our seats as I crossed over the shoulder onto the scrub.

"Where are we going?" shouted Faith over the sudden racket.

"Across!" I nearly took a hand from the wheel to point, but thought better of it.

"Across what?"

"The river!"

She abandoned speech and jumped into my head.

Across the river? Are you crazier than usual?

I let her roam my mind to examine what I generously called a plan while I concentrated on driving. The Jeep didn't have many issues with the flat, marshy plain, but I felt the ground clutching at the wheels. The Conqueror wasn't a light vehicle, and the additions we'd made pushed it over seven thousand pounds. I had the feeling if I slowed, we'd sink into the muddy surface.

I hope you know what you're doing.

Don't I always?

No.

A smile crept across my lips despite the situation. Ah, she knew me so well.

A peek in the mirrors relieved my mind, but I didn't let up on the gas. The truck had stopped, still on the blacktop, and two figures were climbing out. I couldn't make out details, and they were getting more distant by the second, so I put them out of my mind. If we forded the river, we'd be a few hundred feet from a road that would get us back on track.

"Buckle up—no, unbuckle," I corrected. "If we have to bail out, we don't want to be slowed down."

"Kal, there are trees ahead."

I didn't need Dakota's warning; I could see them quite well, thank-you-very-much.

"You're not slowing down."

Again with the obvious statement. "No. If I slow down, we won't make it across the river."

"This better be a small damn river," I heard McKenna mutter. Then, louder, "Faith? You wanna check this out?"

I was equal parts impressed and torn. Impressed that McKenna didn't want to break my concentration again. Torn because I needed to know what she saw, and though I could peek into her mind now, it went against the code of conduct Faith and I had built up over the last eleven centuries.

The code won out. Faith released her belt and turned.

"Where? Oh, shit." She dropped back into the seat.

"What?"

She said one word. "Demons."

My mind raced in a million directions. How did she know? Okay, I knew that answer: we could read auras if we tried. That still left lots of unanswered questions. How had they found us? Why had they rammed us with a truck? Why didn't we pick up on their auras sooner?

Faith was more clearheaded. She opened the moonroof, which slid back into the recessed pocket over the cargo compartment, and climbed into the back. She knelt between the seats and asked our friends to hold her legs. They must've agreed, because her body rose and blocked my view of the mirror.

I felt Faith draw on the *kosmiskorka*, celestial energies, through our bond, and knew what she was going to do. As Thirteens, we had abilities beyond those of other Immortals. One was a controlled form of *kosmiskorka*, called *vashwic urja*, that sent blasts or streams of power into whatever we targeted.

Worked a treat on vampires. Immortals were more resistant, but eventually would succumb.

"You've got about fifteen seconds before we hit the trees!" I shouted.

"No problem!" she shouted back. I felt her release the blasts, paired with the gasps from Dakota and McKenna, and allowed myself an indulgence. I looked through Faith's eyes.

The demons were flying, beating the air hard to catch up to us, and that made them easy targets. One caught the *vashwic urja* squarely in the chest and dropped forty feet to the ground. The other was less lucky, and had a wing sheared by Faith's blast. He tumbled out of the sky, bounced, bounced again, and then slammed into something, a rock or tree stump, she couldn't see.

Whatever it was, he was done for a while, even if he survived. Wings didn't grow back.

I returned to my head, gratified to note we hadn't reached the treeline yet, and made another snap decision.

"Faith, get back in!"

She dropped between our friends and wrapped an arm around each of their shoulders. She saw what I was about to do.

"Sorry." I muttered an apology to the Jeep. I'd have to do something nice for it when this was all over, after this abuse. Then I wrenched the wheel around again and willed more power out of the motors, hoping that gravity and inertia would give us a pass, just this once, and not roll us.

Physics can be flexible, if you know how to manipulate reality.

I wasn't up to that level in my studies yet. According to Ariel, our favorite Archangel, Thirteens could do it, but we'd yet to discover how. Since the only example we knew of—the first pair of Thirteens—ended their existence in a mind-mangling explosion that wiped out several galaxies, fucking around and finding out wasn't in the cards.

I had to rely on Newton, with an assist from some very sticky mud.

I think it was the mud, more than the musings of a surprisingly intense alchemist, that saved our asses.

"You're going back?" It might have been McKenna, but the words were screamed, not spoken.

"I want answers," I growled, straightening out and heading for the injured demon.

"You're insane." Ah. Not McKenna, then.

"You've known me how long, Dakota?"

"And you never fail to surprise me, Kal."

I grinned, though she couldn't see, and slowed. Faith rose from the seat to peer out the open roof.

He's not moving.

I didn't have to tell her to keep him covered; I felt the *kosmiskorka* pulled into her again. I braked to a stop a dozen yards away. Even uninjured, he'd have a hard time reaching us before Faith could blast him into atoms. I turned to the back.

"Stay here."

For once, neither argued with me.

I wished for a sword.

I was familiar with most of the weapons humanity had crafted over the centuries, capable with many, and expert with two: swords and daggers. The idea of sharpening a length of metal and wielding it against another person? Genius, from the perspective of a demon. I could see the horror in the eyes of my victims, the realization that they'd lost and would die, as my blade sank into their guts. Their panicked eyes revealed the state of their soul to anyone with the skill to read them, and I learned quickly.

But I didn't have a sword. I didn't even have Thakumis' Blade. That piece of evil was tucked away in my handbag because I didn't expect to need it driving through freaking *Ontario!* Neither did I have the sanctified blade Faith gave me years ago; that was packed. I vowed to never, ever, *ever* be so unprepared again.

That wouldn't help me now, though, so I fell back on intimidation. When I was a few yards away, I stopped. The demon's injury didn't bleed; *vashwic urja* cauterized when it didn't kill.

"Who are you?"

I was certain he was alive; his aura, red and bronze and streaked with black, flickered and hummed. But he decided to play dumb, or dead, figuring that I was just human and couldn't see his aura.

"Dumbass, get up. I know you're playing. Or should I finish you off?"

He lunged, off-balance but quick, face twisted into a mask of contempt. A half-strength bolt of *vashwic urja* put him on his ass, and I smirked.

"You want to try this again, without the mindless violence?" He groaned, which was more than I'd gotten before, so I stepped closer.

I still wished for a blade.

"Who. Are. You?"

"Valefar." His voice was like ground glass, though I didn't know if that was natural, by choice, or by injury. The name didn't help, either. It was the demonic equivalent of Richard, or James.

"Who is your archdemon?"

He was more reluctant, but my continued glare extracted a snarled, "Lioraeth."

She was bad news. Most demons and archdemons under Lilith's rule and Avareth's oversight had given up evil for evil's sake. Not Lioraeth. She enjoyed causing pain, whether directly in combat or indirectly through her minions. I just hoped this didn't mean what I feared it did.

I had to ask.

"Does she know you're here?"

He laughed, or maybe he coughed. It was hard to tell.

"Know? Bitch, she sent me."

I closed my eyes, wondering again why this was happening now.

Kal!

Faith's mental shout pulled my attention back. I dove left, seeing Valefar's latest attempt through Faith's eyes before opening mine on the roll. Unlike me, he'd brought a blade to the knife fight and had it in his left hand. His right arm hung loose by his side, probably broken in the drop from the sky. Stupid. Immortals could heal most injuries, and he was handicapped enough with a missing wing. One-armed was inviting disaster.

I wasn't going to count on him staying stupid, though.

I concentrated, summoning my connection to the *kosmiskorka*, then clenched my left fist. He froze in place.

"Stupid," I said for his benefit. "You can hang out there while we decide what to do with you." A rustling behind me caught my attention.

My fist still clenched, I turned to the Jeep, then shouted. "What part of "stay here" didn't you understand?"

"We thought you might need help," Dakota answered. She had a set of brass knuckles on both hands, and McKenna had her pistol out, leveled in a proper two-handed grip.

"Yeah, no. This is Immortal shit." I spared Valefar a glance, then turned fully to my friends. "You could get killed out here."

"And sometimes an iron is what you need to calm things the fuck down," McKenna retorted. She gestured with the barrel. "What did you do?"

"*Kaalijaya*. Time freeze. Immortal shit," I repeated, then relented. "We can lock a moment in time for as long as we want if we keep our fist closed." I waved my hand at them. "It's like hitting pause on a movie."

McKenna stopped, listening, but Dakota had continued ahead and prowled around the suspended demon. "Why doesn't he have a tail? Or horns? Or is that all bullshit, too?"

"Trust me, he's a demon. Bodies don't matter; it's what the mind and soul do that makes an Immortal good or evil." I ran though our options. Take him with us? While I wouldn't mind seeing him used as Bandit's scratching post, I couldn't keep him like this forever. Kill him? It was always an option, and spilling blood didn't make me squeamish, but I hated to waste resources. He had information we needed.

There was only one choice.

I agree, Faith thought.

A lifetime ago, when I was one of Lilith's favored demons, she'd created a connection between us. At first, I'd taken it as a badge of honor. I was young and naïve, flattered by the attention the Mistress of Hell showered on a newly awakened demon. It wasn't until well after we'd been revealed as Thirteens that I'd figured it out. Lilith knew I was a Thirteen, or at least suspected, and wanted to keep track of me. She couldn't read me, not like I could read Faith, but she knew my general state.

What did I get out of it? After all, one of the first things a new demon learned was to ask, "What's in it for me?"

I could signal Lilith. I'd say summon her, and maybe it was true now, but it was more of a request when I thought I was a lowly demon. The drawback was if Lilith didn't find my reason for calling her suitable, I'd owe her a favor. I hated owing her, because she preferred to store her favors away, cashing them all in at once. Still, this might be interesting enough so she'd let me slide...

I tapped it now.

This took a fraction of a second, not enough for the humans to notice.

"What do we do now?" McKenna waggled the pistol. "I can cover you if you want to let him out of the bubble or whatever it is."

"I'm good," I assured her, touched by her gesture. "How good are you with that thing?"

"Once upon a time I was rated expert by the USMC, and I've kept it up ever since."

"She placed first in her group in the all-Empire competition last year," Dakota added, pride in her wife plain in her voice.

"Wait. You were a Marine?" I shook my head. "You think you know a person..."

"Yeah, I'll tell you later." She waggled the pistol again. "So?"

I opened my mouth, then clapped it closed. I still didn't know if it was a skill particular to Thirteens, or something specific to me, but I could detect the approach of a few Immortals. Lilith was one of them, and it gave me a few seconds to prepare.

"No need. Don't shoot," I added. This was going to be good.

"What?"

"Don't shoot," I repeated, as a soft *pop* sounded.

"Where in the realms did you drag me this time, Kalili?" The voice was seduction made sound, and her scent reinforced it. That was ignoring her body, which was always alluring, no matter which form she'd chosen to wear. I was more interested in my friends' reaction.

Dakota looked like she'd had about five too many of her bar's signature cocktails. McKenna wasn't much better off, eyes wide, mouth slightly agape. Both women inhaled deeply, then did it again. Dakota recovered first.

"Wh-who is that?" She took an involuntary step forward.

"That's Lilith. You might have heard of her?" I hesitated a heartbeat before adding, "Mistress of Hell? First wife of Adam?"

Lilith snorted. "That's a lie. I never knew Adam, mostly because he didn't exist."

I didn't let her interruption derail me. "These days, she runs Hell, and she's a friend of ours. Lilith, this is Dakota and her wife, McKenna. We go way back."

"A pleasure." She turned to me. "Where are we, and why did you call me?"

"Ontario, and you're here because of him." I waved at the frozen demon. My fingers were starting to ache. Lilith crossed the distance in a few steps.

"Interesting. Your work?" she asked, peering at the wing stump.

"Mine," Faith said.

"Very precise. Who is he?"

"Valefar, and we think he's part of a plot to eliminate us."

"Another one?" Her tone made her disbelief plain, but I didn't have time to explain.

"Ask Avy. Can you take him and the other one back to Hell and see what information you can get out them? We've got to keep moving."

She shook her head, but waggled her fingers. "You can let go. *Kaalijaya*?" I nodded. "You're getting better at it." Valefar remained immobilized, caught in Lilith's majik. "You said there's another?"

"Over there." I pointed to where a crumpled body could be seen. "We haven't checked him out yet. He might be playing possum."

She chuckled with a low, throaty sound that still made my knees weak. "Kalili, I never grow tired of you. Play possum indeed." She laughed again. "Your time with humans has made you more interesting than I thought possible."

She did the finger thing again, in a different pattern, and the body rose and floated over to her.

"I'll have a chat with my Chief of Staff. This sounds like something I ought to know about."

I hoped Avy was as skilled at avoiding the fallout of her decision as she'd always been, without letting it show on my face. "See you soon."

Lilith vanished. So did the demons. The truck was left behind.

"Lilith?"

I nodded to McKenna. "Lilith. Come on, I want to go over their truck, then get back on the road."

McKenna pinched Dakota, who started and fell in beside me.

"Is she always that…"

"Sexy? Devastating? Drop-dead gorgeous? The embodiment of lust? Yeah. Pretty much."

"Holy crap."

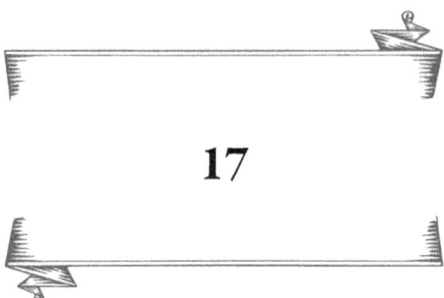

17

We didn't find anything in their truck. Scratch that. We didn't find anything *useful* in their truck. Registration, insurance, fast food wrappers? Yeah, plenty of those. McKenna captured images of everything, including the plates, swearing she'd track down the owner. I was all for an anonymous call to the RCMP, but she vetoed that.

"You might not give your name, but they'll grab your number and then where will you be?"

I couldn't argue, so I left her to it despite my misgivings. Oh, I had no doubt of her abilities, but didn't expect it would do any good. Demons didn't own cars; they stole them, if they needed one. Some poor Canuck would get their vehicle back, but we'd be none the wiser.

None of this took long. While she wrapped up, her prints off, I dug out both the Blade and Faith's sword. I was *not* making the same mistake twice, and I had to admit I felt better with the familiar scabbard pressed against my thigh. We were making miles soon after. Dakota was full of questions, so I put her in the back with Faith while I concentrated on the road. That left McKenna with me, but she was good company for the moment, focusing on the electronic trail the technologically challenged demons left behind.

"Are all demons this dumb?" she groused. I chuckled.

"Dumb doesn't begin to describe them. Out of touch? Prehistoric? You have to realize that most demons are thousands and thousands of years old. They're used to things changing slowly because they've been around long enough to remember shit like dinosaurs and global oceans. You humans, though, you're changing *everything,* and changing it fast." McKenna nodded, but I wasn't done. "A hundred years ago, Faith and I took a trip to Rome, flying on one of the first jet airliners. You know what I read last week?"

She shook her head.

"Some guy named Cochrane, working at CalTech, created what he called a static warp bubble." I snuck a glance at McKenna and saw the blank look as the information zoomed past her. "Yeah, that's what I thought at first, then I read more. It means he separated a piece of the universe from the rest of it."

"That's amazing." Her tone didn't match her words.

"Don't you get it? Didn't you ever watch Star Trek?"

"Maybe? But what does that—oh." I could hear her make the connection. "Warp drive?"

My head bobbed. "Exactly. First steps, at least. It might happen in your lifetime." I reined in my enthusiasm before I started raving. "That's what I mean about humans and change. A hundred years from jet propulsion to faster-than-light travel's pretty impressive. I wonder what Na'le will think of it," I added idly.

"Who?"

I realized my error. "Na'le Vesmiru, the creator of this universe. We mentioned her last night. She's not important at the moment."

McKenna's jaw dropped before she closed it with a clop.

"Right. You hang out with gods."

That provoked a laugh. "Nobody hangs out with Na'le. The Maker's still sulking, but Lucifer can be fun. Get a few drinks into him and he starts with the stories." I shook myself again, remembering the original thread of the conversation. "What about the demons was so dumb?"

"You said they stole this truck, right?"

"That's what I figured, yeah."

"Nope. They rented it. Credit card, tied to a real address. Names, too, one tied to a Social Security number, one Social Insurance number—"

"Pretending to be a Canadian and an American. Naughty, naughty."

Around another laugh, McKenna said, "Right. I'm grabbing every bit of information about them and stashing it in the dark cloud to deal with later."

My answering grin was savage. Whatever those incompetent idiots had put together was about to be torn apart. If they survived Lilith's kindness, they'd be utterly shafted if they tried to step back into their Earthside identities.

McKenna kept at the electronics while I sped down the road.

You don't need to get us pulled over, love.

I glanced at the speedometer. Whoops. I was doing 135 kph in a hundred zone. No wonder the other cars looked like they were standing still. With a grimace I eased off the accelerator.

A sign flashed by. Ten kilometers to the border. There was another reason I had McKenna in the front seat, and I reminded her now.

"McKenna?"

"Already uploaded and accepted." She didn't even look up from the screen. "Over the Point Edward bridge, stay to the far left at the CBP stop, and for fuck's sake, don't run anyone over, mmkay?"

"Only if they're disguised demons—"

"Or angels," Faith added.

"—or angels who mean us harm. And once we're through? I'm taking you all to Hell."

This was something I'd discovered the night before. Much to my surprise, Michigan, and the Northern Imperium, had a road that led directly to Hell. Not the one we were familiar with, but I was tickled by the marketing and decided a detour was in order. It wasn't far off the shortest route and took us through a long stretch of nothing. Right now, that appealed, as did seeing how Hell on Earth compared to the one I was familiar with.

"What?" Dakota gawped at me in the rearview mirror. "Kal, isn't that a little extreme?"

"Don't worry, I have your exit passes all set up."

Dakota turned to Faith. "Don't *you* find this a little worrying?"

She shook her head. "Nope. I was a Prince, remember?"

Dakota groaned. "This is no big deal?"

"I didn't know that Lilith had extended a road system to Earth, but other than that? No." She could see my plan, my idea, and I blew her a mental kiss for playing along. "Though this sounds more like an Avareth thing. She's a demon for efficiency."

That pulled a different groan from both our friends. I concentrated on the road, following the signs for the border crossing.

The Northern Imperium was barely over a decade old and still retained many of the names and procedures of the United States. I had no doubt that, given enough time, new terms would replace the old, but for now? All the baby nations crawling around the continent were still clones of their parent.

Except the damn Collective, which is what landed us in this mess.

I joined the queue for the express pass, obeying the posted rules. Driving through at a brisk 30 mph felt foolish, but that was the direction the overhead signs gave. One run-in with overeager border guards was enough for one trip.

I admit my pulse thrummed as we approached the checkpoint. Even though the highway was well inside the Imperium, until we were officially allowed entry we were in an uneasy no man's land.

"Remember how simple it was to get out of Rome that first time?" I asked Faith, trying to distract myself. She grunted.

"Simple? Sweetheart, your memory is way different from mine, because nothing about it was simple."

Dakota, intrigued, said, "When was this?"

"Nine fifty-two CE," I answered. "And it was simple, love, or would have been."

She grunted again but didn't argue. Dakota was curious and said, "What happened?"

I hadn't thought much of those events in a half century, so I paused, gathering my memories. "It was supposed to be easy. I needed to get us to Ravenna—"

"Why?"

"Because Avy was there, and she was the only person I could think of who might be able to unfuck us. We weren't together yet."

"Yes we were!" Faith objected.

"Well, we'd kissed, but we didn't like each other much, and we were awfully confused about why we felt this unnatural attraction. Angels and demons, you know?" I hurried to add, clarifying the point.

"Why didn't you just, whaddaya call it, jump there?"

"We're through." McKenna's quiet voice was satisfied, her electronic chicanery successful.

"Never doubted you." I accelerated, relieved to see signs in miles per hour. I'd never adjusted to that kilometers crap. Call me old-fashioned.

"Hey, you didn't answer my question!" Dakota was persistent.

As I navigated through Port Huron and headed south, I recounted the tale. Faith wasn't thrilled; it wasn't one of her prouder moments, and she still had occasional moments of regret for the life she took.

"Kal, I think I have a solution."

My mind snapped back to the present with McKenna's comment. "What do you mean? Solution to what?"

"The demon attacks."

"I'm all ears."

"The Conqueror has self-drive, right?"

I didn't see where she was going with this. "Yes?"

"It uses radar or lidar to pick out distant changes in the landscape, matches it to an internal map, uses the cameras to confirm it, and keeps us on the road."

"If you say so." I'd adapted to technology but didn't dive too deeply into how it worked.

"I do. I can tap the car systems with this—" She handed a cable back to Faith, who held it like it was a curious species of snake. "—and use them to look for anything coming at us from above. Even if they're invisible, they're *there*, so we'll get a signal. The car's computer would ignore them, but I won't. I can program an audible alert to ensure we notice."

"Do it."

McKenna instructed Faith while I concentrated on the road. After a few minutes, I heard her satisfied grunt. "It ain't pretty, but it works."

I stole a glimpse beside me. McKenna's pristine laptop was now wired into the Jeep, the screen displaying something that resembled a green Rorschach test.

"What does that mean?" I gestured vaguely at the green.

"That's the car's view of the surroundings. I've combined the radar, visible spectrum, and infrared feeds to a single view."

"Why's it green?"

She shrugged. "I like green."

I threw my head back and laughed, swerving out of the lane and onto the shoulder. "Shit!" The Jeep lurched as I pulled back onto the highway, the tires screeching in protest.

"Sorry," I said to the angry mutters around me.

A sudden squawk from McKenna's computer shut everyone up.

"Does that mean...?"

She nodded. "I've got movement on the grid."

My eyes flicked to the rearview mirror, catching the distant outlines of wings—demonic and angelic alike—closing in. Damn it. They weren't giving us any breathing room. "How close?"

"Close enough," she said, fingers moving. "It looks like they're pacing us."

I cursed under my breath, slamming the accelerator to the floor. The Conqueror roared in protest, but it obeyed.

"Get ready," I muttered, glancing at Faith. Her hands tightened around the seat in front of her, eyes closed, gathering the *kosmiskorka,* spindling it, storing it for use. There was a trick she could use that might give us some cover, but it was a new skill, one we were still learning. I wasn't going to count on it covering our asses.

"It's going to get worse before it gets better," she murmured.

I didn't need her to tell me that.

"They're coming, aren't they?" Dakota asked from the back seat. Beside me, McKenna never stopped working on her terminal, fingers flying across the keys.

"Of course they are," Faith replied softly, her voice taking on a tone of practiced calm. "It's what they do. Keep watch, Dakota. I need to concentrate."

A bright flare in the sky confirmed her words before I could respond. Crap. That was an attack. I pressed my foot harder to the floor, squeezing every drop of power from the Conqueror, hoping we could get out of the open before the attacks grew accurate. I didn't have high expectations.

"Keep them off us!" I barked at McKenna, not sure why.

"Working on it!" she snapped, and I almost jumped in surprise. Hacking into nearby systems, finding anything she could use to block or distract them, sure, and she was invaluable when it came to tech. But hacking angels? This was a new one, even for her.

"McKenna?" I asked, confused.

"Shut up, Kal." She relented almost immediately. "Local air defense systems."

That made sense, though I didn't know what a missile could do to an angel. Guess we'd find out.

"Faith, any ideas?" I asked, not tearing my eyes from the road.

"We need to get to Hell," she said, voice steady despite the growing disquiet in the vehicle. "It's the only place we can get an upper hand."

I knew what she meant. There was a cemetery in Hell, sanctified ground, and nothing but fields between here and there. Dakota let out a soft laugh from behind me, a sound that seemed wildly inappropriate under the circumstances. "Kal, you really know how to pick vacation spots."

"Focus, Dakota!" I growled as another flash of light erupted behind us, closer this time. Faith flinched, her energy surging as she struggled to shield us.

"What the hell is that?!" exclaimed McKenna as a tree to our right burst apart.

"*Vashqar disaat,*" I replied. "Think of it like an angelic rocket-propelled grenade, minus the big metal firing thingy. They're not supposed to use it where humans can see."

"This is bad," McKenna muttered, her fingers still racing across the keys. "I'm doing what I can, but the damn Imperium's not playing nice with me."

I spared Faith a glance. Her face was set in grim determination.

"They're closing in," she warned.

"I can feel them." I jerked the wheel sharply as another blast of holy fire exploded to our right, scorching the asphalt.

We were close to Hell now, and the road twisted and turned. I had to slow, and with each bend, the enemy grew bolder, their attacks more frequent. We were running out of time.

"Brace yourselves," I muttered. We barreled down the final stretch. Hell's welcome sign barely registered in the chaos, but it brought a grim smile to my face.

"We're almost there." It was halfway to being a prayer, my knuckles white on the steering wheel. Another burst of angelic fire exploded to our left, sending a shower of debris across the road. I swerved to avoid it, feeling the Jeep's suspension groan beneath the strain.

"Kal, we need to get onto a straightaway and floor it!" McKenna shouted, her gaze locked on the green blur on her screen. "They'll pin us down if we don't!"

I nodded sharply, eyes scanning for the turnoff I hoped was coming. "Hang on. Cemetery's just ahead."

Faith's voice cut through the moment. "The demons won't follow us onto holy ground. If we can make it to the cemetery, we'll have a fighting chance."

"Big 'if,'" Dakota muttered, but she didn't argue further.

I spotted the iron gates up ahead, the sign for the Hell Cemetery standing as grim confirmation of our destination. I hoped it wasn't a harbinger. Slamming on the brakes, I wrenched the wheel to the right, sending the Conqueror skidding off the highway and through the narrow entrance.

"Hold on!" I barked, the Jeep bouncing violently as we careened over the uneven ground. The gravestones blurred past us as I aimed for the center of the cemetery.

"We're in!" McKenna shouted, her fingers slowing. "We're safe, right?"

"No," Faith answered, her voice quieter but strained. "The angels can still attack, even if the demons can't follow us."

I brought the Jeep to a halt in the center of the graveyard. My pulse still raced in my ears and I exhaled noisily.

"Everybody out," I said, already reaching for the door handle. "We need to set up a perimeter, and we need to be mobile."

We climbed out into the twilight, the cool air of the cemetery a stark contrast to the heat of the pursuit. The graves stretched out in all directions, their silent occupants offering no comfort. McKenna unholstered a pistol and handed it to Dakota, along with a handful of magazines. I was surprised; Dakota hated guns and never used them on a job, but desperate times, I guess.

Dakota took the gun and seated the magazine with an expertise that surprised me. She must have seen it, because she said, "I don't use 'em, but I know how." I raised my hands in surrender as she stretched, cracking her knuckles as she surveyed the area. "So, this is Hell, huh? Gotta say, I expected more fire and brimstone."

McKenna shook her head, muttering as she pulled another pistol from her bag, checking the load. "We're in a cemetery surrounded by angels and demons, and you're cracking jokes?"

"It helps," Dakota shrugged, but her grip tightened on her gun as she scanned the skies.

Faith moved beside me, the *kosmiskorka* she'd stored simmering under the surface, ready for whatever came next. "Kal, they'll hit us soon. We need to be ready."

I nodded, drawing in a deep breath as I centered myself. "We'll hold the line here. McKenna, keep monitoring for movement. Dakota, cover the east side. Faith—"

"I know," she said, her voice soft but steady. "I'll keep them off us as long as I can."

Another flare of light in the caught my attention, and I gritted my teeth. They were coming.

"Let's give them Hell," I growled, gripping my Blade tightly. Between us, Faith was the master of our abilities as Thirteens, but Thakumis' Blade would do for any angel who got too close.

The night erupted in a storm of divine light.

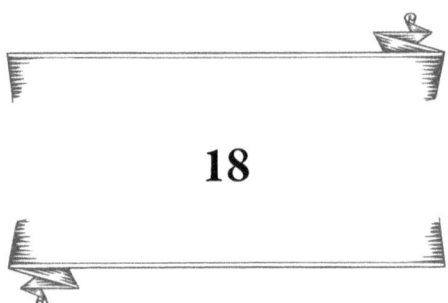

18

The night exploded into chaos, light searing across the cemetery as the first wave of angels descended. Faith was already in motion, her hands glowing with the intense energy of *vashwic urja*. She thrust her palms forward, unleashing a beam of pure power that arced toward the nearest angel.

The blast missed, scorching a headstone instead, sending shards of stone into the air. She cursed under her breath, recalibrating as another angel swooped in from above.

"Faith!" I shouted, the familiar weight of the Blade in my hand like an extension of myself.

Her eyes flashed, and this time her *vashwic urja* hit true. The beam connected with the angel's side, knocking it off course, but it barely slowed. The divine being shook off the hit, its golden armor scorched but intact. It screamed in fury, diving toward us again.

"Dakota, McKenna—now!"

McKenna didn't need to be told twice. She leveled her gun and fired, the bullets slamming into the nearest angel with a precision that spoke to her expertise. The rounds found their mark, tearing through feathers and flesh, but the celestial warrior barely flinched, its wings still beating with furious grace as it descended.

"They're not stopping!" she shouted.

Dakota joined McKenna in the fight. Her first few shots went wide, but then she found her rhythm. The next angel to approach staggered in midair as her bullet tore through its chest. Unlike

McKenna's earlier attempts, the hit seemed to slow this one down—at least for a moment.

"I'll take it," Dakota muttered, reloading swiftly as more angels closed in. "Body shots, not wings, dear."

"Point taken." McKenna shifted her aim and fired again, a triple tap to the chest that dropped the next angel in its tracks.

I had no time to celebrate their small victory. One of the angels broke through the barrage of gunfire, its sword drawn and eyes blazing with fury. It was coming for me.

"Kal!" Faith screamed, but I was already moving.

The angel's blade came down in a deadly arc, but I met it with my own. The metal rang out with a shriek of fury as they collided, the force of the impact jarring up my arm. This angel was strong—too strong to beat in a prolonged fight. I needed to end it fast.

We circled each other, its malevolent eyes locked on mine. Then, with a speed that startled even me, I lunged. The angel parried, but I spun, twisting beneath its guard and slashing downward with the Blade. The razor-sharp edge cut through its armor with a screech of metal, a blazing line of crimson light searing across its shoulder.

The angel screamed—a guttural, primal sound that shook the air. I didn't wait for the Blade to do its job, but followed up with a brutal slash across its back, the Blade leaving glowing crimson lines in its wake. It howled again, staggering forward.

I jumped back, breath coming in ragged gasps, the Blade pulsing in my hand, feeding me images of savagery and destruction. Its will flooded my mind, urging me to finish it. Before I could move, the angel dropped to its knees, hands clawing at the lines of light spreading across its body.

"What's happening?" The moment seemed frozen as Dakota's voice cut through the chaos, her eyes wide as she watched the glowing lines creep faster over the angel's form.

"Celestial death sentence." The crimson light was consuming the angel from within, the gashes widening as its golden skin was divided into ever-smaller segments. Its screams grew quieter, more animalistic, as the light intensified.

"Kal…" Dakota's voice was filled with shock and something close to awe.

In a matter of seconds, the angel's form dissolved into pure light. Then, as quickly as it had flared, it was gone—vanished. Not even a trace remained.

The moment ended and there was no time to dwell on what happened. Another angel was already upon us, its sword raised high. I barely had time to block its strike, my arms protesting under the force of the blow. I kicked and it jumped back, but the momentary advantage was already slipping.

"They keep coming!" McKenna shouted, firing wildly as more angels filled the skies above us, their wings casting shadows across the cemetery.

"Let them!" I called back, gripping the Blade tighter as the angels closed in. This was far from over, and with a feral grin, I threw myself into the fray.

The next wave came down with terrifying speed, their wings creating a gust of wind that sent dust and dead leaves swirling across the cemetery. My body moved on instinct, the Blade raised as the first angel dove for me. Its sword came down, but I met it with a vicious parry.

"Dakota! McKenna! We've got to keep them off Faith!" I yelled, my voice strained as I blocked another strike. The angel's golden armor gleamed in the moonlight. I connected, but not deeply enough, and the crimson lines where my Blade had cut gleamed evilly across its chest. A desperate lunge caught the angel in the thigh, and it howled, collapsing as Thakumis claimed another victim.

"We're on it!" McKenna called back, her gun barking as she and Dakota unleashed a hail of bullets toward the advancing angels.

The shots connected, but like before, they didn't stop the celestial onslaught. Feathers flew, blood sprayed, but the angels pressed on, relentless. I slashed at one's arm, watching as the crimson light spread from the wound, seeping into its flesh like fire. The angel screamed, stumbling back, but not before another took its place, sword raised.

"Faith!" I shouted, eyes scanning the chaos for her. She was still in position, her hands outstretched, releasing yet another blast of *vashwic urja*. The energy slammed into one of the angels, sending it tumbling into a headstone, but the next shot missed, lighting up the sky as it fizzled harmlessly into the air.

"Damn it!" Faith cursed, regaining her stance and trying again, sweat glistening on her brow. She was pushing herself hard, her aura flickering with every blast. I knew she could draw on the *kosmiskorka* to replenish her energy, but it took concentration to start the flow and she might not have time. She hit one angel square in the chest, knocking it to the ground with a guttural cry, but the strain was evident.

I didn't have time to worry. An angel was already in front of me, its sword sweeping toward my head. I ducked, rolling under its swing, and came up with a vicious upward slash. The Blade connected, carving through its arm in a flash of crimson light.

The angel howled, the light spreading faster now as if Thakumis's spirit was enjoying my liberal use of the Blade. It consumed the body before it could drop to its knees. Before I could follow up, another angel was upon me. This time, I wasn't fast enough.

The sword hit my side, cutting through my jacket and sending a jolt of pain across my ribs. I staggered back, my vision blurring as the world tilted. Damn, but I hated pain! The Blade's power surged through me, filling me with savage determination. I gritted my teeth, pushing past the pain, and lunged forward, driving the Blade into the angel's chest.

The familiar glow of crimson lines spread across its form, and I yanked the Blade free as the angel's body dissolved into light, leaving nothing but empty air where it had stood.

"I'm running out of ammo!" Dakota's voice rang out over the chaos, her frustration clear as she emptied another clip into the nearest angel.

McKenna was swapping magazines with practiced efficiency, her shots more precise than before. One of her bullets caught an angel in the wing, sending it spiraling to the ground. She didn't stop to finish it, changing targets and hitting another in the leg. The angel collapsed, but still crawled forward, determined to reach us.

"They're slowing down!" McKenna shouted, her voice edged with exhaustion.

I felt it too. The angels' attacks were growing more desperate, their coordination less focused. The pressure was lifting.

Another wave of *vashwic urja* erupted from Faith's hands, this time catching two angels mid-flight. The blast sent them crashing into the far end of the cemetery, tumbling across the gravestones. They didn't rise again.

I caught sight of an angel retreating in the distance, its wings flickering with the last remnants of divine light. Then another, and another.

"They're falling back!" Dakota shouted, her voice laced with both relief and disbelief.

I pulled the Blade free from another downed angel, its body dissolving into light. My chest heaved as I turned to see the remaining angels fleeing, retreating into the sky in defeat. Their wings glowed faintly against the moonlight as they disappeared into the darkness. The fallen survivors vanished as they jumped away. Where to, I didn't know.

"Is it over?" McKenna asked, lowering her gun, her breath ragged.

"For now," I said, my voice hoarse. I sheathed the Blade, the violent images it had shown me finally fading from my mind. "But they'll be back."

Faith stepped beside me, her energy depleted and nerves afire. "They're regrouping," she said, her gaze fixed on the sky. "We'll need to be ready for whatever comes next."

I nodded, wiping the sweat from my brow. The cemetery was quiet now, save for the crackle of energy still lingering in the air. The ground was littered with feathers and faint scorch marks, but no bodies remained.

As the night settled around us, I couldn't help but wonder how long this calm would last.

I turned my attention to Faith. "How are you?"

She smiled weakly. "Exhausted."

I clasped her forearms and let my *taaqat* flow between us, balancing, restoring her somewhat.

"Thank you," she whispered, leaning her forehead against mine.

"Anything, *arima bikia*."

Faith chuckled. "I didn't spindle enough *kosmiskorka* before the fight. Used it up too quickly."

"We're out of practice," I answered. "Too many years of easy living."

"I hate to interrupt this tender moment," McKenna said from the Jeep. She pointed to her screen. "There's others out there."

"Demons." I nodded, weary and annoyed. "I'll get rid of them."

I released Faith and strode toward the gate, using my depleted *taaqat* to heal the wound in my side. I couldn't heal the jacket, which pissed me off, and I channeled that.

"Followers of Valaferion!" I bellowed, stopping just beyond the gate's protection, in the center of the glow from the lights on the sign. "Show yourselves!"

There was silence for a moment, then I heard a shuffle and a cough.

"Show yourselves!" I shouted again, pulling the Blade from the scabbard. Demons were cowards, but this was ridiculous.

A figure appeared at the edge of the light. Then another, then in twos and threes, until the perimeter was full of shadowy forms.

Faith, I may have miscalculated.

I felt my love pushing *kosmiskorka* into me through our link and my confidence returned. I wasn't the master she was, but these idiots didn't know what a pissed-off Thirteen could to.

Time to educate them.

"Who's in charge?"

Much muttering arose in answer to my question, but nobody stepped forward. Smart.

"I want to negotiate with you." I waved my right hand—the one holding the Blade—at the sky. "The angels have retreated, leaving you on the field alone. I'm tired of fighting and want to leave."

"We outnumber you!" came a voice from the back.

"So what?"

A silhouette separated from the others, edging toward the light. He was about my height, but broader and sported the current fashion in demons: red skin, short horns, goat-slitted eyes, and bat-like black wings. I didn't care for the look.

"We could take you," he said, his voice like honey over gravel.

"That's what the angels thought." I gave him a moment to consider my words, then followed up with, "Are you negotiating for the others?"

He half-turned in each direction, glaring, before facing me and nodding. "I am."

"I'll say this once and make it real simple for your little mind. Option A, we get in our car and drive away, unmolested by you lot, and you leave us alone until tomorrow." I waggled the Blade at them again. "Or, option B, we kill you all." I lowered the Blade and pointed toward the self-appointed leader. "Starting with you."

That evoked a hearty round of laughter, with the leader loudest of all. I grinned widely to show my appreciation for my own joke.

"What's your name?"

"Kyrion."

I idly tossed the Blade, letting it rotate in the air before catching the handle. "Kyrion. Good. Do you agree?"

"We are negotiating, yes?"

I nodded.

"Then I have a counterproposal."

Oh, this ought to be good.

"I'm listening."

"You and the other obscenity come with us, and we let your human pets go free."

I thought I heard Dakota growl, or maybe it was McKenna, but I didn't have time to figure out which. "That's your offer?"

"It is. Option C, you can call it."

I made a show of considering it while I took the *kosmiskorka* Faith funneled to me and transmuted it to *vashwic urja*.

"No." I released the blast from my left hand. Kyrion, barely fifteen feet away, didn't stand a chance. The bolt shattered his body and blew a hole out his back before dispersing. Innards splattered against the closest demons, who were frozen in shock.

I sheathed the Blade and growled, "I'm done negotiating."

I'm not sure which one broke first, but the rustle of rapid footsteps grew into a thunder in an instant. Another instant later, the entryway was clear.

"Come on," I said, heading back to the Jeep and climbing in. "We need to put miles between us. They won't try again tonight, but I doubt the angels will be that easily dissuaded."

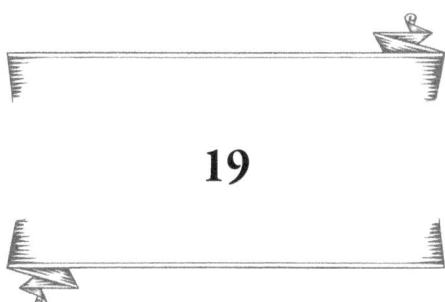

19

The Jeep's motors hummed steadily as we cruised through the last stretch of road toward Kalamazoo, the gale from my broken window whipping through my hair. After the mess at the cemetery, every mile felt like a small victory. Dakota leaned against the side, her eyes drooping but still wary, while McKenna's fingers occasionally twitched as if she were still firing at some celestial target. The confrontation with angels and demons had clearly left its mark on them, but they seemed to be taking the existence of celestials in stride.

We pulled into the city, tired but grateful for the bright neon signs that promised a warm bed and a few hours of peace. After finding an all-night garage and leaving the Jeep for repairs, we checked into a small hotel. It was exactly what I wanted, the kind where the front desk clerk hardly looked at you twice. Dakota and McKenna had kept quiet since the fight, but after the door closed and bags hit the floor, they were ready to talk.

"How long have you two been dealing with all of this?" Dakota asked, hands on her hips as she looked from Faith to me.

"Longer than you'd think," I replied, choosing my words carefully. They deserved some understanding of what they'd faced tonight, but I didn't want to overwhelm them. "This isn't our first encounter with angels and demons gone rogue. With the Maker sulking and the change in management in Hell, they don't always stay where they're supposed to."

McKenna leaned back, processing everything with a calm that belied the night's events. Her tone was casual, but the slight narrowing of her eyes told me she was piecing things together. "You've got enough to deal with as it is, don't you? Angels? Demons? This whole battle between worlds?"

Faith and I shared a look, and we decided to give Dakota and McKenna as much honesty as they could handle without tearing the veil back entirely.

"It's complicated," Faith said slowly, her voice laced with a weariness that only a few hundred years of dealing with celestial politics could bring. "These worlds—angels, demons, all of that—don't always stay separate. They intersect in ways most people never see, ways that should never be, and someone has to put things right."

"That's what you two do? Just handle it?" Dakota's eyes shifted from Faith to me, brows knit in curiosity and eyes flickering with disbelief.

"More like try to contain it," I replied. "Think of it as maintaining balance. When rogue Immortals decide to act out on their own, Faith and I sometimes get involved. Or, in this case, we're the targets."

"So, you're like celestial law enforcement?" McKenna asked, and I couldn't help but laugh.

"Not exactly," Faith interjected, amused. "We turned that down centuries ago. Think of us as mediators with big sticks. Rogues tend to ignore Immortal laws, so if they step out of line, we try to minimize the damage. Word gets around; Immortals are as prone to gossip as humans. As a result, this isn't the first time they've come after us, but it's the most serious attempt."

McKenna gave a slow nod, and Dakota raised a brow as she cut in. "And what we saw tonight? Was that normal?"

"Define 'normal,'" Faith said, her smile widening. "But, no, rogue angels and demons joining forces isn't a usual occurrence, and not one we're thrilled about, either."

McKenna leaned forward, exchanging a look with Dakota before asking, "You knew it was coming, didn't you?"

"We suspected it," I admitted. "You heard Avareth back in Niagara. We didn't know how coordinated they'd be, though, or how many would come at us. I expected they'd act in ones and twos, not dozens. That's why I thought we'd be able to handle it, even without our friends as backup."

"You're like some ancient, otherworldly clean-up crew." Dakota said.

"Pretty much," Faith replied, shrugging. "It's what we do."

Dakota nodded slowly, glancing at McKenna. "We're along for the ride—"

McKenna looked at her, then back at us, finishing the thought. "Until they're done, I guess."

"That's a fair way to put it," I said.

They looked at each other, a silent conversation passing between them, almost as if they were testing the boundaries of this new understanding. I felt the buzz of their thoughts, a remnant of the connection formed in the jump, but couldn't tap it. Finally, Dakota looked back at me, arms crossed. "There's more of them out there, right?"

Faith and I nodded, and McKenna picked up the thread. "So it's going to get worse before it gets better. They're not going to leave us alone, are they?"

"No, probably not," I replied, and Faith sighed, adding, "But we'll be there to keep things in check if we can. Eventually, we'll have help, if Zophiel can catch up to us. We're kinda off the beaten path, and since they have to stick to the human realm, they're dealing with human limits. Physics works on Immortals, too."

Dakota exhaled, her brows raised. "Well, guess we'd better get some sleep, then. Gotta be fresh for whatever apocalypse tomorrow holds."

She gave a wry grin, but her eyes lingered on Faith and me, the weight of what we'd shared settling between us. McKenna pulled Dakota toward their room, their exhaustion obvious. As the door clicked shut, Faith and I were left alone, the silence thick with the unspoken knowledge that the lives of our two allies had been irrevocably changed. The quiet broke as the air shifted with a *pop*. Faith stiffened beside me before a smile tugged at her lips. Avareth stepped toward us with the graceful ease that was uniquely hers.

"You're still alive," she said, her tone as dry as ever, but I caught the gleam of concern in her eyes.

"Barely," I replied, then filled her in on the ambush, the pursuit, and the uneasy retreat of our opponents. With each detail, Avareth's expression darkened, her concern transforming into something sharper, more dangerous.

"Why the fuck didn't you call for help?" she snapped.

"Because I was busy!" My retort was hot off my lips. "I didn't exactly have time to call you, and you know that signaling Lilith takes concentration. There weren't two seconds where we weren't fighting to stay alive until it was all over, and what then? Hmm? Besides, I got the feeling that Lil wasn't entirely happy to have been kept out of the loop. How did that go?"

"She's pissed," Avy agreed. "I think we've worked it out, but she wasn't happy that this has erupted now."

"What do you mean?" Faith asked.

"You need to understand," she began, pacing in quick, controlled strides, "our hands are tied. Lilith and Ariel can't act openly, not without risking their authority. If they go after the rogues directly, it'll look like they've lost control. I don't know what it is, but some of the other Princes and Archangels are muttering, looking at Lucifer's reign as the good old days. If word gets to them of Valaferion's rebellion?" She mimed snapping a twig.

A flash of irritation ignited in me, and I could feel Faith's frustration echo my own. Faith's tone turned clipped as she spoke. "That's because they *have* lost control, Avy. If they hadn't, we wouldn't have fought off rogue angels and demons three times today!"

Avareth's eyes sharpened, her gaze cutting as she turned toward Faith. "Lilith and Ariel are holding the line as best they can. If they push openly, they'll provoke a backlash that could collapse what fragile balance remains. Remember, Lucifer is waiting for an opportunity to reclaim his power."

Faith shook her head, exasperation written across her face, and before either of them could escalate further, I stepped between them. My voice was gentle as I took on the unfamiliar role of peacekeeper. "Enough," I said, glancing at each of them in turn. "This isn't on you, Avy. We're all feeling the strain here."

Her shoulders eased, and she let out a breath that softened her stance, her usual composed exterior fading for a moment. She looked at me, then at Faith, with a depth of understanding that felt like warmth radiating through the room. "I know. It's just complicated," she admitted. "And I'm biased. I want to smash them flat, now that they're in the open, but I can't. In fact, Lilith doesn't want me Earthside for fear that I'll go rogue and do exactly that."

Faith's expression softened, frustration yielding to acceptance. "And we love you for it, Avy." She squeezed Avy's shoulders. "So far, we haven't run into anything we can't handle. Dakota and McKenna have been huge for us. If we keep moving, stay off the radar as best we can, we ought to be fine." Her tone changed from reassuring to commanding. "Promise me, Avy, if you hear anything, *anything* that might give us an edge, tell us. We'll take all the help we can get."

"Speaking of help," I added. "Where's Zophiel?"

"Delayed," Avy admitted. "It seems that our rebellious cohort have sympathizers. A number of the angels and demons we requisitioned for support were recalled by their superiors for missions in the human world. We can't rescind them without tipping our hand."

"Fuck, Avy. Any idea when we can expect anyone?"

She shook her head at my exasperation. "No. I'm sorry, Kal. I'm doing what I can, but..." Avy shrugged helplessly. "Bureaucracy exists to slow decisions, and I'm caught in it."

I sighed. "I know. Who invented it? I want to string them up."

Avareth nodded her agreement, a rueful smile on her face. "Speaking of help," she began, her voice careful. "Dakota and McKenna—there's something unusual about their bond, isn't there?"

I hesitated, feeling the faint echo of their connection in the edges of my mind. It had only been a few hours, but it was weakening, fading like a distant melody. "Yes," I admitted. "Their connection is strong, but my perception of their bond is slipping."

Avareth's frown deepened, the gleam in her eyes now one of worry. "You can't feel them as clearly?" Her tone betrayed a concern beyond mere curiosity, and I realized her worry wasn't about our safety—it was about Dakota and McKenna's unpredictability. Humans added an element of chance to anything they touched, and with my ability to see their thoughts disappearing? The potential for disaster grew.

"It's fading," I said, meeting her gaze. "Whatever they share is unlike anything I've encountered in a human, and without a clear sense of it, I don't know how to manage it. Or them."

Avareth's mouth tightened, her gaze drifting to Faith as if looking for answers she couldn't find. "Kal, if you're losing touch with them, it's a huge risk. If it strengthens or evolves unchecked, they could become..." She trailed off, the unspoken consequences heavy in the air. Humans with transmitting minds would be a beacon to anyone looking, for one thing. Faith and I routinely masked our bond from prying eyes. Dakota and McKenna wouldn't have a clue.

Faith laid a hand on Avareth's arm, her touch grounding us all in a way only she could. "They're not alone," she said gently, her gaze filled with the love that flowed between us, even now, amidst the tension and worry. "They have us, and if we have to teach them how to mask their bond? We'll try. They're tough, Avy, and flexible. If anyone can adapt to becoming telepathic, it's them."

For a moment, all of our frustrations, fears, and doubts melted into the quiet understanding that bound us together. I looked between them, the two women who had stood by me through centuries of conflict, who loved me as fiercely as I loved them. Even here, in the middle of a battlefield that spanned realms and loyalties, that love was a constant—a warmth that wrapped around us and held us steady.

Avareth sighed, her posture relaxing as she allowed herself to lean into Faith's touch, a rare vulnerability slipping through. "I don't like feeling this out of control," she whispered, glancing at me. "But you're right. They've proven themselves stronger than I'd have thought."

"We'll keep them close," I promised, my voice steady. "For now, they're managing."

Avareth gave a final nod. "I have to get back before Lilith notices I've gone."

Faith kissed her. "Be safe, love."

"I ought to be saying that to you."

"Safe? Us?" I forced a laugh. A smile echoed on Avy's face, but the worry lingered in her eyes even as she jumped out, returning to Hell. I felt Faith's hand slip into mine, her fingers warm and reassuring, and I held on, grounding myself in her presence, in our unbreakable bond. We sat in silence, the weight of Avareth's warnings settling over us. In that quiet moment, I knew how powerfully our love anchored us, steady and unwavering in a world that had long ago lost its certainties.

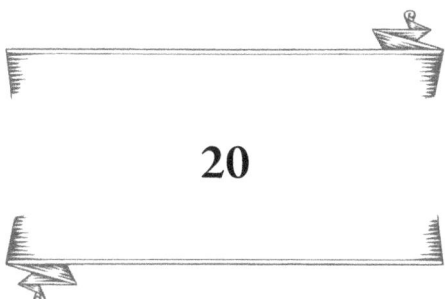

20

The morning was cool, a deceptive calm after the chaos of the night. I leaned against the Jeep, scowling at the shiny new glass in the driver's window. "They charged me a small fortune for this one window! I swear, it's more than the Jeep itself. And it's not even the same material, just what they could come up with overnight!" My outrage wasn't feigned, but it calmed quickly. After all, it was a thing, and things could be replaced.

Dakota snorted, clearly enjoying my misery. "Maybe that's sticker shock from the 21st century, huh, Kal?"

I glared at her, but a reluctant smile tugged at the corner of my mouth. "You wouldn't last five minutes in the markets I'm used to."

Once we'd loaded up and checked out, we hit the road, following the signs toward Chicago, capital of the Northern Imperium and one of the new powers on the continent. As the miles disappeared beneath the wheels, my mind drifted to the complexities of this fractured world. Militarily, the U.S. still held a narrow lead over the Northern Imperium and the New Confederacy—just enough to keep an unstable peace. On the economic front, the California Confederacy and the Republic of Texas led the way, with the Northern Imperium and Empire of New York fighting for third. All of which meant the Imperium had power, and we were heading for the heart of it.

When Illinois and Michigan declared independence back in 2040, it wasn't a quiet withdrawal, negotiated in smoky rooms between genteel politicians. No. They'd fought hard and taken Wisconsin and Minnesota with them. Now the Daley family ruled, minting their own currency, creatively named the Daley, and keeping a tight grip on power. In the seat of this empire stood the grand Imperial Palace, a converted Venetian-style mansion with baroque terra cotta that gleamed like old money. Perfect for a man as ruthless as Emperor Richard Daley V.

Despite this, as we pulled into Chicago and found a place to stop for a few minutes, McKenna was already brimming with excitement, practically bouncing in her seat. "Come on, we're here. We can't pass by without seeing the Palace up close!"

Faith glanced at me, clearly sharing my reluctance. We had a history in the Imperium, and not on the side that was in power. It was unlikely we'd be recognized, but unlikely didn't mean impossible. "McKenna, this isn't some roadside attraction. We can't just walk up and ask to see where they keep the jewels—"

"Yes we can. They run tours," Dakota supplied. I glowered at her.

"Besides, you might be fine, but we're not exactly welcome here."

McKenna rolled her eyes, undeterred. "Oh, come on! It's the *Palace*. Don't you want to see how the Daleys live? You can't tell me you're not even a little curious."

I raised an eyebrow. "Curiosity isn't worth risking getting on Daley's radar. Besides, we have more important things to do," I finished, an unsubtle reminder of our pursuers. We hadn't seen any today, which suggested they were planning something big. I wanted to be mobile when that happened, not trapped in a marble and concrete pile.

Dakota leaned forward, eyes gleaming as she threw her weight behind McKenna. "Kal, you're being way too cautious. When's the last time we had a little cultural enrichment?" She smirked, clearly amused. "We're blending in as tourists—it'll be fine."

Faith shook her head, but there was a hint of a smile. "It's more complicated than that. Do you think Daley doesn't have contingencies for people snooping around? It's asking for trouble."

McKenna gave a dramatic sigh. "Listen, we're not planning on knocking on his office door. We're blending in with the crowd like any other gawking visitor. You both know how to keep a low profile." I crossed my arms, not entirely convinced. Taking my silence as an opportunity, McKenna's eyes lit. "Look, we're already here. What's the harm? Didn't you say those celestials won't attack when humans can see them?"

Dakota nodded, egging her on. "Exactly. Come on, Kal, you always say we need to 'know our enemy.' Let's do a little recon." At my puzzled look—I had no beef with the Daleys any longer, except on general principles—she explained. "Maybe we can draw one of those rogues into making a mistake, trying something in public, and we can capture them."

I admitted it was a possibility, and Faith sighed, glancing at me with a resigned look. "Kal, they're not going to let this go."

I let out a long breath, finally conceding. "Fine. But we're in and out, no detours."

McKenna grinned. "Knew you'd come around. Let's go see the Emperor's little slice of paradise."

The palace tour was even more lavish than I'd expected. Every room we passed seemed more decadent, more absurdly decked out in historical artifacts and over-the-top opulence than the last. McKenna and Dakota had their eyes on the glitter, which in this place was practically everything.

"Look at this, Kenna!" Dakota whispered, nudging her. She pointed to an elaborate bronze statue of Athena. "I'll bet that's worth more than my old apartment."

"More like it's worth more than your old *building*," McKenna shot back as she gazed at a gilded antique clock on a nearby table.

The docent, a prim woman with perfect posture, paused in front of an enormous oil painting. "This is an original from the French Revolution, painted by Jacques-Louis David himself."

Faith leaned toward me, her voice low. "David? And this guy has it hanging around like it's nothing? We should have done a better job on them."

"Maybe," I agreed.

The docent continued, oblivious. "Emperor Richard Daley IV personally acquired this piece for the collection when he assumed the throne in 2040, as a symbol of triumph over the old American government."

Dakota leaned close to McKenna and whispered, "Pretty sure *acquired* is rich person code for *stole*."

I smirked and whispered, just loud enough for the docent to hear, "Wouldn't be the first time the Daleys laid claim to something that wasn't theirs."

The docent gave me a stern look and McKenna stifled a laugh, clearly enjoying the scandalous thought. We moved into another room, this one filled with intricate tapestries and gold-framed mirrors.

"This mirror," the docent said, gesturing to a tall, ornate piece, "once belonged to Louis XIV and was later transported to Chicago for display at the Art Institute. In recognition of the Daleys' contribution to the history of the city and Imperium, it was donated in 2045."

"Donated," I muttered, rolling my eyes. "Guessing the Institute didn't exactly lend it out willingly."

The docent paused, as though deciding whether to hear me or not before continuing. "The Daley family believes in honoring the cultural heritage of our world by preserving these items."

Dakota leaned over to McKenna and muttered, "Preserving, huh? I think I'd like to get into preservation."

McKenna bit her lip, suppressing a laugh as the docent led us further into the palace. We passed into the Imperial study, and I could feel Dakota's interest shift, her eyes darting to a collection of small items on the Emperor's desk. Most of them were engraved, jeweled, or otherwise valuable and portable – a bad combination for someone with sticky fingers. I didn't have to have a connection to smell trouble brewing.

The docent waved toward a large, heavy mahogany desk that dominated the center of the room. "This desk was once owned by Franklin Delano Roosevelt. Emperor Daley IV had it transported here from the White House, a gift to symbolize the lasting peace between these two great nations."

I leaned over to Faith, whispering, "I'm sure he used *persuasive diplomacy* to get his hands on that."

Faith snorted, and Dakota's fingers brushed the small letter opener on the edge of the desk, her eyes lighting up with an unmistakable glint that always made me nervous. I looked around, hoping that everyone else was distracted. When I turned back, the opener was gone.

Shit.

We moved to the throne room next, where the docent gestured proudly at the extravagant chair on a raised platform. "And here is the throne of Emperor Richard Daley V himself, a symbol of the Northern Imperium's strength and continuity."

McKenna nudged Dakota, whispering, "Bet that throne would look pretty good in our apartment."

Dakota grinned, her eyes locked on the throne with a look that said she was already picturing how it would look with *her* in it.

Just then, two guards entered the room, their eyes landing directly on Dakota. "You there! Stop!" one of them barked at her. The other strode forward, eyes locked on us, taking in every detail.

Dakota threw me a quick, innocent look, as if to say, *Who, me?* I plastered on my best poker face; no point in giving away the game. But it was too late—they'd spotted the letter opener in her pocket, its outline visible through the fabric.

"Care to explain this?" the guard said, holding out a hand.

Dakota shrugged, feigning nonchalance while she dropped it in his hand. "What? It's a souvenir. I picked it up in the gift shop."

The guards weren't amused. Within moments, we were being hauled down the grand corridor, past the stunned tourists, and brought directly into the Emperor's private offices. Emperor Richard Daley V himself sat behind a surprisingly functional desk, a look of dark amusement on his face.

"Your Majesty," one of the guards announced, "we caught this one attempting to steal from the Imperial study."

Dick the Fifth's gaze was cold and calculating as it fixed on Dakota. He wasn't a large man, but the way he held himself—rigid, chin raised—suggested someone who demanded absolute obedience. His face was hard, almost chiseled, but his eyes—sharp, dark, and unrelenting—betrayed something feral. I thought of the leaders I'd met across centuries: generals and kings, tyrants and visionaries. Some had carried an undeniable presence, an aura that demanded respect or awe. Daley, by contrast, seemed to enforce his authority through intimidation alone. There was nothing inspiring in his gaze, only the cold calculation of a man who viewed everyone around him as pawns, holding himself with the practiced arrogance of someone who had clawed his way to power and didn't plan on relinquishing it.

He raised an eyebrow, his lips curling as he gave the order. "Execute her." The words came out low and indifferent, as if he were ordering coffee rather than the end of someone's life.

A surge of panic hit me. I took a step forward, instinctively ready to intervene, but stopped when I noticed McKenna's hands moving with purpose, her fingers tapping rapidly on a small handheld device she'd discreetly palmed. She wasn't even looking up, her focus entirely on her screen as she worked furiously, her eyes flitting from lines of code to search results and back. I caught a glimpse of the Imperial Seal and muffled a grin. The connection between her and Dakota was an invisible current that buzzed in my mind—an insistent hum of communication I couldn't interpret but relieved my tension.

Dakota's expression shifted, an almost playful gleam entering her eyes as she held Daley's gaze. She seemed to draw confidence from whatever McKenna was silently feeding her, her demeanor shifting from alarm to a cat-and-mouse game, with Daley as her unwitting prey. Her chin lifted, and she took a half-step forward, hands open in a casual display of innocence.

"Your Majesty," she began, her voice light, almost offended. "I'm not sure where this *misunderstanding* has come from, but I assure you, I'm as baffled as anyone. Why on Earth would I want to take anything from your lovely palace?"

One of the guards stepped forward, holding the letter opener. "We found this on her, Your Majesty. In her pocket."

Dakota gave a small, disbelieving laugh, waving a hand as if dismissing an absurd notion and picking the opener from the guard's unresisting hand. "This? Oh, please. I must've picked it up by mistake! You know how easy it is to get distracted by the beauty of one's surroundings." She glanced around, feigning admiration for the rather pedestrian room.

Daley's mouth tightened, his gaze unwavering. "Enough. I'm not in the mood for games, girl," he replied, disdain dripping from every syllable. "Your pitiful excuses won't save you."

Dakota's face shifted to mock contrition, her hands clasped in front of her. "I'd hardly call it theft. It's a letter opener—barely anything." Her expression turned earnest, her eyes wide. "Can you really hold that against me?"

Behind her, McKenna's fingers moved even faster, her eyes darting back and forth as she dove deeper into Daley's files, skimming through whatever skeletons were hidden there. I could hear her breath quickening, feeding Dakota's confidence as she stalled for time.

Daley's lip curled in disdain. "I'm not some fool for you to charm. *Anything* in this palace belongs to the Imperium, and we do not tolerate theft."

Seeing his growing annoyance, Dakota let out a dramatic sigh, smoothly shifting tactics. She met his eyes, her voice now daring. "Are you sure, Your Majesty? You wouldn't want me to start discussing certain sensitive details about your personal life, would you? And while I'm here, under your control, you know the old saying: information wants to be free."

Daley's eyes narrowed, a dangerous light flickering behind them. "Bluffing won't save you, girl," he snarled, his voice low.

Dakota tilted her head, unperturbed. "Bluffing? Who said anything about bluffing?" She looked Daley dead in the eye, her expression hardening. "If you want to risk it, go ahead. I'm sure some of your loyal subjects would be fascinated to learn about a particular indiscretion." She let the words linger.

Daley's bravado slipped for an instant, his face tightening as his glare shifted from Dakota, to the guards, then back to her. He was clearly rattled, but his pride wouldn't let him back down so easily.

"You think you can intimidate me?" he sneered, though the hard edge in his voice was starting to crack. "You're not the first to try, and you won't be the last."

Dakota smirked, tilting her head slightly as she met his gaze. "Oh, I'm not bluffing, Your Majesty. But I get it—it's hard to take my word on this. Maybe I should lean in and make it clear."

Daley hesitated, his gaze flickering with a mix of suspicion and curiosity. He shot another quick look at his guards, then gave a curt nod. "Fine. If you've got something important to say, let's hear it."

Behind her, I felt McKenna's glee as she stole the final piece of the puzzle. A surge of mental satisfaction told me she'd found exactly what she needed. Dakota's face betrayed nothing, but I knew she sensed it too. She stepped forward, closing the distance to Daley, her confidence as solid as Gibraltar as she leaned in. Dakota whispered a few quick words into his ear.

Whatever McKenna had unearthed, it was enough to give her the leverage she needed. Daley's reaction was immediate. His face drained of color, his mouth tightening into a thin line as he processed what she'd said. For a long, tense moment, he didn't speak, his expression caught somewhere between anger and poorly concealed fear. Finally, with barely controlled rage, he snapped his fingers, gesturing sharply at the guards.

"Let them go," he said, his voice rough, every word laced with frustration.

The confused guards stepped back, releasing us without further question. We walked briskly out of the throne room, holding our pace steady until we'd put some distance between ourselves and Daley's gaze. The trek to the nearest exit took moments but felt longer. I was sure some guard would 'accidentally' fire upon the 'fleeing thieves.' Only when we were safely back in the Jeep did I relax. As I sped away from the Palace, heading anywhere but here, Dakota flashed a triumphant grin, pulling the letter opener from her pocket with a flourish.

Faith arched an eyebrow, clearly exasperated. "Dammit, Dakota!" I snuffed out a giggle. Faith didn't swear much. When the errant laugh was firmly quashed, I asked the important question.

"What did you say to him?"

Dakota shrugged, tucking the letter opener into her bag. "A girl's gotta have some secrets," she said as McKenna suppressed a knowing grin beside her.

I groaned. "We are getting you out of the Imperium before we run into trouble McKenna can't hack our way out of."

I checked the sun. West. We wanted to go west. I'd figure out the details once we were beyond Imperial justice.

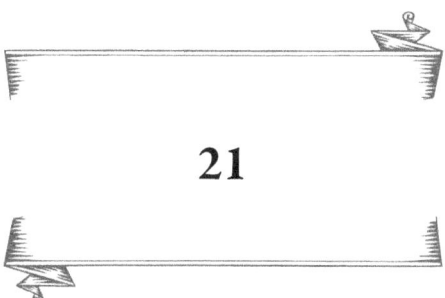

21

As we left Chicago in our rearview, I felt the tension loosening around us. The city's cold, steely skyline faded into the distance, and the unnerving encounter with Daley became another chapter in our endless game of whack-a-human. Dakota was still practically glowing with triumph in the passenger seat, toying with the letter opener like it was a trophy from a victorious hunt.

"So," Faith murmured beside me, her voice barely audible over the hum of the road, "where to now?"

"South and west," I said, eyes on the road ahead, letting the steady rhythm of the drive settle me. "There are better roads, but I'd rather stay out of Daley's reach for the next leg. I'm dead certain that Imperium agents are tailing us; I would, if I were him, if only to be sure we left the country."

"But staying isolated plays into Valaferion's hand, doesn't it? Your idea was good, Dakota," Faith admitted, drawing her in, "but he's obviously not going to try again in a public place. Daley and his minions are second-rate compared to celestial forces."

Dakota shrugged, sliding the letter opener away. "Maybe. I don't know about angelic and demonic crap, but as for Daley's goons? They'd have to know we're worth chasing first." I could see her scanning the horizon as carefully as the rest of us. "Besides, McKenna has them covered, right?"

McKenna's mouth quirked into a smile, and she patted her laptop affectionately. "Yeah, I hacked into their systems before we left the city. I don't want to shut them down and disappear, because that would make them sus, but I'll make sure they have a harder time tracking us than they're used to, and they're gonna have a hell of a time sharing any information. We'll be fine as long as we make the border."

"We'll make the border." I was certain of that, which meant we were down to a one-dimensional threat again. We could handle them. I hoped.

For miles, McKenna kept an eye on her laptop, tracking the NI agents as they shadowed us. Despite our bravado, we were on high alert, each of us glancing at the side mirrors, eyes sharp on the road behind us. Finally, after what felt like hours, the Imperium car slowed and pulled off the road, shortly before we hit the bridge to cross the Mississippi and enter the United States in Davenport.

"They've turned around," McKenna announced with a grin, closing her laptop with a satisfied click. "In a minute, they'll discover that their computers have suffered a catastrophic wipe. That will keep them from having any kind of proof. Better still, nobody on the US side's picked up on us being persons of interest. Looks like we're in the clear."

A breath of relief passed through the Jeep. Dakota stretched, her triumphant grin back in full force. "Guess they figured out we're not worth the chase."

"Oh, we're worth it," Faith said with a half-smile, "but they know when they're outmatched."

The banter flowed. For the first time since Daley's throne room, the weight of what lay behind us—and what might still lay ahead—felt manageable, like a challenge we could handle. The road stretched wide and empty, and for a few peaceful hours, everything was quiet.

Then Nebraska opened up before us, the seemingly endless plains stretching beneath an ominous sky that darkened unnaturally as we drove. I shifted, the initial ease melting into something more tense, a familiar coil tightening at the base of my spine. The flat landscape offered a perfect, unobstructed view of the road ahead, but somehow it felt more suffocating than freeing. The sky hung low, a storm gathering at the edge of our vision, and the looming clouds heralded the arrival of another type of storm.

A prickle ran down my arms, a creeping sense of foreboding that was too powerful to ignore. I glanced at Faith, catching her expression. Her gaze darted upward, her jaw set. She felt it too—that faint, buzzing tension, like static building before a lightning strike.

I scanned the horizon, my fingers tightening on the wheel as I saw a flicker of movement. A shadow cut across the sky then disappeared into the clouds. Dakota's easy grin faded as she, too, sensed the shift in the air. The encroaching silence thickened as more shadows danced across the darkening sky.

Something was coming. Somethings. And I had a sneaking suspicion I knew who they were.

More shadows flickered across the sky, too swift to be clouds, too close to be aircraft. My fingers clenched around the steering wheel, and I felt the familiar surge of Faith spindling *kosmiskorka* beside me, her energy coiling and gathering like the spark before a storm.

"They're here," she said, opening the moonroof again and standing.

Ahead, the horizon blurred as figures gave up the subterfuge, drifting down like feathers in the wind. Angels and demons, their wings a cold, blinding white, moved together in an unnatural alliance. Their combined presence made my nerves sing with an electric tension.

I shouted a warning, but the words were barely out before they attacked. The first angel dove from above, its blade glinting like a comet. I swerved as it sliced past, narrowly missing the Jeep. Faith didn't hesitate. Her hands pulsed with energy as she struck back, a brilliant, blinding arc of *vashwic urja* streaking through the air.

The angel recoiled, its wings singed where her blast had grazed it, but it wasn't enough. A demon swooped in, shifting into a mass of dark fire, and Faith spun, deflecting its strike with a shield of light that sparked and shimmered. The collision of energy cast a strange glow over the plains, bathing the landscape in a cold, otherworldly light.

We weren't going to outrun them, and there wasn't any shelter to be seen. If we were going to make a stand, here was as good a place as any. We screeched to a halt, gravel spraying as I leapt out, taking a moment to unearth the sanctified blade Faith had entrusted to me, the others bailing out behind me. Unlike Thakumis's Blade, this one hummed with a purity that pulsed against my palm. The power coursing through it felt like light forged into steel, a sharp contrast to the darker energy of my usual weapon.

An angel swooped toward me, descending in a deadly arc, its eyes devoid of anything remotely human. I barely had time to brace as it struck, its blade crashing against mine. I parried, twisting the blade upward as it hissed and staggered back, wings flaring wide in anger as it flew up to regroup. I barely had a second to catch my breath before another form closed in, this one wreathed in shadows that writhed and shifted, claws extended as it lunged. Oh, that wasn't good.

Demons had a primary form, like an angel, and a secondary form, like the red-skinned, bat-winged form in pop literature. This, though, was a gift from their master or mistress, a transmutation of their *taaqat* into a form designed to strike fear into humans. Still, I'd seen it before and didn't scare easily. A quick thrust with the sword connected, and it dropped to the ground, dead.

Out of the corner of my eye, I saw Dakota and McKenna weaving through the chaos, trying to add what firepower they could, their movements cautious but focused. Another winged figure appeared, its form shrouded in shadow but with wings as bright as any angel's. McKenna hesitated, her gaze fixed on its wings, lowering her weapon.

"Demon!" I shouted as it lunged toward her. "They're all out for us, so shoot!"

McKenna's eyes went wide, her body tensing as she reacted, barely dodging its strike. Dakota fired a round straight into the demon's chest, the force driving it back momentarily, but it recovered with terrifying speed, snarling as it swiped at them both. I pushed forward, swinging between McKenna and the demon, the edge of my sword catching its chest and dropping it.

Beside me, Faith moved like flowing water, her powers gathering and pulsing outward. She directed a brilliant arc of energy toward a trio closing in on her, the light erupting into a blinding burst that sent two of them staggering back, their wings singed and blackened. But the third, wreathed in shadows and wielding a blade twisted with dark energy, resisted, pushing through her *dhakshan* with a snarl.

"Faith, watch out!" I called, swinging the sanctified blade toward the attacker, slicing through its shoulder and sending it tumbling back with a shriek that cut off abruptly. No demon could stand against the sanctified blade. An angel would be hurt by it, yes, but no worse than being hit by a sword crafted by mortal hands. The fatal wound smoked with an acrid stench, like burning metal and sulfur.

Dakota and McKenna positioned themselves back-to-back, firing with precision, their movements instinctively synced. They adjusted their positions to cover every angle, their focus unbreakable despite the chaos around them. I could feel the echo of their connection in my mind, their link sparking with each new threat they took down together.

Dakota's shots rang out oddly, with intermittent gaps as she found a new target. McKenna's fire was relentless, her stance solid as she kept a steady barrage at the oncoming attackers. Her accuracy allowed her to take head shots, which were temporarily fatal for both angel and demon. Dakota's hits, while painful, were generally torso shots, survivable but irritating.

The attackers didn't relent, pressing us with a brutality that sent a chill through me. These weren't chaotic rogues or rabble, thrown together to take an opportunity. No, they were trained, unified, each one moving as part of a single, lethal force. Where did they get this training? I wondered, but then I wrenched my mind back to now. Another angel dove toward me, and I brought up my sword, the clash of metal sending a shockwave through the air. Golden light blazed along the edges in that contact, fading when I broke away and swung wildly. I connected, a glancing blow that seemed to surprise the angel. It shrieked and fell back, but more figures emerged from the shadows.

Faith's *vashwic urja* flared as she blasted a demon mid-lunge, scattering it into wisps of dark smoke. It left her momentarily drained, her reserves growing low. I moved to shield her, standing as another wave of figures surged forward, allowing her to channel *kosmiskorka* through me to replenish her.

I was out of practice. Too many years dealing with human threats, human problems, and too little time sharpening my skills were taking their toll. *I need to find a gym when this is all over,* I thought to Faith, earning a mental chuckle despite the situation.

It wouldn't help me now. My human body didn't have the endurance it once had, though the muscle memory was intact. Each strike felt heavier than the last, each block took more effort, each step slower. Sooner or later, we'd succumb, the weight of our combined powers straining under the assault.

The next wave crashed against us, relentless, a blur of wings and claws tearing through the air. Faith leaned against me for a heartbeat, *kosmiskorka* flowing through me as her energy replenished, giving her the strength to rise and face them again. Together, we pushed back, her *vashwic urja* blazing bright, striking down one attacker after another. Beside us, Dakota and McKenna fought with skill born of a lifetime on the wrong side of the law, adding their firepower to the fight. The field pulsed with light and shadow, our combined forces barely holding the line against the tide.

Finally, the assault began to slow, the remaining forces hesitating as the ranks of their fallen littered the field.

"They're thinking," I said. "They're scared. Faith?"

I felt her nod.

"Dakota, McKenna, watch for leakers."

"We've got you," Dakota said. I sheathed the sword that had done so well for me and tapped the *kosmiskora* for myself. Faith might be more skilled in using *vashwic urja,* more precise, but I was capable. We needed to get distance between us, not engage at arms length. Playing with a sword wasn't going to win this battle.

Long seconds stretched out, seconds they shouldn't have given us. I felt full to bursting with the energy stored in me when Faith shouted, "Now!" and released a gout of power across the shortened field. I followed suit, my blasts crashing into our foes. Demons and angels fell before our whirlwind. Soon, too soon, surprisingly soon, we drove them back, watching as they melted into the shadows and retreated, their snarls fading into the distance. The air hung heavy with the aftermath, thick with the scorched scent of earth and the lingering tang of metallic blood. Every breath felt like breathing fire, but we'd held.

McKenna and Dakota, still alert, headed to the Jeep to reload. Faith and I stood a little distance away, and I was drained. I couldn't spindle as much power as Faith, and our continuous efforts had exhausted my reserves. Still, the field was clear, and a flicker of relief washed over me.

A dark energy surged on the edge of my senses. I turned, my right hand gripping the blade's pommel, to see her—Lioraeth. She stood tall, her silhouette imposing, her eyes gleaming with a merciless fire that sent a chill through me. Her form flickered and became beast-like, hands growing claws that were easily four inches long. The ground seemed to reverberate with power as she approached, her steps measured but her gaze promising bloodshed.

"Faith!" I wanted her by my side, but her reply dashed that hope.

"We've got more company."

"Angels?" I couldn't turn to look, as Lioraeth continued to close on us.

"No."

I didn't have the extra second to ask what she saw.

"Well, well," Lioraeth said, her voice a low growl laced with evil humor. "I didn't expect to see you up here, *Kalili*. You've been causing so much disruption? You were always a disappointment to Beelzebub, never meeting your potential."

I hadn't thought of the unlamented Prince of Hell in decades. "Glad to hear it, Lioraeth. Makes me feel like I've done something positive with my life."

She waved off my jibe. "And that's the problem, Kalili. You're a demon—"

"No, I'm a Thirteen," I snapped. Lioraeth and I had a history, but it was ancient history, and I didn't feel like being seen as less than I was.

"Demon, Thirteen, whatever," she scoffed. "You're weak, and you always have been. I was hoping for a challenge, but it seems I'll have to settle for killing you."

I met her gaze, drawing the sword and shifting my weight, feeling the hum of the blade pulse in response to her taunt. "Careful what you wish for, Lioraeth," I shot back, my voice edged with venom. "You might choke on that arrogance."

She laughed, a guttural sound that sent a ripple of power skittering across the ground. "I've been sent to put down mortals and celestials alike, Kalili. You're another tally, one that I'm going to enjoy."

With a snarl, she lunged, her claws sharp and swift. I raised the sword, meeting her with an upward slash that forced her to pivot, but that was the end of my initiative. She moved with predatory grace, her attacks calculated and controlled. Each blow she struck felt like a shockwave, her strength monstrous as she drove me back, step by step. I parried her strikes as best I could, borrowing power from Faith through the blade she'd given me. I hadn't realized that using a sanctified blade would deepen my connection with her, and I put it aside to tell her later.

If I survived. Lioraeth might not have the same celestial powers as me, but she far outclassed me in physical combat. Even if I had the *kosmiskorka* to spare, I couldn't retreat far enough long enough to use my powers as a Thirteen. She'd forced me to battle her on her level. I couldn't show weakness, though, not if I wanted to prevail.

"Is that all you've got?" I taunted, catching her claws mid-swipe with the blade, the sanctified energy sparking against her dark aura, sparks flying from her claws on contact.

Her eyes narrowed, fury flashing. "You're starting to annoy me, Kalili." She struck with renewed force, her movements faster, her strikes aiming to slice and tear. Each step we took ground the earth beneath us to dust, and I could feel the energy between us seething like a storm barely contained.

Out of the corner of my eye, I glimpsed Faith's battle and gasped. Our company was another archdemon, Azariel, and they were a right bastard. If there was a demon in Hell who could contest Lilith's mastery of majik, it was them. I didn't know how Faith would fare against this kind of opponent.

I found my attention torn between fending off Lioraeth's attacks and my concern for my love.

Azariel stood, their form shifting like smoke, eyes cold and filled with scorn as they regarded Faith. She held her ground, her *dhakshan* a shield of light around her, but I could sense her hesitation as she met Azariel's gaze.

"Why are you doing this?" Faith's voice was steady, persuasive. "Angels and demons fighting together? This alliance goes against everything you stand for."

Good girl, I thought. *Make them doubt their allegiances.* I parried Lioraeth's swipe and took a fast step toward her, blade outstretched, forcing her to retreat.

Azariel let out a soft, derisive laugh, their tone dripping with contempt. "You still cling to that naive morality, Faith? You never understood the true power of darkness. This isn't an alliance—it's survival."

Faith's brow furrowed but she raised her hands, summoning the *vashwic urja*. "That's not power, Azariel. It's fear." Her voice carried a quiet strength that pierced the darkness surrounding them.

Azariel smirked, dismissing her words with a wave of their hand. "You can spout your ideals, but in the end, you're still a single celestial—a flicker in the grand scheme." They shot a bolt of dark energy toward her, and she countered, *vashwic urja* flying outward, meeting the darkness with blinding light.

As their powers clashed, I caught Lioraeth sneering in my direction, clearly reveling in Faith's struggle. Interesting. She was distracted too. Maybe this was my opening. Taking a quick breath, I tightened my grip and forced Lioraeth back, pressing her with all I had, summoning the memories of battles long past.

"Still think you can put me down, Lioraeth?" I snarled, driving the blade forward, slicing through her defenses and forcing her into a reckless dodge. Her eyes blazed with fury, but she faltered, her expression betraying a flash of doubt. Her strikes grew more frantic, each blow carrying her desperation. She snarled, her anger flickering in her eyes, but I could sense the cracks in her resolve. Still, I wasn't going to beat her with my swordwork, not with arms that felt like limp noodles.

It was time for something new. I opened myself to the *kosmiskorka* and let it flow into the blade, hoping the angelic nature of the sword would keep it from vaporizing from the power pouring into it. I blocked one of her slashes and then pressed forward.

I didn't know if it was the added power or my increased confidence, but I had her on her heels. Her defense was her attack, forcing her opponent to react to her moves. When the tables turned, she was vulnerable, and I could sense her growing fear.

"Something wrong, Lioraeth?" I growled, driving her back one more time. "You thought you could crush us, but you're not even close."

Her face twisted as she stumbled, barely holding her ground. With a last, desperate scream, she shot me a look of pure hatred, but I could see the retreat in her eyes. I made a lunge toward her but was too slow. She turned sharply, her form blending into the night, vanishing with a frustrated hiss as she disappeared.

As Lioraeth fled, my gaze snapped to Faith, who was still locked in a fierce struggle with Azariel. Their forms clashed, light and darkness swirling in a dizzying storm. Faith's *vashwic urja* surged, but Azariel's dark majik pushed back, their face twisted into an expression of deep contempt.

"Faith," Azariel sneered, "do you still believe in that pathetic light of yours?"

Faith's face was set, her eyes blazing with unshakable conviction. "I don't believe in light, Azariel, or darkness as powers to rule the cosmos. I've seen the whole, every inch of its glory, and know that it's a balance. It's you whose belief is faulty. It's everything you've forgotten—everything you've twisted into darkness."

Azariel let out a low, mocking laugh. "Your ideals will die with you, like every other fool who cannot see the power of darkness."

But Faith didn't flinch. Instead, she raised her hands, gathering a concentrated pulse of *vashwic urja*. In a split second the energy grew brighter, more intense, radiating from her like a miniature sun. The brilliance drowned out Azariel's shadows, her light consuming the darkness as she summoned the full force at her command.

Azariel's smirk faded, replaced by a flash of fear as they realized what was coming. They raised their arms in a futile attempt to block, but it was too late. Faith unleashed the *vashwic urja* in a massive, searing wave that tore through the dark aura around Azariel, breaking them apart piece by piece. The power surged forward, and Azariel let out a final scream as they were engulfed, their form disintegrating in a blaze of light. A blast of celestial energy washed over us: Azariel's *taaqat*, released back to the cosmos. It was both a beacon and a warning to any Immortal nearby, signaling the death of the archdemon.

When the light faded, Faith staggered, her face pale but her gaze fixed on the spot Azariel once held. I moved to her side, steadying her, and together we looked over the battlefield, now cleared of any remaining threat. The dust settled around us, the unnatural darkness receding, leaving the clean evening behind.

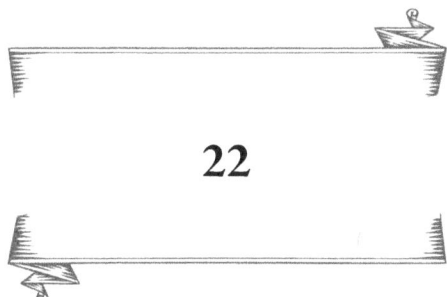

22

"Where the hell are we?" Dakota's voice cut through the quiet of the Jeep, her tone flat with exhaustion. The night stretched on around us, darkened cornfields rushing by in a blur as we hurtled down the empty highway.

I shrugged, too tired to give much of an answer. "Damn if I know, Dakota."

We'd fought hard, and though we'd made it out, every part of me ached. After defeating Azariel and driving off Lioraeth, we'd scrambled back to the Jeep, fleeing west, putting as many miles as possible between us and our latest encounter. It had been hours since then, and the adrenaline had long worn off, leaving only bone-deep weariness.

McKenna didn't look up from her laptop, her eyes focused on the screen as she tracked our location. "We're about ten miles from a wide stretch of highway called Maxwell," she said, her voice low and almost detached.

Faith gave a tired sigh from beside me, glancing at Dakota, then at McKenna, her eyes showing the same exhaustion I felt. "Maybe we should stop for the rest of the night. We need a few hours to get ourselves back together."

I couldn't argue, so I pulled off the highway and onto a secondary road, reassured by McKenna that I was still going the right way.

The lights of a run-down motel flickered in the distance, a beacon of shabby promise against the dark highway. The parking lot was mostly empty, and the place itself looked like it'd seen better decades, but it would have to do. We checked in without ceremony, nodding our thanks to the clerk who barely took her eyes from the television. After dropping our bags in our rooms and setting Bandit free from the carrier, the four of us met back in the parking lot, drawn by the neon glow of an all-night diner across the road.

The diner was nearly deserted, the buzz of the fluorescent lights filling the empty spaces between us as we settled around a table. A server brought us coffee and water, and I relished the peace, broken by the distant clatter of dishes in the kitchen and a few murmured conversations. We ordered whatever was quick and easy without engaging in more than perfunctory small talk.

Faith and I exchanged a look, while Dakota and McKenna sat across from us, nursing their own frustrations. The weight of what we'd been through hung in the air, with nobody willing to break the quiet.

When the food arrived, we ate in near silence, the clinking of silverware the only sound between us. Tension crackled like static in the air, growing thicker with each passing minute, until Dakota finally looked up and broke the moment.

"So," she said, her tone sharper than usual as she set her fork down. "We said we're with you, and we meant it. Mean it. And you've tried to explain what's going on, and we get it, there are things we don't, or can't, understand. But when does it stop? You faced a couple of big bads tonight. Does that end it? Are we through? Or are we supposed to keep rolling with this until one of us doesn't make it out?"

Her words hung between us, her gaze leveled at me. McKenna nodded, her mouth pressed in a tight line as she looked between us, waiting for an answer.

I took a steadying breath, glancing at Faith. She nodded, her expression gentle and encouraging. I knew they deserved answers—or whatever bits of them I could offer—but exhaustion and stress twisted inside me, and I strained to keep my tone even.

"We're handling it—" That's all I managed before Dakota cut me off.

"Kal, you keep saying we're handling it. What does that mean, exactly?" Her voice carried the edge of someone who was reaching her limit. "How much more of this is coming? Are we pawns in some cosmic feud with no say? Because right now, that's what it feels like. You say you're taking care of it, but every time we turn around, we're barely making it out."

Beside her, McKenna looked at me, her expression softer but just as insistent. "Kal, we know it's angels and demons. We know it's some unholy alliance coming after you two. We know you're fighting back, but we don't know how or where we fit in. We're trying to help, but we don't even know what helping looks like right now."

Their words struck hard, their raw frustration and humanity clear in every syllable. They weren't asking for explanations out of ignorance; they wanted to understand what role they were playing and if it mattered. Dakota's gaze didn't waver as she continued, "We can't keep moving blindly through all of this, wondering if the next battle is the one we don't survive. You can't ask us to risk everything without at least giving us a sense of what's coming. We deserve to know that much, don't we?"

McKenna nodded, adding quietly, "Look, Kal, we're fighting, we're doing our best, but we can't do this if we don't know what we're up against—*really* up against."

Their questions hit like blows, one after another, each one heavier, each one weighing down on me with a crushing pressure. I wanted to give them answers, something concrete to make them feel safe, but the truth was, I had no guarantees to give. My hands curled into fists under the table, the words spilling out harsher than I intended before I could temper them.

"You think I have the answers? We've told you all we know. You heard what Avareth told us! That's it, that's everything, there ain't no more for us to give you! Faith and I are just as much in the dark as you are. We're doing everything we can, but there's no guidebook for this. No promises, no guarantees."

Dakota's expression darkened, the hurt in her eyes unmistakable. "So that's it?" she said, her voice edged with carefully controlled anger. "We keep going? You're not the ones risking everything out here, Kal."

"Do you think I don't know?" I snapped back, struggling to keep my tone in check, aware of the few curious eyes from across the diner. "Do you think I don't understand the danger? Faith and I have been dealing with this for longer than I care to remember, and every time, we're making it up as we go. We're trying to survive, same as you."

McKenna leaned in, her voice a hushed but intense whisper. "That's the thing, Kal. We're *not* like you. We don't have whatever cosmic powers and celestial instincts you and Faith have. We're here, doing our best to keep up and getting hit by stuff we barely comprehend. My God, Kal! What you're doing, what we're seeing? It's straight out of the churches my mom tried to drag me to."

"You think I don't feel that?" A part of me softened, seeing the raw fear in her eyes. "Believe me, I'd give anything to have a better answer for you. But this isn't some grand plan. We're not getting handed the rules either."

Dakota's jaw clenched, her voice tight. "We can't be the ones tagging along at the edges, the comic relief, the characters wondering if they'll survive to the final curtain, wondering if this is the time we're not fast enough or strong enough."

I felt a pang of guilt, which flashed into irrational anger. "Look, it's not that simple. I wish it was, but it isn't, and I can't change that.

You want out? Fine. Go. Run back to Brooklyn and your bar, stick your heads in the sand, and hope we can handle this. If we can't? It's going to be Hell on Earth, once the old ways come back." My voice dropped, my fury spent. "But we can't get out. Don't you understand that? We're trapped in this. It's *not* over, it's *not* easy, and I don't know if we'll survive. But we have—no—choice!"

Dakota pushed her plate away, her voice like crystal shattering. "If you don't want us here, we won't stay. Maybe we'll find our own answers, figure it out ourselves. And maybe we should have stayed home. At least then we'd know we were fighting humans. I understand people." She paused, and I thought she was done. Then she crushed me.

"Do you?" She let the question hang between us. After an eternity that was only a few seconds, she stood, McKenna rising beside her, their chairs scraping softly against the floor.

Their retreating figures left a hollow silence in their wake, and the sting of my words lingered. As Dakota and McKenna walked out, guilt twisted in my chest, the sting of regret gnawing deeper with each second. I stared down at my plate, appetite long gone, feeling every word and misstep weigh on me. All the tension I'd been holding back—the exhaustion, the fear, the frustration—seemed to unravel at once, and before I could stop it, a wave of helplessness surged forward, swallowing the last remnants of my composure.

A hand slipped into mine, grounding me. Faith's warm touch pulled me back from the edge. She leaned in close, studying my face. Her fingers wrapped tightly around mine and another arm slid around my waist, pulling me into her.

"Kal," she whispered, her voice a soft anchor. "They're here because they trust us. They're scared—like we are—but they're still here. Don't push them away."

Her words broke something loose, and it all came crashing down. My breath hitched, a raw ache tightening in my chest as the flood of emotions spilled out, years of strain I'd been carrying. The pain of battles we hadn't asked for, of friends thrust into dangers they couldn't possibly understand—all of it surged up, tangled and fierce.

"It's too much, Faith," I whispered into her shoulder, barely holding it together. "Every time I think we're a step ahead, something else blindsides us. I don't know how to protect them anymore. And now... now I've driven them away."

Faith's golden eyes shone with understanding, acceptance, and her love. She gently brushed a stray tear from my cheek, her expression warm. "Kal, you're an idiot."

"I know. You don't have to rub it in."

I felt her smile, soft against my hair. "Not that way. You've always seen yourself as the leader, even when you ran as fast as you could away from it. From our first meeting, you've called the shots." I inhaled to argue, but she placed a finger over my mouth, shushing me. "You've done it out of kindness, and duty, and love. You've listened, and learned, and have always made me feel I had an equal say. I wouldn't be here if you hadn't," she added in a whisper, and my reality trembled. A world without Faith? Unthinkable.

"But you've always borne the brunt of your decisions. You carry all of the burden, and try to take mine, because somewhere, deep down, you still see me as that naïve angel who didn't know any better than to fall in love with a demon. In some ways, I want to be her, let you hold all the responsibility, but I can't. I won't. And it's time you realized it, too."

She moved her head away and turned me to face her. "I love you, my *arima bikia,* and can't imagine not loving you. But I'm not going to let you kill yourself under a weight you don't need to bear. If it's too much for one, then let's find out if it's too much for two. Or four. Kalili, whatever troubles you, you don't have to carry it alone. You don't always have to be the strong one. That's why I'm here. And they are, too, if we let them in."

I closed my eyes, letting her words settle, the knot in my chest loosening as her words washed over me. Her hand in mine felt like an anchor, pulling me back piece by piece. She didn't let go as the emotional hurricane gradually faded into something more manageable.

When I finally met her eyes, she gave me a small, reassuring smile. "We'll go to them," she said gently, squeezing my hand once more. "They need to hear the truth—even if it's hard. Let them see how much we're counting on them, how much we depend on them. Trust them to carry some of it with us."

I nodded. Faith was right. We couldn't afford to let this break us apart. Taking a deep breath, I squeezed her hand back, the beginnings of a plan taking shape, one step at a time.

"First, grovel. Then explain."

Faith grinned at me. "You're good at groveling."

"I've had a bit of practice," returning the grin automatically. I knew what she was doing, trying to keep my mind occupied with happier thoughts, and I let her do it as we walked across the road to the motel. All too soon, Faith and I stood outside Dakota and McKenna's room, the air heavy with every ill-chosen word. I gave a light knock, and after a moment, Dakota opened the door, her expression guarded, her gaze flickering between the two of us before she reluctantly stepped aside.

Inside, bags lay open on the bed, half-packed with clothes and gear. McKenna was sorting through their things, her movements brisk, her shoulders tense. The sight of it—their quiet, stubborn preparation to leave—made my throat tighten.

"That's it?" Faith asked softly, her voice breaking the silence as she looked between them. "You're leaving?"

Dakota's jaw tightened, but she didn't meet our eyes. "You made it clear, Kal. You two don't need us holding you back."

McKenna's expression softened as she glanced at Faith, but her resolve was as solid as her wife's. "We're not Immortals, Kal. We don't have celestial power to keep us safe, and if all we're doing is slowing you down..."

"You really think that's what you're doing?" I stepped forward, keeping my voice low, fighting to keep the rawness of my emotions from slipping out. "Yes, Faith and I have been through more battles than you'd believe, and we're powerful. But do you know what we don't have? What we *can't* bring to the table?" I met McKenna's eyes, taking in her words, showing her that I understood, or was trying to. "Your humanity. You two bring a perspective, a resilience that we don't have—and that changes everything."

Dakota paused, her hands lingering over her half-folded jacket, her face unreadable, eyes still not meeting mine. "You mean you need a couple of rookies to add a touch of chaos to the mix?"

"No." Faith stepped in, her voice firm. You could have built a monument on the solidity of her words. "Your presence keeps us grounded. You remind us of why we fight, of what's worth saving. You two have a strength that doesn't come from powers or weapons. You see things in ways we can't, *feel* things we've forgotten how to feel. We're not asking you to fight *like* us; we're asking you to keep fighting *with* us."

McKenna looked down, her hands falling still. "But... all of this... angels and demons, celestial wars... It's beyond anything we've ever faced. It's terrifying." Her voice was a whisper, but the fear behind it was raw and open for all to see.

"That fear? That's what keeps us going." I willed them to understand as I searched for the right words. "Faith and I have been doing this for so long that sometimes we forget what it means to be truly afraid of losing everything. But you two? You remind us every day. That humanity—the drive to survive against impossible odds—it's what makes you irreplaceable."

Dakota finally met my gaze, her expression softening, her resolve wavering. "We're not liabilities?"

I shook my head. "Not at all. You're the part of us that knows how to hope, how to connect. The part that isn't fighting for survival but for something bigger. Immortals fight to survive against a more powerful foe. Humans fight because it's the right thing to do, because they want to keep a dream alive. You fight for something larger than yourselves. If you walk away, we lose that. We lose... us."

The silence that followed was thick, but it wasn't heavy this time. It was a quiet, shared understanding, and I felt something click into place as the weight of my earlier outburst fell away.

McKenna closed her bag, glancing at Dakota with a small, hesitant smile. "Well," she said, "if you're serious about needing us, I guess we're not going anywhere."

I grinned. "Good. Because I have a plan. And they hardly ever fuck up."

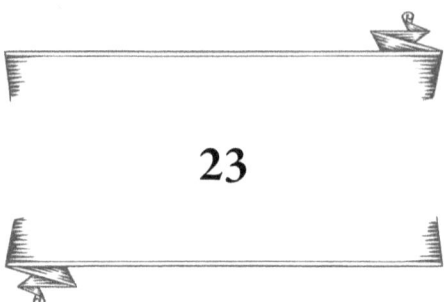

23

As we drove into Denver, the tension in the Jeep was a constant undercurrent, each of us glancing out the windows, watching the city lights with wary eyes. Dakota was quiet in the passenger seat, her usual sharp humor subdued, her fingers tapping a restless rhythm on her knee. McKenna's face was lit by the glow of her laptop screen as she scanned through various feeds, muttering status updates to herself.

"Are we sure this is safe?" McKenna finally asked, breaking the silence. "I'm not picking up anyone tracking us, but that doesn't mean they're not."

Faith leaned over. "We're taking precautions by masking our auras with ones that look human. Denver's big enough that they won't pick us up easily." We'd explained about our ability to alter our auras. After a few pointed questions about why we hadn't done so earlier—the thought never occurred to us—they accepted the logic.

Dakota scoffed softly. "Yeah, well, let's hope they're not already here, blending into the crowd. I'd rather not have another ambush waiting by the front desk. Didn't you say that demons regularly hid themselves among humans?"

I didn't need the reminder. Every block we passed felt loaded with unseen threats, each shadow holding potential enemies. I gripped the wheel a bit tighter, a knot of tension lodged in my chest. The Brown Palace finally came into view, its lights glimmering, an oasis of calm amidst the city's bustle. Even that sight didn't ease the worry that tightened each of our faces.

Inside, the lobby was a strange juxtaposition on our situation: polished wood, crystal chandeliers casting soft light, and an elegant silence. The calm felt almost surreal, and for a second, it was as if we'd stepped into an entirely different world—one where battles didn't wait around every corner.

At the reception desk, Dakota shot a look over her shoulder, her voice barely above a whisper. "Feels a bit too nice, doesn't it? Like someone set the stage."

"It does," I agreed.

"What about our friends? What if they show up?" She spoke carefully, avoiding naming the Immortals who were after us.

I smiled wearily. "Well, if they're planning an attack, they're in for a surprise. I don't know about you, but I'm ready to be off the road for a while. Immortal or not, my ass hurts. It's going to take more than a few demons to get between me and a comfortable bed, so if they want to throw down here? Let's go."

McKenna snorted, but the smile didn't reach her eyes. We finished checking in, each of us scanning the lobby as if expecting an ambush from behind a potted plant.

Once in the suite, I barely set my bag down before Dakota and McKenna sprang into action, their unease fueling their focus. McKenna slid into the small desk's chair, laptop open and screen flickering to life, diving into OutLook's IT structure. Her fingers flew over the keys as she wormed her way through the system. Across from her, Dakota settled into an armchair, phone in hand, her voice a low murmur as she connected with contacts McKenna had dug up, aiming straight for the assistants in OutLook's C-suite.

Faith and I exchanged a glance, our exhaustion giving way to admiration as we watched them work. They might have been as weary as us, or wearier, but their simmering fear and stubborn resilience kept them going, each of them using their talents to chip away at the enemy's defenses. Or, in this case, our target's defenses.

I had enough money to buy OutLook a thousand times over, but money wasn't always all a situation required. That was a lesson I'd learned long, long ago. A company like OutLook, which spent most of its time in the shadows, could slip away and disappear if I didn't apply the right pressure, or use the right leverage. That's what Dakota and McKenna were finding for me now.

Dakota's voice flowed smoothly, her words carefully chosen as she played her part with effortless charm, almost like a game. There was genuine laughter here and there, her tone shifting to match whoever was on the other end of the line, each conversation carefully nudged to reveal critical connections. Her smirk was unmistakable as she pieced together details.

McKenna, on the other hand, was the picture of focus. She hunched over her laptop, the light reflecting off her face, jaw clenched, eyes flicking across the screen. Her fingers waltzed across the keys, each click purposeful as she scanned OutLook's internal structures, searching for even the smallest vulnerability. Her quiet intensity was broken by occasional exclamations as she found another piece of the puzzle.

I nudged Faith. "Look at them," I whispered.

Faith chuckled, her eyes bright with pride as she watched them. "They're naturals," she murmured. "We couldn't have picked a better pair. What brought you to them all those years ago?"

I shrugged. "A hunch? A message from Na'le? Who knows?" I finished with a grimace. "Maybe it was all coincidence."

"And maybe it was meant to be. Like us, *arima bikia*."

The words hung in the air between us, filling the quiet room with a warmth I hadn't expected. In the midst of the fear, there was something profoundly grounding about having these two alongside us.

Faith's pride mirrored my own, and for a moment, it felt like we were back on steadier ground, stronger than before.

Even as the feeling settled, the air shifted, a familiar hum prickling at the edges of my senses. I shot Faith a glance and fed her my peculiar gift. There was no mistaking it; we felt the familiar pull of celestial energy. Before either of us could react, the space in the center of the room shimmered, and then Avareth and Lilith *popped* into reality, standing side by side. Dakota and McKenna glanced over, but neither stumbled or skipped a beat.

Lilith's gaze was as penetrating as ever when she locked eyes with me, a faint, cold satisfaction in her expression. "Valefar is dealt with," she said, her tone leaving no room for ambiguity, no doubt about his fate. "He broke, spilling every drop of information he had before I sent him to the Lake of Brimstone. Their unholy alliance is confirmed, as Avareth suspected, but it's more intricate than she'd imagined."

She glanced sidelong at Avareth and her mouth tightened into something between a smile and a warning. "Perhaps if certain trusted advisors brought things like this to my attention sooner, we wouldn't have been blindsided by this little scheme."

Avareth's expression stayed calm, but I caught the way her shoulders tensed. The anger pulsing through our link was a dead giveaway, too. "With respect, my Lady, Kalili and Faith are the constant targets of cracks and nutters. We had no reason to suspect this was anything but another half-baked rumor until recently, albeit with more powerful players."

Lilith grunted, either in acknowledgment or assent, and Avy continued. "Since you broke Valefar, we've been intercepting demons cycling through the soul queue as they've been killed, interrogating them as to the where and when of their death." Demons who weren't killed by an angel or angelic object—like a sanctified sword—were regenerated. It was a closely monitored process, and since there was only one such queue, easy to intercept.

Demons who died by heavenly powers didn't regenerate, nor did victims of Thakumis's Blade. Which meant every one I'd killed was one which wouldn't be spilling secrets. Faith's victims, as well as ones who fell to Dakota and McKenna, would regenerate.

Avy finished with, "Ariel tells me that she's done the same in Heaven, and between us, we have already neutralized several who requested new bodies to circumvent exposure."

Lilith's smile didn't reach her eyes. "Good to know that at least the interception went smoothly. Still, Avareth, I trust you're aware of the importance of *proactive* action—bringing these issues to me more frequently, not less." She folded her hands, the irritation plain as she looked between Avareth and me. "This situation requires direct handling, and we've already let it run its course too long."

Avareth dipped her head respectfully, though I could tell the reprimand had hit its mark. "Yes, my Lady," she replied evenly.

Satisfied, Lilith turned back to me, her mouth curving slightly as her tone edged into dark satisfaction. "Valefar's information, while useful, isn't the end of it. We felt the death of Azariel when their *taaqat* was released, but Valaferion, Lioraeth, Seraphina, and Zadkiel remain. According to some of the regenerated demons, they planned to gather their forces for a final assault. We're not yet certain of their timing, but I'm closing in on their location."

The enormity of what we were up against hit me all over again. We were looking at a Duke of Hell, an archdemon, an Archangel, and a principality—some of the strongest beings in the celestial and infernal realms. It would take every shred of strategy we had to face this lineup and make it out intact.

As I nodded, taking in Lilith's words, Avareth looked back at me, her mask fully in place, but I could feel the turmoil beneath the surface. Her love for us, her worries, clashed with her ironbound commitment to her duty to her liege.

"As soon as I know more, I'll tell you. Avareth." Our lilac-haired love turned to her mistress. "I will expect you in Hell… by morning." Was that a twinkle of understanding in Lilith's eye? Surely not. Then again, she surprised us on occasion.

"I'll be there, my Lady," Avy said, and I couldn't resist adding, "No guarantees on how coherent she'll be," before Lilith vanished.

Lilith's departure left a charged silence in the room. Avy's mask fell and her concerned gaze lingered on Faith and me. She approached us, her usual confidence softened, her eyes shadowed with thoughts she hadn't yet voiced.

"It's only going to get harder from here," she said, her voice meant only for us. "You've already risked so much." Her hand reached out, and before I knew it, I had taken it in mine, reassuring her with my touch.

Faith leaned into her other side, her hand resting on Avareth's shoulder as she replied, "That's the nature of things, isn't it? We wouldn't know what to do if life was easy."

Avareth's lips quirked into a pained smile, her fingers tightening in mine. "Leave it to the two of you to turn a business trip into a chance to flirt with disaster," she said affectionately. I felt the weight of her care for us in the way her eyes held mine, and I couldn't resist brushing my thumb along her hand, pulling her closer.

"Danger is what brought us together, Avy," I replied softly. "I wouldn't change it. Neither would you."

Faith wrapped an arm around Avareth's shoulders, resting her head against Avareth's. "Besides, it gives us more reason to keep holding on. To each other."

Across the room, I could tell Dakota and McKenna were doing their best to look away, pretending to be completely engrossed in their tasks, but I saw the faintest smile tugging at Dakota's mouth as she shot a sidelong glance our way. McKenna tried to hide her amusement by coughing into her hand, but I could sense their barely contained grins.

I met Faith's gaze, a glint of laughter in my own as I leaned in to brush a kiss against Avareth's cheek, feeling Faith's hand slip into mine, closing our circle. Faith chuckled softly, her breath warm against Avareth's hair. "Guess we're giving them a show," she whispered, glancing over her shoulder at Dakota and McKenna, whose exaggeratedly innocent expressions didn't fool any of us.

Avareth's smile softened as she regarded Dakota and McKenna. "Let them watch," she said with warmth in her voice, eyes glinting with a familiar teasing edge. "Maybe they'll pick up a few tips if they see it all the way through."

I caught Faith's amused glance as I replied, "Later. And honestly? For humans, they've had quite the run together. Not sure we could teach them anything new about handling a relationship."

Faith chuckled. "If they haven't learned by now, they've certainly found a way to make it work," she added, with an approving nod toward the duo.

I turned my head to Dakota and McKenna, who gave up the subterfuge and were watching us with undisguised interest. "We're all in this together," I said, my voice steady as I turned back to Avareth, who nodded in silent agreement. "No one is turning back."

A gentle smile graced Faith's face as she added, "You two have held up better than most would. I don't think we'd be here without you."

Dakota shifted in her seat, exchanging a look with McKenna, her usual sharpness softened, almost shy. "Yeah, well." She brushed off the compliment as her eyes met mine again. "We're still hanging in there. Now that we know where we stand, what the stakes are? We're not gonna flake on them now."

I let the words settle, then probed for the bond that had tethered us so closely. To my surprise, I felt only a faint echo, like a whisper on the edge of hearing. Whatever had linked us had faded, but I could still sense the tie between Dakota and McKenna.

"That's odd," I said.

"What?" Avy asked.

"Well..." I hesitated, suddenly embarrassed. I hadn't told Dakota and McKenna that I could feel their bond, and I worried that bringing it up now would hurt the new understanding we'd reached. But I'd spoken aloud, and it was too late to pretend I hadn't, so I'd have to bull through.

"Remember that curious sensation I was telling you about?" I sent a mental plea to Avy to play along.

"Yeah. You said it felt like your link to us, right?"

I nodded, playing my part. "Exactly! Well, I think I figured out what it was."

"Don't keep me in suspense, Kal."

"It was my perception of the link between them, but now it's almost gone." I pointed to Dakota and McKenna.

Avy didn't say it, but her body screamed relief. "I was hoping it was a temporary effect. Linked humans would be difficult to explain away."

I shook my head. "No, not their link. My connection to them."

Faith got it first. "You can't feel them—"

"Not as strongly, no."

"—but they can still feel each other?"

Avy stiffened, and I reached out with my mind. *Wait. Don't explode. This could be good for us. It has been already, and if it can continue...*

"I think so." I turned to Dakota. "I'm right, aren't I? You two still feel it?" I studied their faces. "The link?"

McKenna nodded slowly, casting a sideways glance at Dakota. "It's there. Maybe stronger. It's easier, smoother, now." She looked back at me, uncertainty in her eyes. "We thought it'd fade by now, but it's permanent, isn't it?"

Avareth nodded thoughtfully, her expression considering, calculating the odds, figuring the best angle to take. "Looks like it. May I?" She separated from us and approached Dakota, extending a hand but stopping before it touched her forehead. "I'm not going to do anything to hurt you. Kal and Faith wouldn't like that."

Dakota nodded, and Avy closed the last inches. The touch lasted seconds, and she returned to our side of the room before speaking. "It's permanent. This sort of bond is rare in humans, and powerful. Sometimes it means there's celestial blood in your veins, but I couldn't detect any. You're unique among humans, as far as I know." Half-turning to us, she added, "It's the *arima bikia* bond, like what we have."

"*Arima bikia*?" McKenna stumbled over the celestial words.

"The closest human term is soulmate. It's a bond that transcends time," Faith explained.

Dakota shot another glance at McKenna, then back at us, her face softening as she took in the gravity of Avareth's words. "Alright, then," she said, half to herself, half to us. "Telepathy. Soulmates." She snorted. "I coulda told you that thirty years ago. Still... Damn, this could be useful!"

I knew where her thoughts went without reading them. "Heists? Dakota, are you serious?"

"What? No radios to get picked up or go haywire. It's perfect!"

I shook my head and Faith laughed. "I'm not bailing you out," I said, but we all knew I didn't mean it. Faith's hand found mine again and she drew Avy in with her other arm. The warmth of her touch, the comfort of being connected, strengthened all of us.

Dakota rolled her eyes, an echo of her planner persona breaking through. "Alright, you three. Let's not get too cozy. Some of us still have work to do." Her tone held no bite, just fondness from shared battles and the camaraderie forged through fire.

An hour later, we were all flagging, so we decided to put our tasks aside and check in. We gathered in the suite's sitting area, drinks in hand. Dakota perched on the edge of a plush armchair, one leg crossed over the other, idly twirling a pen between her fingers. "So, here's the gist," she said, voice all business. "I've reached out to everyone McKenna identified and managed to get a couple of the assistants chatting, but it's like peeling layers off an onion. OutLook's C-suite plays things close to the vest, and that extends to their help."

"They're smart, and probably scared," Faith said, leaning forward with her elbows on her knees. "I can't imagine the various governments are happy about their existence."

Dakota nodded. "Right. They're holding back, but I can tell they're more than corporate suits. There's something fortified about their defenses, even in conversation."

McKenna looked up from her laptop, where she'd been running a scan of OutLook's digital defenses. "Their IT security backs that up. I've cracked through the first firewall, but they're running some serious redundancy. Whoever's pulling the strings at OutLook didn't slap on a few firewalls and call it a day. They're smart, and they're cautious. I'll need more time to get to anything worthwhile."

I nodded, my mind racing through our options. "I have to say I'm encouraged by your lack of progress." At their confusion, I added, "They're in the intelligence business. If we could get them to drop information with some phone calls and minor hacking, they wouldn't be worth the effort." They nodded, and I continued. "McKenna, can your automations work without you supervising?"

"Not as effectively, but yeah."

"Good. We all need rest, but we need to be in their systems. Anything we can get on them, even if it seems harmless, might be enough for me to work with." I glanced at Faith, who met my eyes with a spark of inspiration.

She turned to McKenna. "Do you think you'll have access to the department calendars by morning?"

McKenna shrugged, her fingers tapping a rhythm on the edge of her laptop. "If I can slip past their internal barricades, yes. Why?"

Dakota gave me a look that was almost conspiratorial. "What's the plan, boss? You walk in there and buy them out?"

"More or less, yes. That's exactly it." I leaned back, a sharklike smile breaking through. "I'm going to walk in, drop a platinum credit line on their desk, and tell them to sell. OutLook will never see me coming."

McKenna chuckled softly. "Simple and classic. Here's hoping their drive for money outweighs their caution."

"I've never gone wrong betting on greed."

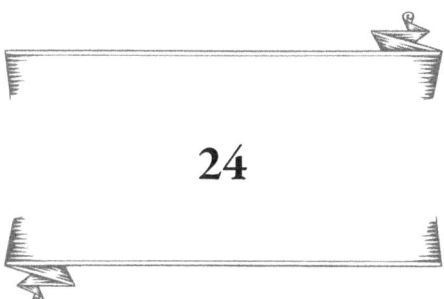

24

As we pulled up a block away from OutLook HQ, I took in the building's sleek design, all glass and steel. The sharp lines hinted at wealth and influence, somehow blending into the city's skyline rather than dominating it. Futuristic without flaunting it, like OutLook wanted to convey power with subtlety.

Dakota and McKenna hunkered down in the back, McKenna doing her magic with her keyboard, the screen's glow flickering over her face. Dakota was leaning back, her phone in hand, swiping through contacts and muttering as she readied for the social engineering tactics ahead.

"Look at that place," she complained, eyes lifting to the looming glass structure. "You'd think with all the money they dropped into their building, they'd have nothing left to put into security." Her tone was tinged with annoyance. "Nope. It's like they're *expecting* us. Whoever set up OutLook's system deserves a raise… and a punch in the face."

McKenna chuckled without looking up. "Careful, Dakota. Your flair for social engineering might get you an offer to join their security team."

"Doubtful," Dakota replied. "I don't think they'd take kindly to my methods. But hey, anything's possible."

Faith looked at me with amusement, and I couldn't hide a grin. "You two have this under control, right?" I asked.

Dakota rolled her eyes. "Kal, please. I could do this in my sleep." Her fingers drummed against her thigh as she added, "We'll send what we find your way through Faith."

That was a wrinkle Dakota presented to us after we'd caffeinated. "There's no way they let you inside with any electronics, no matter how innocent you try to look, but we don't need them. You and Faith, you can talk to each other like we can. That's what you said, that arima thing, right?" I'd nodded. "So we stay behind and keep working, and Faith feeds you what we discover. They'll never pick up on it, and they can lock you in a lead box and you'll still know what's going on."

"What's this about a lead box?"

She gave me a look of pity. "Didn't you ever read Superman? Never mind."

That also decided whether one of my companions would play the role of my assistant. As a big-money player, I'd be expected to have at least one flunky. On the other hand, appearing alone was a statement of confidence. In the end, it came down to numbers. I needed Dakota and McKenna to keep working their magic with security, so they were out. Faith was out, because she was our link. If it all fell in the shitter—always a possibility, with an organization like OutLook—it would be simpler for me to self-extract than worry about additional bodies. Avy, who'd returned to Hell before breakfast, was a phone call away and was our hole card.

McKenna glanced up, nodding to Faith, her face serious again. "I've got the third layer of the firewall cracked, but the fourth one's tougher. I'll keep digging."

"Don't forget to put me on their calendar."

McKenna's response was a distracted nod.

Faith reached out to squeeze my hand, easing the vultures circling in my chest. "Don't worry, my love," she said, her voice low and steady. "You can do this."

"I love your belief in me."

"I've believed in you since the day I met you."

I gave her a sideways look. "You mean when you were assigned to kill me?"

"Even then."

Before my treacherous mouth could say anything else, I leaned over and kissed her, then stepped out of the Jeep. Faith's telepathic link was a lifeline, helping me focus as I crossed the street to Out-Look's headquarters. Without glancing at the Jeep, I could feel their presence filling my mind, adding stature to my steps as I walked into the lobby with confidence that said I belonged there.

The first layer of security was standard, almost amusingly so. Two guards stood at attention, their gaze flicking to me as I approached the minimalist checkpoint. A metal detector framed the entrance, and a small glass booth housed another guard monitoring cameras. I was greeted by a smartly dressed attendant behind a desk who offered a polite but guarded smile.

"Good morning, ma'am. May I have your ID and reason for your visit?"

I gave her a warm smile, handing over my passport and the sleek business card Dakota had helped me perfect: *Kalili Keoka, Principal Investor, Keoka Global Ventures.* The card itself was heavy in the hand, understated yet luxurious, giving off the impression of discreet wealth and power. We used it when I was the beard for her long cons, but there was reality behind the illusion.

I introduced myself, my tone friendly but firm. "Kalili Keoka. I have a meeting with the CEO." I added a small, knowing smile as if we shared a secret about how money moved in these circles.

The attendant's brow furrowed slightly, glancing at her screen. "I don't see an appointment here, but perhaps it's a recent addition. Could you share a bit more detail?"

Dammit. McKenna must not have gotten into the calendar app for the building. I'd have to bluff my way past.

I leaned in, lowering my voice with a practiced intimacy that conveyed trust and urgency. "I'll tell you what I can. It's all about the 'currency of the future'—information. Our firm has considerable capital ready to put behind OutLook's operations, and I'm here to see if we can come to an arrangement."

I felt Faith's amusement and nearly blew the game by giggling. The attendant didn't notice, her gaze shifting to assess me carefully. I could see her interest piqued by the phrase Dakota had insisted I use: information as currency. It practically screamed of exclusivity and importance. After a beat, she gave a slight nod.

"Understood, Ms. Keoka. If you'll step through here for a quick screening, we can get you set up."

I passed through the metal detector without a hitch, allowing a guard to search through my mostly empty bag while sending a message to Faith to stop laughing at me. Once I was through, I was directed toward a glass elevator that took me on a silent, smooth ascent to the C-suite's floor.

As I stepped out of the elevator, I was met by an assistant seated behind a polished hardwood desk, his nameplate reading *Marco Alvarez*. He gave me a practiced, courteous smile, but I could see the slight arch of his eyebrow, the tension in his posture. He knew exactly who belonged here—and it wasn't me.

"What are you doing here?" he asked without preamble. I had a provisional pass, having cleared security downstairs, but his smooth tone carried his suspicion. His gaze swept over me with the subtlety of someone trained to spot intruders. I knew that if I gave the wrong answer I wouldn't get another foot into the building.

As I was framing my response, Faith's presence in my mind nudged me. *McKenna's still working on the schedule, but Dakota found something on him. Stock dealings—it's a gray area at best. The timing is sus. He probably used some insider information he shouldn't have access to.*

I allowed a slow, predatory smile to curl my lips as I leaned in, keeping my voice low. "Marco, may I call you Marco?" He nodded, the frozen smile as fake as a politician's honesty. "Let's not waste my time. I doubt your boss would appreciate the fallout if we had to discuss certain investments you're holding on the side. Ones you made using certain corporate assets that you oughtn't have, if you know what I mean."

His eyes widened a fraction, enough to betray the fear beneath his calm exterior. I saw the muscles in his jaw clench, his hands tightening momentarily on the tablet in front of him. The mask slipped and I could practically see the calculations running through his mind.

"I don't know what you're talking about," he replied for the benefit of any microphones listening, his voice carrying a barely noticeable tremor. "But I'll let you through. This time."

"Much appreciated," I replied smoothly, giving him a small nod as I lazed past, catching the way his shoulders sagged with relief the second he thought I was out of view.

The hallway leading to the CEO's office was quiet, every sound swallowed by thick carpet, every view muffled by soft, ambient lighting. It felt like walking through a gallery where everything had been designed to impress but not overwhelm. As I approached the final door, another assistant stepped in front of me. She was poised, with a polished, detached demeanor that told me she'd turned away her share of overconfident visitors.

I can't bluff this one, I sent to Faith.

She's almost there.

I stuck my hand out. "Hello."

She took it, an automatic reaction, and I stripped her name from her memories. Lina Chen. I sent that to Faith, just in case.

"Do you have an appointment?" she asked, releasing my hand. Her eyebrow lifted slightly, her tone impeccably polite but skeptical.

"Yes, of course I do," I replied smoothly, keeping my tone calm as I waited for McKenna's trick to settle into place. "Kalili Keoka. Check your calendar," I added, giving her a knowing smile as if I'd been expected all along.

The second I finished speaking, Faith sent me a message. *McKenna says it's in. You're fashionably late.*

Lina's eyes shifted to her tablet, her confident expression faltering as she scrolled down, a frown creasing her brow. She didn't look up immediately, and I didn't push.

"Yes, you're on here. We've expected you," she said finally, her voice taking on a slightly clipped tone as the lie slipped out. She stepped aside with a practiced smile that didn't reach her eyes.

I walked past her, letting her close the door with a soft click, and found myself in the office of the CEO. I'd noted his name on the door, Oskar Lindgren, and the furnishing matched his name. It was everything I'd expected—calculated, minimalist, each piece of furniture a testament to the company's wealth. The only exception to the less is more theme was the desk. It dominated the room and was empty except for a tablet and a slim stack of precisely placed documents.

Behind the desk sat a tall, composed man, his pale hair neatly styled, his ice-blue eyes studying me with an intensity that bordered on chilling. His expression remained unreadable, an impassive mask that betrayed nothing, though I felt he was sizing me up. That was fine; I was doing the same to him, and I already had him pegged.

He inclined his head slightly, his gaze sharp. "Miss...?"

"Keoka. Kalili Keoka," I replied, taking the seat across from him without being invited, meeting his gaze evenly. I could tell he was used to power games, to people bending under his scrutiny, but I wasn't here to play by his rules. "I'm here to make an offer, Oskar."

He leaned back, fingers steepling, his eyes narrowing a fraction. "An offer," he echoed, though he held himself with an almost exaggerated calm.

I kept my eyes locked on his. "Information is the currency of the future, and I'm a buyer with unlimited resources," I said, letting the words settle between us before dropping my bombshell. "How much for OutLook?"

His eyebrows lifted, and for the first time curiosity flashed in his eyes before being shuttered by his professional demeanor. Oskar's fingers tapped slowly against the desk, his expression never shifting from that practiced calm. "You seem confident, Miss Keoka," he said, drawing out each word as if tasting it. "But I'm not sure confidence alone is enough to purchase OutLook."

I leaned forward, meeting his calm with a knowing smile. "Confidence is the beginning, Oskar. Let's not pretend this is about whether I have the means. We both know I wouldn't be here if I didn't."

He arched an eyebrow. "True. However, OutLook is more than another business asset. It's a carefully built network—one that's deeply integrated into markets that might not be amenable to a change in ownership."

"Oh, I wouldn't be so sure about that," I replied smoothly. "In my experience, most markets are surprisingly adaptable when the right *encouragement* is applied."

His expression remained unmoved. "I don't think you understand, Miss Keoka. It's a delicate ecosystem that requires understanding beyond mere financial means. We're talking about an organization that is, essentially, a gatekeeper of information. We're selective with our partnerships."

I allowed myself a small, amused chuckle. "Selective is one way to put it. Another would be cautious to the point of limiting growth.

Paranoid? That might go too far. I wouldn't be here if I thought Out-Look had reached its potential."

"Or if you didn't think you could profit from it," he countered, a faint smile emerging as he folded his hands neatly. "OutLook's growth, Miss Keoka, is a carefully calculated strategy, not something to be recklessly inflated for personal gain."

I tilted my head slightly, amusement in my tone. I hadn't had this much fun in years. "Isn't that exactly what a company like OutLook is for? To create value?" I let the words hang in the air. "If it isn't, then maybe you're not the visionary you think you are."

Oskar's mouth tightened almost imperceptibly, his fingers tapping once against the desk before he responded. "I suppose I should appreciate your directness, Miss Keoka," he said, his tone colder now. "My duty to OutLook's vision extends beyond profit margins. We don't respond to pressure."

"Then maybe it's time you considered a new approach," I replied, keeping my tone light but not hiding my irritation. "One that embraces both growth and innovation. A forward-thinking approach that a company with the right investor can fully realize."

His eyes narrowed, studying me with an intensity that suggested he was weighing every word, every inflection. "You present an interesting perspective," he said at last. "One which may be most enlightening to examine further. However, OutLook is not for sale. If that's all you came here to discuss, I'm afraid we're done."

I crossed one leg over the other as I met his gaze. "That's where you're wrong, Oskar. OutLook is *entirely* for sale," I replied, my voice firm. "It's a matter of the right number."

I took out a pen and paper, scribbled a figure that would make most CEOs drool, and slid the sheet across the desk to Oskar. His expression shifted as he read the figure. I could see the flicker of genuine surprise in his eyes—maybe even the faintest touch of admiration. Still, when he looked back up, his face was set, a mask of resolve.

"That's impressive, Miss Keoka, but I can't accept it," he said, folding the paper in half before creasing it firmly. I noticed he didn't return it, keeping it in front of him, his fingers resuming their tapping. I was getting a read on his tells, and this screamed uncertainty. "As I said, OutLook is not for sale. It's not about the money, but a duty to our clients and suppliers. We've built a unique foundation here. You understand why I'm reluctant to let it go."

Just then, Faith's voice touched my mind. *No leverage yet. Keep him talking.*

"Fair enough," I said, the picture of relaxation. "But you're a businessman, Oskar. You know everyone has a price—OutLook is no exception. You say this isn't about money? Fine. Let's talk motivation." He didn't shut me down, so I continued. "I need the best, most up-to-date information available. My interests are broad, and I require full control over how that information is sourced and used."

He tilted his head, eyes narrowing as if he were trying to read beyond the words. "Full control, you say? I'm afraid it's out of the question. If it's access to quality information you're after, I could bring you in as a client—at a considerable level of access, of course. We'd even custom-tailor data reports for your specific interests. That way, you'd have the information without all the administrative baggage."

I couldn't help but chuckle at his volley. When I answered, I let feigned impatience color my tone. "Appreciate the offer, Oskar, but a client relationship isn't what I had in mind. I prefer control over dependency. I'm not in the business of asking permission when I need intel."

Our eyes locked, and for a moment, we were at an impasse. I could feel his pride urging him to hold his ground. Then I felt a sudden rush of excitement from Faith in my mind. *McKenna's in,* she relayed. *Sierra's lending a hand remotely. They've locked OutLook out of their servers. Nothing on Lindgren, but...*

Information was the currency of the future; more accurately, *access* to information. Wasn't that what I'd been saying? I guessed it was time to prove it. I reached across the desk, reclaiming the paper. Without breaking eye contact, I struck through the original number and wrote a new one—half the initial offer. I pushed it back across, watching his expression as he took it in, the corner of his mouth twitching in amusement.

Oskar laughed softly. "Dropping your bid? Miss Keoka, that's not how negotiations are supposed to work."

I smirked. "Then maybe you're not as up-to-date on current events as you thought. Why don't you pull up some exclusive data—say, regarding the current war in the New England Collective? I'd love to see what you have that isn't already public. I'll pay, of course. Whatever your client rates are. If you can do that, I'll drop my offer and walk out. If not..." I let the implication dangle.

He turned to his desk and tapped a button I hadn't noticed. A monitor rose from the surface, and another panel slid aside to reveal a keyboard and touchpad. "Pretty slick," I said, but he didn't respond. His fingers flew over the keyboard, accessing the secure server. A moment later, his brow furrowed, frustration flashing across his face as he tried again, only to be met with error after error. He glanced up, his mouth tightening. "What...?"

I shrugged, satisfaction blooming in my chest. "Information is only valuable when it's accessible. Maybe OutLook isn't the best, Oskar. But I'll give you another chance to say yes. With my offer, OutLook *can* be the best. You need to choose... wisely."

He hesitated, processing his loss of access. "This isn't a decision I can make on my own," he finally said, straightening up. "The board would have to approve the transfer of ownership after a thorough evaluation of any offer and the financing behind it."

I pointed to my offer. "I've done my research. For what you do, the network you've created, the infrastructure you've built? That's triple what the company would be worth on the open market. As for financing? This is a cash deal, Oskar. No banks, no middlemen. And the board is entirely an advisory committee. They don't hold any real power, and their approval is a formality," I replied, dismissing his excuse. "They'll do as they're told if the CEO says yes. So, Oskar—do we have a deal?"

He held my gaze, the mask slipping as he weighed his options. After a moment, he sighed, resignation settling into his expression. "Yes," he said, the word clipped. I could hear his worry about his future in the syllable and hurried to reassure him.

I retrieved another of the *Keoka Global Ventures* business cards and placed it on his desk with a light tap, my voice warm. "I don't anticipate making changes in leadership, Oskar. Why fix what isn't broken? I wouldn't be here if I didn't value what you and the company offered." I paused to let that sink in before adding, "I'd like this to be as smooth as possible. A binding memorandum of understanding would be ideal, something to get the ball rolling. Today. If you could draft that, Oskar, I'd appreciate it."

"I'll need access," he said. "I assume you were responsible for this?"

"Me?" I put on as innocent a face as I possessed. "How could I do such a thing?"

"I don't know," he growled, "but it would be worth teaching us."

"A woman has to have some secrets, Oskar. Without admitting anything—purely hypothetically—I might have a few connections that would interest you. After we're in business together, we can talk about a meeting."

Let Oskar back in, I sent to Faith. A few seconds later I felt her affirmation.

He didn't notice my distraction and turned to his computer, typing up the document with swift keystrokes. I adopted a friendlier tone. "OutLook has built something exceptional. I'm looking forward to seeing it reach its potential."

Oskar glanced up, his guarded expression softening slightly, his tone curious. "You've got unconventional methods, Miss Keoka. I'd be lying if I said it wasn't refreshing. Most people with power are far more formal. Stuffy. Full of their own importance." He managed a small, reluctant smile, finally giving in to my charm offensive.

I returned the smile, unflappable. "Well, I'd hate to be predictable, Oskar. That's a weakness I can't afford."

The printer below the desk hummed to life, producing two crisp copies of the MOU, and he reached to grab them. "You don't seem to miss much, I'll give you that."

"Glad to hear it," I replied with a glint of humor. "Consider this the start of a strong, mutually beneficial relationship." I reviewed the document, noting the simplicity and the lack of legalese. "Thank you for sticking to the bones, Oskar. I'm sure all the legal vultures will get their pounds of flesh, but there's no need to start now."

He called in his assistant to witness the signatures, and as we signed on the dotted lines, I could almost feel the air shift to a sense of cordial professionalism. Lina, after scanning and copying the documents, gave me a respectful nod as she exited. I slid my original of the MOU into my bag, casting a final, pleased look at Oskar.

"I'll expect the board's approval within two weeks," I said, my tone leaving no room for argument.

He chuckled, a low, reluctant sound. "I suppose it's best not to keep you waiting, Miss Keoka."

"No. Patience isn't my strong suit."

Not in this lifetime, Faith added and I suppressed my smile. With a final nod, I left the office and made my way to the elevator, my pulse humming with satisfaction. The moment I was outside, Faith's voice buzzed through our mental link. *Did you get it?*

We got it!

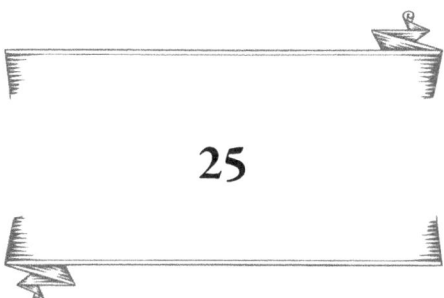

25

The suite buzzed with an electric, post-victory high, each of us holding glasses as we toasted the purchase. There was a lightness to the moment as we realized that, for once, things had gone exactly as planned. Faith stood close, her eyes bright with pride as she raised her glass to meet mine.

"To the best investor I know," she said, a grin spreading across her face as we clinked glasses.

"Only the best for the team," I replied, letting the champagne fizz on my tongue, the bubbles matching the excitement in the room. "And let's face it—having real-time intel means no more surprises, right?"

Dakota snorted, dropping into an armchair. "Congratulations. You have your private CIA. Now you can spy on the entire human world."

"Not spying," I corrected with a shrug. "Staying aware. Connected."

She raised an eyebrow. "Uh-huh. And I'm sure this is purely for *informational* purposes, right?"

I waggled a finger at Dakota. "Exactly right. Don't get any sneaky ideas about using OutLook as your personal search engine for your next job." She feigned an innocent look, which fell flat, and everyone laughed. McKenna perched on the arm of the chair, laughing harder than anyone else. "Besides, I thought you were retired from that life?"

Holding her wife's hand, Dakota answered, "Mostly."

I laughed, setting my glass down as I leaned back in my seat. "I'm serious, Dakota. Staying one step ahead is how we'll survive the rest of this century. I don't think this country is finished crumbling, and what happens then?" I glanced at McKenna, who gave me a nod of agreement, understanding the bigger picture.

Faith laced her fingers with mine. "We don't have to live here, but we choose to. We like being around people, and now we won't be taken by surprise by *anyone,* celestial or human." Dakota looked confused, so Faith explained. "Most Immortals operate in the shadows of the human world, making ripples that turn into waves. Even if we can't pinpoint them directly, we ought to be able to triangulate their point of contact among humans based on odd effects. We feed that information to our friends—" She jerked her thumb down, then up. "—and let them take care of the rest."

Sobering us, McKenna said, "Speaking of Immortals, what about the unholy host?"

Shit. In the excitement of the moment I'd forgotten about the forces aligned against us.

"I think our best bet is to get home fast. They'll take time to track us down, and we'll be back on our home turf. Our building's not perfect, but it's as close to invisible to the Immortal realms as we can make it," Faith said, pausing before finishing with, "And I think we ought to jump there."

"Jump?" It burst out of me before I could stop it. "Remember what happened last time?"

Dakota and McKenna shared a look before McKenna said, "Yeah, I do. We ended up with a gift we wouldn't trade for anything."

Okay, so I wasn't going to get anywhere with that argument. I tried another tack. "I don't know," I started, glancing around the room. "What about the Conqueror? We've been through a lot with that Jeep. It's like part of the team." I met Faith's eye, hoping for backup, but her face held the thoughtful look that told me she wasn't convinced.

Dakota huffed from her armchair. "Kal, it's not the Jeep that worries me. It's Bandit. What's going to happen to her if we jump? We don't know if she can handle it, and I don't want to risk it. Shoving her into a void between time and space?" She turned to McKenna. "You remember what happened when we had to move out for a week when we redid the kitchen?"

McKenna nodded solemnly and turned to me. "She was a wreck, Kal. She's handling the driving fine. Why change?"

"Exactly!" I crowed, glad for allies.

Dakota looked down at Bandit, who was blissfully napping in her carrier, completely unaware of the debate about her next move. "Honestly, she's handled worse." Then, meeting my gaze, she added, "You know, I just thought of something. We don't know what's going to hit us next. If they're as powerful as they're supposed to be—"

"Then maybe we don't have the luxury of taking it slow," McKenna finished. I had the sneaking suspicion that they'd coordinated their argument, but didn't have any proof.

"Exactly," Faith agreed, throwing my word back at me. "It's a *car*, Kal. We can get another one. We can't putt across the countries and risk another run-in with our enemies because you're feeling sentimental."

I sighed, running a hand through my hair. "Look, I get it, but jumping feels like it's asking for trouble. A fast, direct drive, and we're there in two days. No stopping to sleep, we'll switch off drivers and blast our way home."

Faith met my eyes, her look gentle. "Kal, I know you love that Jeep. But getting home fast is the smartest move here. We'll be safer together, on familiar ground, where we can protect each other. Besides, Bandit didn't mind the first jump, did she?"

"What first jump?" exclaimed two voices, so I had to explain what happened at the Border office. It calmed their minds that Bandit could survive the jump, but didn't convince them. Before I could gather my thoughts for another round of debate, we heard the now-familiar *pop* of displaced air, and Avareth stepped through. She wore a knowing smile that said she'd been listening to our argument for a while.

"Your debates are as lively as ever," she said, casting an amused glance around the room.

"Glad you're entertained," I replied dryly, lifting Bandit from her bag to emphasize our latest dilemma. She drooped over my hand in the boneless way only cats could manage. "What do you think, Avy? Can a cat handle a long jump?" I fed Avy our memory of the earlier jump.

She gave a soft laugh, tilting her head to consider her. "Bandit, is it?" Her eyes held gentle warmth as she reached out to let Bandit sniff her hand. Apparently, she passed, as Bandit turned the sniff into a full-on head rub against Avy's fingers. "Quite a companion you've got here. If it's an issue, I can take her through a portal myself. Denver, through Hell, and then back to Brooklyn. No jumping involved."

McKenna looked relieved, her face lighting up. "You're serious? That would be incredible, Avareth. Bandit's tough, but I'd rather not put her through anything that'll freak her out."

"Tough?" Dakota laughed. "She's a marshmallow! Remember the mouse?"

McKenna's cheeks flushed. "Oh. Yeah. Maybe."

Dakota pivoted to our confused looks. "A couple months ago, a mouse got into the apartment. Not unusual, right, not in Brooklyn, but they don't usually come out of the walls and scurry across the floor. This one—" she gestured to Bandit. "—followed the mouse around until the critter turned and came at her. Then the big, brave hunter fled. Fled!"

"She's not used to mice," McKenna explained weakly. "But she's handled everything so far, hasn't she?"

We couldn't deny that, and Avareth gave her a respectful nod, clearly impressed by McKenna's dedication. "Of course, McKenna. I know how important she is to you both. It's refreshing to see such loyalty and resourcefulness in your world. You two are quite the team."

Dakota grinned, clearly pleased by the praise, and gave McKenna a nudge. "Hear that? Avareth thinks we're impressive."

McKenna chuckled, but her gaze stayed serious as she met Avareth's eyes. "We want to keep her safe. And you're making it easier, Avareth. Really."

Faith nudged me encouragingly, her hand resting lightly on my arm. "Well, that settles it, doesn't it? Bandit's portal-hopping with Avareth, and we're down to the last choice: drive or jump."

Dakota said, "Wait, wait! What's a portal?"

"Portals are like doors. Hell uses them to shuttle demons around places on Earth, since they can't jump."

"Not allowed to jump," Faith corrected her.

"Semantics."

"It's an important point, Avy!" Faith insisted. "If Lilith wants to—"

Dakota cleared her throat, stopping them both. "Can we use them? Wouldn't that be safer than jumping?"

"Oh." Avy considered, then shook her head. "Yes, you could use them; it doesn't take any effort or skill. But humans aren't often seen wandering around Hell, and these two shouldn't be seen there. Not until we've dealt with this issue."

"That sucks." Dakota crossed her arms and leveled a look at me, arching an eyebrow. "Then I guess it comes down to you, Kal. You gonna let go of that Jeep, or do we need to debate it all day?"

"What about your booze?" It was my last, weakest argument. The padded box had survived our misadventures without any breakage, surprising me, but nothing in it was irreplaceable.

"What about it? It's booze, Kal. I'll bet you have at least half of them in your penthouse."

I pressed my lips together, knowing that was a bet she'd win.

"I thought so. We're not abandoning the Jeep, Kal, just leaving it parked. You can get one of your new OutLook flunkies to drive it back when all this shit's settled."

I couldn't fault the logic, but when did logic win an emotional argument? I glanced at the key fob on the table, feeling a small pang in my chest as I picked it up. There it was, solid and familiar, tied to a few tons of metal and leather with memories woven in. The fob felt heavier than it should, like I was leaving behind more than a vehicle.

After a long, reluctant pause, I let out a resigned sigh, setting the fob back down. "Fine. It's a car, after all."

Dakota flashed a grin of victory. "That's the spirit. Pack it up, people. New York, here we come."

Avy's gaze lingered on each of us in turn. "You know, I think you all might be exactly what we need in this fight," she said softly, almost to herself. Then, a little louder, "Travel safely. I'll meet you in Brooklyn—with Bandit, of course."

"Manhattan, Avy. Our home. Wards."

"Of course. I'll take down the defenses Faith put in place before you left, so you don't go splat."

"Thanks. See you soon, love."

She packed Bandit in her carrier and walked to the door. "Love you both. Be safe." Then she closed the door behind her and was gone.

It was time to go home.

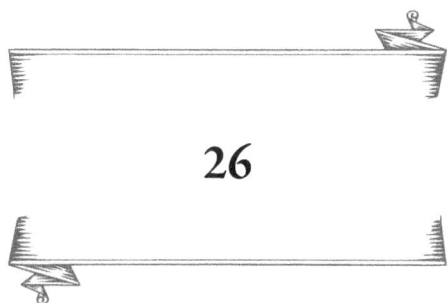

26

We took only what was necessary. When I insisted that included weapons, I was relieved that neither Dakota nor McKenna argued. Faith knew better and had already strapped a pair of short swords to her thighs. As for me, Thakumis rode at one hip, and my borrowed sanctified blade rode on the other. McKenna had a brace of pistols holstered, and a bag filled with magazines; Dakota settled for the one, but she carried an equal amount of ammo. Feeling a bit foolish, but comforted by the weight of the steel, I said, "Let's go."

Faith moved to the center of the room, her expression outwardly serene but with an undercurrent of worry. Dakota and McKenna, despite everything they'd been through, looked more relaxed than I'd expected. Dakota's eyes met McKenna's, and a quick, amused glance passed between them—a look that said they were both ready to tackle whatever Faith and I had planned.

Faith raised her hand to get our attention, her voice focusing our attention on her. "Alright, let's go over it one more time. Concentrate on the penthouse in Manhattan. Picture it as clearly as you can—the light coming through the windows, the layout of the living room, even the sound of the traffic below."

Dakota let out a small laugh, interrupting Faith's explanation. "Can we imagine the coffee machine making us something good, too? The coffee we had last night tasted like battery acid."

McKenna elbowed her lightly, but she couldn't keep the grin off her face. "Priorities, Dakota," she teased.

Faith chuckled. "Go ahead, picture the coffee. Anything that makes the place feel more real will make it easier for us to land exactly where we need to be."

McKenna closed her eyes, nodding thoughtfully. "Got it. I can see it: the living room, the glass windows, that table covered in Kal's never-ending stack of notes... and yes, Dakota, the coffee machine."

Faith took a step forward. "Good. Now hold onto that picture. The clearer we make it, the more smoothly the jump will go. Kal and I will focus on anchoring everyone while you keep your minds on the penthouse."

I took a deep breath, feeling everyone's focus. "Ready?" I asked, squeezing Faith's hand reassuringly. Dakota and McKenna mirrored each other, eyes closing, looking unexpectedly serene.

Dakota took a deep breath. "I'm picturing it," she said, her tone calm. "Expensive coffee machine included. I want a double shot of the good stuff waiting when we land."

McKenna's stance was relaxed, hands resting loosely at her sides. "Got it. I can see it—the best penthouse in the city."

Perfect," Faith said. "Keep that image steady. Kal and I will handle the rest."

The link to Dakota and McKenna, having faded to almost nothing, sparked as their minds sought ours. The moment we all joined hands, the connection between us flared back to life, the connection stronger and more vibrant than it had been since Niagara. I could feel their energy merging, syncing with ours like gears clicking into place.

McKenna's thoughts slipped into the link, clear and steady. *And what about the landing? Do we get, I don't know, a soft touch-down or should we brace for a bit of a rough stop? Superhero landing for the win?*

Faith's gentle laugh filled the connection. *We'll try to make it soft, but that depends on you. Keep your focus on the penthouse. Trust us—this isn't our first jump.*

Right, McKenna replied, her mental tone as steady as her grip. *Not ours, either.*

Faith's focus sharpened, gathering energy through me, using our combined abilities to wrap all of us in a protective cocoon. She sent a final nudge through the link. *Alright, we're ready. Let's go home.*

As Faith's voice flowed around us, I could feel each of us lock into the visualization, the energy shifting, preparing to carry us across space and toward the familiar setting we held firmly in our minds.

Faith's voice echoed her thoughts. "Let's go home."

I felt the familiar tugging pull of energy that marked the first step into the space between. Dakota and McKenna gripped our hands, their connection with Faith and me at full strength as the room faded from sight.

Dakota's voice drifted into my mind, her curiosity stronger than her usual wariness. *What's actually happening right now? Are we moving? Teleporting?*

I sent back a wave of reassurance. *Think of it like passing through a tunnel, but without walls or even distance in the usual sense. We're between two places, in a space that doesn't quite exist in our reality.*

Between realities, McKenna echoed, a sense of wonder mixing with her thoughts. *That's surreal. And no offense, but are you sure we're gonna land in one piece?*

One piece, guaranteed, I replied with a grin. *The jump space may look strange, but as long as we stay focused, it's all smooth sailing.*

The world around us shifted again, and in an instant, the suite vanished, replaced by a vast, swirling expanse that stretched in every direction, as if we were suspended within a living, breathing being. Shadows and lights flickered across an endless horizon, shimmering in colors that didn't quite belong in the human spectrum. Silence enveloped us, profound and absolute, yet I could feel the steady thoughtbeat of each person's presence—strong, calm, connected.

Dakota's voice came through, her mental tone tinged with awe. *Whoa... it's like... floating in a dream. How does this place even exist?*

It's a space outside space, I explained. *It's the potential for places, rather than a place itself. It doesn't have fixed dimensions or rules. We shape it by focusing on where we want to go.*

Faith's voice slipped gently into the link. *Stop chattering! Keep your minds on the penthouse. Picture it as clearly as you can.*

I felt McKenna's mental focus sharpen, her energy locking onto the image of the penthouse. *I've got it—right down to the annoying hum of the elevator.* Her tone was amused, and I could feel her energy stabilizing alongside ours.

Good, I sent back. *It's working—hold on a little longer.*

The jump space flickered, the colors around us merging and bending in waves. The pressure of moving through this unreal corridor pressed against my imagined senses. Dakota and McKenna's energy pulsed strong and bright, the comfort of home pulling us closer with every heartbeat.

So, Dakota asked, *what happens if we get distracted? You know, wander off in here?*

That's one way to get lost between worlds, I replied lightly, trying to downplay the very real possibility. *But don't worry—Faith and I have done this plenty of times. As long as we keep steady, you'll get back in one piece.*

The familiar pull of the jump grew stronger, the penthouse drawing closer, shimmering in our minds, just an arm's reach away...

And then, abruptly, the connection snapped, like a tether cut from the other side. The warmth and light vanished, replaced by a dark, cold emptiness. My grip on Dakota and McKenna tightened instinctively, and I felt Faith's energy flare, stabilizing us, but wherever we were, it wasn't home.

Shapes began to emerge through a thick, swirling mist, but they held none of the comforting familiarity of our penthouse. Instead, towering, jagged rocks loomed around us, piercing a sky stained with shades of crimson and ash. The landscape was desolate, utterly devoid of life or any sign that humanity had ever touched it. The ground was dark, scorched, and cracked, as though it had borne witness to an ancient, endless agony.

McKenna's hand tightened in mine, her thoughts pushing through our link, sharp with the sting of panic she was struggling to control. *Kal, this... this isn't New York. What's happening? Where are we?*

Dakota's voice slipped in, calmer but strained. *Did something go wrong with the jump? Are we stuck here?*

I took a steadying breath. *I don't know. But stay close. We'll figure this out.*

I scanned the area, looking for anything recognizable, any hint of where we were, but the landscape stretched endlessly in every direction, dark, broken terrain beneath a heavy sky. The silence pressed against my ears, thick and oppressive. I muttered, "Where the hell are we?"

A deep, rolling voice answered, low and resonant, dripping with amusement and malice. "Exactly."

The voice carried unmistakable authority, each syllable echoing off the surrounding rocks, filling the empty space with its presence. "Welcome," it continued, the words like the scrape of iron against stone, "to my demesne, I don't think. No. You are not at all welcome. You have been far more trouble than I bargained for, and I am finished with half-measures."

A chilling realization settled over me as the figure materialized, taking form in the shadows, dark and imposing. Horns arched back from a forehead ridged with deep furrows, and his eyes, like two glowing embers, settled on us with cold satisfaction. His figure was shrouded in layers of dark, metallic armor that seemed both fluid and solid, like shadows forged into steel.

It could only be Valaferion, Duke of Hell.

Faith's hand squeezed, her gaze locked on the demon. Dakota and McKenna, while holding their ground, cast nervous glances around, their hands hovering near their weapons. I didn't tell them a demon of Valaferion's rank wouldn't be bothered by bullets.

Valaferion's lips curled into a sharp, predatory smile. "You're quite far from your little sanctuary, I'm afraid. But rest assured, you've made it to a place where survival is a rather flexible concept." He tilted his head, eyes glinting. "And here, *I* make the rules."

The air around Valaferion thickened. A dark, twisting energy coiled at his sides, and three figures materialized out of the shadows, each as distinct as they were terrifying. I had a pretty good guess who they were, and in the next instant my guess was confirmed.

To Valaferion's right, Lioraeth settled into place, her presence as sharp and menacing as a drawn blade. She'd shifted form again, but I recognized her towering, sinewy form clad in nightmare-black armor, every movement fluid and lethal. Her eyes met mine and I read her predatory gaze, daring me to show a flicker of fear. She tilted her lips into a smile that promised pain. Despite the thundering of my heart, I forced myself to hold her eyes, refusing to give her the satisfaction.

Faith gasped, pointing to Lioreth's right. "An Archangel!"

I broke my stare with Lioraeth. It had to be Seraphina.

The figure was surrounded by a cold, blinding light. Seraphina's radiance was piercing, her massive, perfect wings stretched wide, each feather shimmering with an almost unreal purity. Her clothes, a cream-colored suit that wouldn't be out of place on the fashion runways, showed she was in touch with the mortal world. Gold highlights gleamed, a tribute to the armor an archangel would usually wear, each detail meticulously crafted and flawless. Despite the beauty of her flawless body, her eyes held a hollow darkness, as if her inner light had long been extinguished. She regarded us with detached disdain, the kind reserved for beings far beneath her notice. I resisted the impulse to stare into her dead, soulless orbs, tearing my eyes away and immediately regretting it.

"What the fuck is that?" I squeaked, pointing to a figure that phased in and out of reality.

Faith leaned closer, her voice wary. "That's a Principality. Avareth called it Zadkiel. Principals are higher order celestials—more concept than physical form. They're powerful, Kal, and very hard to pin down if they choose not to manifest in our reality."

A memory tickled my mind. "You ran into one in Rome!"

She nodded. "But he was on a mission that required physicality."

To Valaferion's left, Zadkiel hovered, flickering like a mirage, their figure ethereal, shifting as though they were only half-present in this realm. Their form pulsed with translucent layers of light, each glow like the beat of a heart. Their face, when it came into focus, was smooth, androgynous, and utterly unreadable. They watched us with a serene detachment, a quiet calm that sent a shiver down my spine. It was as if we were mere pieces on a game board, and they were calmly deciding our next move.

I straightened, grounding myself, chin held high and stance locked in a defiant front as my mind raced. This was different from anything Faith and I had faced in ages. Four opponents, each powerful beyond measure, and every instinct told me we were in deep, over our heads in a way I hadn't felt in centuries.

Faith, I reached out through our link, doing my best to keep the rising panic from bleeding into my thoughts, *we're in serious trouble. They're all here. And they're not here to chat.*

Faith's response came like a steady heartbeat, easing the raw edge of my fear. *What happened to the woman who took on Lucifer twice?*

She got older and wiser!

We'll handle it, Kal. Despite her brave front, I felt the doubt behind her words, and a cold weight settled in my stomach. These four wouldn't be retreating. Either they survived, or we did, and the outcome was far from certain.

I felt Dakota and McKenna close by, their presence a reminder of why we were on this path. They edged partially behind Faith and me, Dakota's fingers brushing my arm in silent reassurance. Her voice slipped into my mind, *We've got your back, Kal. Just tell us what to do.*

A thread of strength moved between us. They believed in us, even now.

Valaferion's eyes swept over us, and his mouth curved into a deliberate, cruel smile. "Ah, such resolve... and such delicious fear," he drawled, his voice low and rumbling, echoing across the barren landscape like a distant storm. "Tell me, little mortals and stray celestials—do you truly believe you stand a chance against us?"

I forced a smirk, digging deep to find a memory of confidence, letting my voice ring with steel I barely felt. "I don't believe anything, Duke," I replied, putting a brave face on every syllable. "I know it."

Faith took a step forward, a sword in hand but angled downward, a clear sign she wasn't here to attack—yet. I shot a mental pulse her way, more alarmed than I cared to admit. *What are you doing?!*

Trust me, she replied, her focus locked on our enemies before us.

Of course I do, arima bikia. Her determination made my heart skip a beat. *I'd still like to know...*

"Look, if there's something we did," she began, her voice calm, "something we can undo to stop this bloodshed, then let's talk about it. There's no point in fighting a war for the sake of chaos. This road leads to death and destruction. Irrevocable. Permanent. Are you certain that's the choice you wish to make?"

Valaferion's eyes glinted, amused and dangerous, his mouth pursing as if he were readying a response that would end the discussion altogether. Before he could speak, Faith raised her sword, the tip aimed unflinchingly at him. "Not from you, Duke. I want to hear it from the rest."

A flicker of irritation crossed his face, but he inclined his head, gesturing to the others with an open hand. "As you wish, you deluded Immortal. Perhaps my companions would care to share their motivations."

Seraphina's gaze landed on Faith, her wings shifting, casting an ethereal glow that contrasted starkly with the scorched landscape around us. Her voice, when she spoke, was cool, almost mournful, as if she were pronouncing a long-neglected truth. "I want what was lost—the order that existed before you meddled in things beyond your comprehension. A time when every being knew its place and served as ordained." Her words cut like shards of ice, each syllable laced with centuries of resentment. "It was a world of purity and purpose. And I will see it restored."

Faith held her gaze, unflinching. "A return to the old ways? At the cost of how many lives?"

Seraphina's silence was answer enough. Lives were the poker chips that scored the game, no more.

To her left, Lioraeth chuckled darkly. "Power," she said simply. Her voice was a low purr, vibrating with a hunger that could consume the world. "Nothing more. Nothing less. Power isn't meant to be wasted. It's meant to be wielded by those who know how to use it—and I intend to wield all of it." If Valaferion cared about this blunt challenge to his supremacy, he didn't show it. She let her gaze linger on me, sparking a twisted smile. "It's a pity, really. You're almost strong enough to be interesting, Kalili."

"It's a pity I don't find you the same," I shot back, hoping my bravado masked the cold fear that ran down my spine.

Then, all eyes turned to Zadkiel, who gazed back at us with a calm that was somehow far more disturbing than Lioraeth's power-lust or Seraphina's coldness. They regarded us as if we were children, their face smooth and expressionless. When they spoke, it wasn't in words that could be comprehended, but a strange, layered intonation that seemed to resonate from within their core, twisting through the air like a foreign melody woven with shadow.

A soft, hollow echo of intent came through, a sense rather than a clear answer: not power, not restoration, but an idea of control and chaos merging, balanced like two sides of a single coin, incomprehensible yet essential. It was a motive that made my skin crawl, its alien logic twisted and inexorable.

Faith's eyes flickered to me, her grip tightening on her sword, and I gave her the smallest nod, a silent agreement that we'd gotten our answers—and that, somehow, we'd have to survive this knowledge.

As the reality of their motives set in, one thought took over—the safety of Dakota and McKenna. I turned to Valaferion, my voice unwavering even as a knot tightened in my stomach.

Go ahead and try, Faith urged. *There's nothing to lose.*

"Send them home," I demanded, waving at our friends. "This is between us—between Immortals. They have no place in this fight."

Valaferion's gaze settled on me, a cruel spark dancing in his eyes. "Oh, Kalili," he murmured, each word a deliberate mockery. "You misunderstand the rules. Everyone here is part of the game." He waved a dismissive hand in Dakota and McKenna's direction. "Why should I deny myself the pleasure of watching your precious humans break under our power?"

My jaw clenched, fury igniting a fire deep within. "Coward," I spat, the word dripping with contempt.

A dangerous smile spread across his face, his eyes gleaming. "Now, let's have some fun."

With a wave of his hand, the air shifted, vibrating with the crackle of raw energy. Shadows materialized, twisting and solidifying into forms—angels with pristine, blinding wings and demons wreathed in darkness and flame. A double score of them, all trained, all deadly, surrounded us in a tightening circle. I felt Dakota and McKenna shift behind me, bracing themselves. Surprisingly, all I got from Faith was immense frustration. At what, I couldn't tell, and didn't try, my blood suddenly boiling, my nerves at a breaking point. I raised my blade, my voice booming through the desolate landscape with a roar that tore from the depths of my being. "You want a fight? Come and get it!"

Without waiting another second, I launched myself forward, every muscle and ounce of energy driving me toward the nearest enemy. Faith, Dakota, and McKenna followed, a wall of defiance against the endless darkness surrounding us.

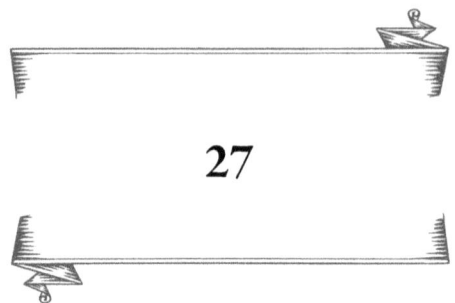

27

It wasn't my smartest move.

The air ignited with energy as I charged into the fray, the sanctified blade in my grip humming with power, its light flaring like a beacon against the encroaching darkness. Demons and angels, taken by surprise, recovered and rumbled toward us, their feral eyes locked onto Faith and me. I swung the blade, carving a wide arc that sliced through the first demon's shoulder. A blinding line seared from shoulder to chest before he stumbled back and collapsed.

I noticed Faith slashing at an angel and goggled. Why wasn't she using her powers? For that matter, why wasn't I?

Faith, I sent out as I sidestepped another strike, *why aren't you frying them with* vashwic urja? *Is something wrong?*

She grunted in frustration, her thoughts crackling through the mental link as she took a defensive stance. *It's the* kosmiskorka, *Kal. It's being blocked—something's been set in place here, keeping the* kosmiskorka *out.* Her voice was tinged with fury. *Looks like I'm back to basics.*

That sucked. Without access to *kosmiskorka,* her *vashwic urja* was useless in this place. Our *taaqat* would serve to power it, but only for two, perhaps three blasts. Against this array of enemies? Best to save it for when we had to have it; healing, perhaps, or manifesting our wings if we had to fly.

She drew both short blades, one in each hand, spinning them with a deftness that betrayed her centuries of experience.

You've come a long way since Rome.

She glanced at me with a grim smile before leaping to engage a nearby angel, moving with ruthless efficiency.

You've been practicing, I teased, unable to resist.

A little.

Just keep close. I deflected a spear thrust aimed for her side and kicked a demon who lunged for me. *We've handled worse with less.*

And without two humans to guard, she replied dryly, her mind as clear and sharp as her blades.

I stole a glance over my shoulder, catching sight of Dakota and McKenna as they sprinted for cover. Smart. They'd realized they couldn't stand toe-to-toe with Immortals, and found a narrow rock formation. From there, with something sturdy to put between themselves and the advancing horde, they scanned the battlefield, pistols ready, firing with calculated aim at anything that came close. Despite their efforts, our attackers were largely ignoring them.

Good, I thought, grateful for small mercies.

Faith's voice slipped into my thoughts. *Don't look back—focus on keeping us alive here. My blades aren't spelled or imbued with power, so I'm counting on you to handle the big ones.* She ducked low, her twin blades flashing as she brought them up in a deadly arc, slicing through the wings of an angel that dove for her, feathers scattering like embers. *I'll handle whatever else gets in close.*

A snarl broke the air as two demons closed in on me, their eyes gleaming with fury. I shifted my grip on the sanctified blade, swinging in a tight arc that cut through the first with an explosion of light and energy. The second demon hesitated enough for me to press forward and drive the blade home, the blade's power burning through him. Another wave surged forward, two angels leading a half-dozen demons.

Faith, I called out, *brace yourself—more incoming.*

Faith shifted closer, and we stiffened, our shoulders just shy of touching, moving instinctively into a tight, defensive formation. My focus narrowed, each of the oncoming attackers appearing with chilling clarity. The angels led the charge, wings spread wide, gleaming with a cold light, while the demons formed a tight wall of shadows and flame behind them.

Faith's grip tightened on her twin blades, her voice pulsing through our link. *Looks like they're trying to overwhelm us with numbers. Guess they aren't underestimating us anymore.*

I huffed a dry laugh, sweeping my blade as one of the angels veered to the side, its sword slashing down toward Faith. *About time,* I thought back, deflecting its blow with a fierce upward block. The clang of metal rang out and I swiveled away from its return swipe.

Faith lunged, bringing her short blades up in a crisscross motion, intercepting the other angel's strike with fluid precision. She moved like a whirlwind, her arms a blur of silver as she parried each blow, driving the angel back one careful step at a time. *Any time you want to lend a hand, Kal,* she sent, her tone teasing.

I'm admiring the show. Clang!

Bitch.

A demon dove towards me and I speared its outstretched hand. *You wouldn't have me any other way.*

Restored by our banter, I threw myself at the demons, driving them from Faith's back. The other angel abandoned its attempt to reach Faith and turned on me, but I was already attacking. Instead of an overhead swing, I chopped down at its ankles, hoping to cripple it. It dropped its weapon to block, but the sanctified blade cut through with a burst of light that sent it staggering back.

The respite was brief. The demons behind surged forward, filling the gap left by the angel, clawed hands reaching out and fire flaring in their eyes. Dakota and McKenna's gunfire rang out from the shelter of the rock formation, harassing our attackers, bullets striking two demons squarely in the chest. The demons dropped, badly injured and out of the fight for the moment.

"Nice timing!" I yelled over my shoulder, swinging the blade to intercept another demon that lunged at Faith.

McKenna's voice echoed across the field, fierce and confident. "We'll keep them off your backs!"

The demon closest to me slashed with a set of serrated claws, each swipe faster than the last. I met its attack with a parry, my blade moving almost by instinct, each strike deflecting just enough to keep the claws from tearing through flesh. A streak of dark energy grazed my arm, a searing heat flaring across my skin, but I forced myself to ignore it, driving my blade upward in a swift counterattack that caught the demon under its chin. Its head snapped back as the blade cut through and it dropped.

Another demon lunged forward, eyes wild with fury, a low growl rumbling from its chest. Faith took a step forward, her expression fierce as she struck, both her blades whooshing through the air in perfect sync. The blades sliced through flesh, cleaving the luckless demon in two, and the halves fell.

Through the haze of battle's fury, I felt her frustration pulse through our link. *Damn it, Kal—this would be a lot easier if I had my usual powers.*

I know, I sent back. I glanced toward Dakota and McKenna. They were holding their own. *But we make do with what we have. Stay close, and we'll keep pushing.*

Faith's jaw tightened as she deflected another blow, her voice whispering through my mind, *Like we have a choice.*

At least the others haven't stepped in.

As if on cue, Zadkiel edged toward the fight. Maybe it was because we'd whittled them to a handful, or maybe they simply wanted to be part of the action. Either way, it was bad news for us. How do you kill a being that barely existed in this plane?

The realization hit me like a hammer: I had everything I needed to end Zadkiel. In my left hand I held Faith's sanctified blade. It gleamed with Heaven's power and radiated purity and light. At my side, Thakumis's Blade hummed with malevolence, forged from a Prince of Hell's primary feather, imbued with the essence of his soul. Pure good and pure evil, contained within two weapons.

The thought of wielding both sent a shudder through me. I knew what the Blade would do to my mind once I unsheathed it. How would it react to the presence of the sanctified blade? It was something I'd have to face; this wasn't going to be easy, and the timing would have to be exact. It would take both strikes at once, perfectly balanced, to bring Zadkiel down.

Faith, I shot through our link, *keep the others busy. I'll handle the Principality.*

Her response was as sharp as a blade. *Right, because keeping us alive out here is just another Tuesday. Have fun!*

Not my usual idea of fun.

As if cued by our exchange, Zadkiel edged forward, their form shimmering with a surreal light that made them seem only half here. They closed in, those eyes—ancient, unreadable—fixed squarely on me.

Before I could react, Zadkiel struck, extending a hand with an elegance that made the moment feel timeless. Their fingers phased through my clothes and brushed my shoulder. I hissed in pain, a wound opening that was somehow both searing hot and freezing cold, the agony sharp and disorienting.

I darted back, gritting my teeth against the pain, trying to buy time. I needed to feint, to keep Zadkiel off-balance, until I could line up the perfect strike. They watched me closely, their gaze betraying nothing, as though humoring my attempts at resistance.

Another attack came, fast and precise. I sidestepped, raising the sanctified blade and letting it catch their hand, which sizzled against the holy energy, though they betrayed nothing. Zadkiel tilted their head slightly, a mockery of a smile ghosting their lips, and then lunged forward again, their movement as seamless as water.

I deflected with Thakumis's Blade, feeling the dark energy flare up at the contact, the spirit of the Prince eager to claim a new type of soul, and I saw hesitation flicker across their expression. It was a tiny tell, but I latched onto it. They could sense the danger, even if they weren't showing it.

Just one more opening, I thought, willing myself to stay focused.

Zadkiel pressed forward again, unfazed by my defenses, their movements faster, bolder. I misjudged and their fingers grazed my side with a touch that spread a sharp, prickling ache through my entire body. But my mistake had forced them into an error, a vulnerability, and this time I was ready.

I feinted with Thakumis's Blade, swinging it in a wide arc that Zadkiel dodged with ease. It was the exact reaction I wanted. In a smooth motion, I twisted my body and drove both blades in arcs, one in each hand. The sanctified blade and Thakumis's Blade sunk deep into Zadkiel's sides, Heaven and Hell colliding in a pulse of raw, explosive energy.

Zadkiel's eyes widened, their expression shifting from serenity to shock as both powers tore through them, clashing within, the battling powers wreaking havoc on their body. Their form flickered, wavering like a candle in the wind, and then the light imploded inward with a piercing shriek that resonated through the air, shattering in a blinding burst of energy that forced me to stagger back.

And then... silence.

In the empty space where they had stood, a faint glow dissipated, leaving nothing but a fading echo of their presence.

I didn't have a chance to celebrate my victory. Two angels and a demon closed in on me, their weapons glinting as they moved in sync. I tightened my grip on the sanctified blade, the weight of both it and Thakumis's Blade grounding me as I stepped forward. I wasn't as skilled with paired blades as Faith, and the balance was off, but if it made my attackers think? It was a win.

With a quick lunge, I drove the Blade into the first angel's chest, its light flaring in protest as it dissolved in a haze of blinding gold and red. I twisted to meet the second angel's charge, still leading with the Blade. My hand arced through the air to sever its wing, sending it crumpling to the ground. I didn't linger to watch its dissolution in a shimmer of red, hellish energy, turning to the remaining opponent. The demon hesitated, but only for a heartbeat before it lunged. I met it with a downward slice, the power of both blades clashing and obliterating it in a burst of dark, acrid smoke.

"Impossible!" Valaferion's voice thundered across the battlefield, rage twisting his face. His burning gaze locked onto me, and a chill shot through me. I felt the intensity of his fury as if it were a physical weight pressing down. "Seraphina! Finish them."

The Archangel's eyes gleamed, a slow, feline smile spreading across her lips. "My pleasure."

As she stalked toward us, her wings spread wide and her form radiating an almost unbearable light, I forced my *taaqat* to heal my wounds, drawing from my limited reserves. It wouldn't last long, but it was enough to keep me on my feet, at least for now.

Without hesitation, Faith stepped in front of me, her twin blades glinting, her stance unyielding. *My turn,* she sent, her tone leaving no room for argument. *Cover me. Finish the last of the lesser Immortals.*

I gave her a quick nod, catching the anticipation in her eyes. Seraphina had been a thorn in Ariel's side for centuries, provoking and prodding but never crossing the line. She'd also taken a dislike to Faith in the days when Faith thought she was an angel. My sweet, gentle love tolerated most attacks, but Seraphina had gotten under her skin. Faith had been waiting for this moment, and I knew better than to try to hold her back.

Seraphina's gaze locked onto Faith, her lips curling into a sneer. "You've fallen so low, Faith, to fight with these *lessers* by your side."

Faith's grip tightened on her swords, her voice frozen. "I fight alongside them by choice, Seraphina. Something you wouldn't understand."

Seraphina's laugh was chilling, her eyes narrowing with contempt. "Choice? You delude yourself, Faith. You're clinging to weakness." With a sudden, sharp flick of her wrist, Seraphina's sword appeared in her hand, glowing with a fierce light that made the air hum. "Let me show you true strength."

The Archangel lunged, her movements fast, her blade striking out in a deadly arc aimed straight for Faith's heart. Faith twisted, her body moving with a lethal fluidity. She parried the strike with one sword while angling the other for a counterattack, forcing Seraphina to dodge.

I circled around them, dispatching the last lesser Immortals who dared approach. Faith's concentration was absolute, each move flowing into the next as if they were steps in an intricate dance, her swords spinning, blocking, slicing, the clash of metal reverberating in the air.

Keep going, Faith, I sent, the words almost a prayer.

Seraphina's expression shifted, a flash of irritation breaking through her calm façade as Faith forced her back, her twin blades striking without cease. The Archangel snarled, her eyes flashing. "You dare defy me? You, who once served Heaven?"

Faith's voice was unwavering. "That was a long time ago, Seraphina. I've learned strength isn't defined by subjugation. Didn't Ariel teach you that?"

Seraphina let out a furious scream, her wings flaring wide as she launched another assault, each blow more forceful than the last. Faith met her attacks with a skill that astonished the Archangel, her movements finely controlled, her blades a seamless extension of herself. She was far removed from the naïve angel who didn't know one end of a gladius from the other.

But I could see her flagging. Each of Faith's blocks came a fraction slower, her breath quickening as Seraphina's relentless attacks pressed her harder. I could feel her fatigue echoing through our link, but her arms held firm. For now.

Hold on, Faith. I shared some of my *taaqat*, probably more than I could spare. If Faith fell... I didn't want to consider it. I racked my brain for something else I could do, clenching my fists in fury, feeling Thakumis's soul echo my darkness.

Thakumis. I looked at the hand holding the Blade. Wrong hand—I'm a natural righty—but desperate times, desperate measures or whatever.

I flung the Blade at Seraphina, hoping for a blow that would end this. The Blade spun through the air, wobbling, missing Seraphina by inches, but it served its purpose. Her gaze snapped to it, a flash of confusion in her eyes, and Faith seized the opportunity. She lunged forward, her twin blades flashing in the muted light.

Faith angled her right blade low, forcing Seraphina to parry downward. But Faith didn't stop. Her left blade struck like lightning, slicing upward in a clean, brutal arc that cut across the Archangel's chest, severing cloth and flesh alike.

Seraphina gasped, her mouth open in shock, her hands reflexively clutching at the wound. A blinding light spilled from the gash, but Faith pressed on. She swung with the right blade, embedding it in the open wound, stepping closer as she drove it deeper, her expression hard.

"You never understood," Faith said, her voice barely audible over the scream of celestial energy escaping from Seraphina's form. "Strength isn't about domination. It's about the will to protect."

With a final wrench, Faith twisted her blade, the light surging, exploding outward in a wave that forced me to shield my eyes. The air trembled, and Seraphina's figure fractured, breaking apart in beams of pure, blinding light, each fragment scattering like shards of glass. They were embers of eternity, vanishing into the hellish landscape.

When the brilliance faded, Faith was standing alone, her chest heaving, her blades raised, while the remnants of Seraphina's presence dissolved into the air. A heavy silence fell over the battlefield, the power of the moment settling deep into the ground beneath us.

Faith turned to me, exhaustion lining her face, but her gaze was steady. *It's done,* she sent, her voice a quiet triumph that resonated through our link.

No, I corrected her. *It isn't.*

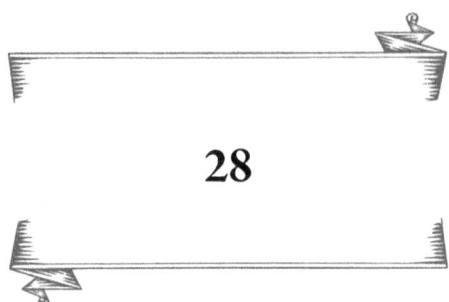

28

My chest heaved, each breath sharp and raw, and though Seraphina's light had faded, the air still crackled with energy, thick with the scent of scorched earth and blood. Darkness surrounded us, an oppressive shadow cast by jagged rocks and twisted ground that seemed to shift beneath our feet. A chill lingered in the air, biting through even the heat of battle, a reminder that this place was a domain designed to drain and weaken us.

Into the cold stepped Lioraeth.

She moved forward, every step calculated with lethal grace. Her armor gleamed, dark and organic, as if it pulsed with its own malevolent life, shifting and tightening with every movement. Her eyes, sharp as blades, found mine, and the faintest curl of satisfaction touched her lips, a silent promise of pain to come. I forced myself to hold, but the dread coiled in my stomach, a cold weight that seemed to grow with every step she took. Lioraeth wasn't here to fight—she was here to savor the kill.

Behind her, Valaferion's voice thundered, his rage spilling across the battlefield in harsh, echoing rants.

"How could this happen? How could these pretenders—" His voice was venomous, laced with scorn, and his eyes burned, flickering from Faith to me with an almost feral intensity. Maybe it was insanity. "Seraphina, fallen? Zadkiel, defeated?" He shook himself as if casting off doubt. "You insignificant gnats—do you think this changes anything?"

I tried to tune him out, focusing instead on Lioraeth, but his words dug in, amplifying the nerves radiating from Faith and me as we stood our ground. He raged on, his voice booming, "Lioraeth, show them the price of their impudence. Make them *suffer.*"

Faith stepped to my side, her face pale, her twin blades held steady despite the exhaustion evident in her stance. *We have to do this together.* I felt the weight of my fatigue, every muscle protesting as I gripped the sanctified blade. *I don't have enough strength on my own.*

Faith's reply was exactly what I needed. *I'm with you.* She met my gaze, and in her eyes, I saw the same determination I felt. *Let's finish this.*

Lioraeth stopped a few paces away tilting her head as if considering us, her gaze traveling slowly from Faith to me, assessing. She raised a hand, her claws extending, shimmering with energy, and a low, mocking laugh escaped her lips.

"Two against one?" Her voice was dismissive. "You truly think that evens the odds?"

I forced my stance to steady, drawing a long breath and willing my legs to stop trembling. The fear receded, but she could sense it—I knew she could. Lioraeth's smile widened as she took another step, the satisfaction on her face deepening as if savoring the scent of our desperation.

Faith's grip tightened on her blades. I could feel her mind reaching out, her strength interwoven with mine, pushing back against the darkness around us. As Lioraeth advanced, her movements predatory, her eyes gleaming with intent, I clung to that connection with Faith, grounding myself in it, preparing for what would be the deadliest dance yet.

Lioraeth's blade gleamed as it cut through the dim light, a flash of murderous steel pirouetting in malicious circles faster than my eyes could track. Her gaze flicked from me to Faith, noting every hint of fatigue, every faltering movement, selecting her first target.

With a feint at Faith, she chose, lunging toward me, her form blurring as she closed the gap, her blade coming down with deadly precision. I barely had time to twist my body, raising Thakumis's Blade to parry. The impact almost wrenched the Blade from my grip.

Without missing a beat, Lioraeth turned her attention to Faith, frozen in place. Her blade slashed across in a brutal arc. Faith intercepted it, crossing her twin blades just in time, but the force of the blow drove her back, her boots sliding against the rough, scorched earth. Lioraeth sensed the advantage and pressed forward, engaging us both, moving with a vicious elegance that kept us on the defensive.

Each time I raised a blade to block, her strikes seemed to get heavier, her movements sharper, forcing me to focus on staying upright. She pivoted, thrusting toward Faith before swinging back to me with a downward strike aimed for my shoulder. I sidestepped, avoiding the blade, but the narrow miss left my balance unsteady, and I nearly toppled before recovering.

"Is that all you've got?" Lioraeth sneered, echoing my earlier words, her voice contemptuous. She spun, her blade arcing in a swift upward slash that Faith barely dodged, the steel grazing the fabric of her sleeve. A swatch of fabric fluttered to the ground.

Faith's face was pale, her eyes fixed on Lioraeth as she moved in closer, launching a rapid series of strikes meant to disrupt the archdemoness's rhythm. She swung one blade low, forcing Lioraeth to dodge back, then followed up with a second, angled toward her side. But Lioraeth blocked both strikes with a flick of her wrist, her movements effortless, her laughter ringing out as she countered with a quick thrust that forced Faith to retreat.

Lioraeth's smile widened, her eyes flicking between us with a triumphant gleam. Her strikes were relentless, forcing us back, step by step, her blade a blur as she lashed out, aiming for any gap in our defenses. I swung Thakumis's Blade upward, hoping to break her momentum, but she anticipated the move, sidestepping and bringing her blade down in a blinding arc that caught my shoulder at an angle. I screamed at the pain, but my arm was still attached, the sword slicing through flesh instead of cleaving bone.

I fell back, needing to heal, to stop the bleeding at a minimum, and Faith lunged forward, her twin blades aimed for Lioraeth's exposed flank. But the demoness was faster, twisting her body to avoid the strike and retaliating with a brutal kick that sent Faith sprawling. My heart lurched as Faith hit the ground, her weapons clattering beside her, and Lioraeth took the chance to press her advantage, raising her blade high, ready to bring it down in a killing blow.

Only half-healed, and without thinking, I leapt forward, swinging Thakumis's Blade in a desperate attempt to intercept her strike. The blades clashed, and the shock reverberated through me, agony from my damaged arm nearly forcing me to my knees. Lioraeth's gaze snapped to mine, her eyes gleaming with fury.

"Persistent, aren't we?" she hissed, twisting her wrist and breaking the lock, her movements fluid as she pulled back to deliver another strike.

I kept up. Somehow, I kept up, staggering away from Faith, shuddering under each blow. Each block was harder than the last, my arms trembling with the effort as I struggled to keep up with her speed and precision. Faith was back on her feet, moving to flank her, but I could see her breathing was labored, her stance unsteady. We were both tiring fast, while Lioraeth seemed to revel in every moment, her attacks becoming more aggressive, her smile growing as she watched us falter.

She's toying with us, I thought, my grip tightening on the blade. It wouldn't be long before—

A gunshot cracked the silence, sharp and unforgiving, and Lioraeth staggered, her eyes widening in shock as she clutched her shoulder. Thick, dark blood seeped between her fingers, staining her armor. For a moment, her composure faltered, her gaze darting around, trying to locate the source. Another shot rang out, this time hitting her in the side, sending her reeling as her lips curled in a snarl of pure rage. Another shot, and another hit, this time to her thigh, and the demoness was down on one knee.

McKenna.

With Lioraeth thrown off-balance, an opening appeared, a brief, precious sliver of time where her defenses were down. Every muscle screamed in protest, exhaustion pulling at me like weights dragging me under, but I forced myself forward, tightening my grip on Thakumis's Blade in one hand and the sanctified blade in the other. They were two forces of pure, opposing energy, and I let their power surge through me, drawing it into me, stealing it to bolster my flagging reserves.

Lioraeth's eyes narrowed as she saw me approach, a flicker of realization crossing her face as I drove forward, the sanctified blade aimed squarely at her chest. She tried to raise her weapon, but her movement was sluggish, her balance compromised by McKenna's shots. With a final surge, I struck, burying the sanctified blade deep into her chest. Its divine energy flared upon contact, searing through her armor and burning with a brilliant, unforgiving light.

She gasped, her face twisting in fury and disbelief, her body convulsing as the sanctified energy pulsed through her, sending jagged cracks of light racing along her skin. But she wasn't done. With one last, desperate move, she swung her blade in a wide, deadly arc. I managed to duck, feeling the rush of air as her weapon skimmed past me, but Faith—

Faith let out a sharp cry, her voice filled with pain, and I turned to see her crumple to the ground, clutching her leg, blood pouring between her fingers. The sight was like a spark to dry tinder, igniting a fury that blazed through me, hot and wild, pushing away the exhaustion for one final act, reminding me that I was a demon for six thousand years.

I met Lioraeth's defiant, hate-filled gaze, her lips pulling back in a sneer even as her body shook with the effects of the sanctified blade. Her breath came in ragged gasps, the light from the blade consuming her bit by bit. I took a step forward, my voice low and venomous, filled with every ounce of anger and protectiveness left in me.

"You don't get to touch her," I snarled, my words a death sentence.

I swung Thakumis' Blade upward. The Blade met her neck, cutting clean through. Her body, already being consumed by the power of the sanctified blade, released a blinding flash of light. Her head fell, her expression frozen in shock and rage, before her body flickered, dissolving into twisted shadows, her form unraveling until she was nothing more than a faint, lingering darkness, dissipating into the air, leaving only a blackened form on the ground.

The sound of Lioraeth's body crumbling to nothing was swallowed by the silence that followed, an eerie quiet settling over the battlefield. I had no time, no attention to spare for it, as my gaze went immediately to Faith. She lay on the ground, her face pale and drawn.

"Faith!" I dropped to my knees beside her, gripping her shoulder as my heart thundered in my chest. I could feel her pain, sharp and unrelenting, echoing in our connection.

She managed a weak smile, her voice barely a whisper. "Took... long enough to bring her down, didn't it?"

I let out a rough laugh, swallowing back the panic clawing at my throat. "Don't try to talk. Just let me—"

I closed my eyes, summoning the energy I'd stolen from the blades, transmuting it to *taaqat*, willing it to flow into her, to knit the torn muscle and stem the bleeding. I knew it wasn't enough, but I tried, gods, I tried. My strength was waning, slipping through my fingers like sand. The energy I sent her way was faint, barely enough to dull the pain. I forced more, feeling the strain twist through me, but it was as if we were both standing at the edge of an empty well.

Faith's hand found mine, her grip weak but steady. *You're spent, Kal.* Her voice came through our mental link, soft and reassuring despite the pain. *It's enough.*

"No," I whispered, my voice hoarse with frustration, my fingers pressing against her leg, trying to stop the bleeding through sheer will. "It's not enough. This is—" I swallowed, feeling the bitterness of helplessness clawing at me. "This is nothing. I need to do more."

She squeezed my hand, a faint warmth against the cold dread creeping into my heart. "You've already done enough. We both have."

I couldn't bring myself to agree, couldn't accept that all I had to offer was this feeble trickle of healing energy. My hands trembled as I continued pressing against her wound, frustration simmering beneath the surface.

Behind us, the sound of footsteps approached, and I glanced up, catching sight of Dakota and McKenna, their faces etched with a mixture of relief and worry. McKenna still held her gun, her hands steady, while Dakota's gaze darted between me and Faith, her face hardening as she took in the blood staining Faith's leg.

"You two really know how to make a mess," Dakota muttered, her voice rough with forced bravado. She stripped off her blouse and wrapped it around Faith's leg, tying it tight by the arms and eliciting a moan from Faith.

McKenna knelt beside us. "Anything we can do?" she asked.

I shook my head, guilt pressing against my ribs. "Not unless you've got a few centuries' worth of power stashed somewhere," I replied, my tone harsher than intended. I took a shaky breath, softening. "We're drained. I can't even manage basic healing."

Dakota's face tightened, her hands pressing against Faith's wound. "Hey," she said softly. "You did what you could. Let us help from here."

Faith's fingers squeezed mine one more time, her eyes meeting mine with an exhausted look. "We'll get through this, Kal. Just take a breath."

I nodded, swallowing back the sharp, raw edge of panic.

A slow, mocking clap echoed through the barren landscape, slicing through the silence left in the wake of Lioraeth's death. My gaze snapped to Valaferion, standing beyond the battlefield, his hands meeting in an exaggerated, sarcastic applause. His eyes gleamed with cold amusement, a smirk twisting his lips as he surveyed the carnage we'd left behind.

"Well done," he drawled, his voice dripping with condescension. "Truly, it's a marvel to witness such perseverance from celestial castoffs and their mortal pets." He glanced at the disintegrated remains of Lioraeth with mild distaste before turning his icy gaze back to us. "It's almost impressive. Almost."

I clenched my fists, every fiber of my being alight with the need to strike him down. Exhaustion pressed down like a lead weight, and I could feel the last of my *taaqat* dwindling with every ragged breath. I staggered, steadying myself, feeling the ache in my bones, the strain from every wound and every blow that had brought us to this point.

Valaferion took a slow, measured step forward, his expression growing darker, his amusement replaced by something cold and merciless. "I'm afraid playtime is over. You've wasted enough of my resources—no more distractions. It's time I end this little farce."

I forced myself upright, ignoring the searing pain that shot through my side, summoning what was left of my strength as I met his contempt with my own. My knees threatened to buckle, and my vision swam for a moment, but I stood. This was it—the final showdown.

Before I could take a step forward, two figures moved beside me, flanking me, Dakota on my left, gun raised and stance firm, and

McKenna on my right, her eyes narrowed, her jaw set with that familiar stubbornness.

"What are you two doing?" I hissed, my voice barely more than a whisper. "This isn't your fight—"

"No. It is. We can't let third-rate trash like that turn our world upside-down," Dakota shot back, her gaze locked on Valaferion with a taunting focus. "We're here. That makes this our fight, too."

McKenna nodded, a smirk quirking her lips. "Besides, you're our ticket home." She glanced at the landscape. "This shithole makes the Bronx look good. No way am I staying here."

A surge of gratitude and protectiveness flared within me as I looked at them, my heart pounding. We stood together, battered and bloodied but unbroken, ready to face whatever came next.

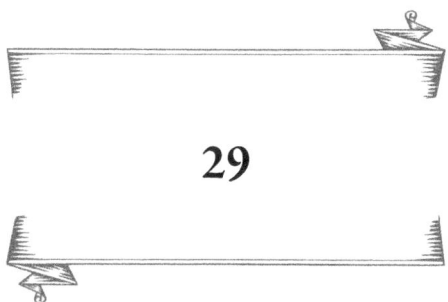

29

The air was charged with the battle we'd fought, the field littered with the fading traces of those we'd struck down. My grip tightened on Thakumis's Blade and the sanctified weapon, every nerve screaming for rest, yet I forced myself to keep steady, to project the confidence I no longer felt. Beside me, Dakota and McKenna stood tall, mirroring my resolve, though I knew they, too, must be nearing the end of their endurance.

Valaferion's gaze swept over us as if our very existence offended him. His lips twisted in a smirk, an expression dripping with contempt, and he let out a low chuckle that sent a chill down my spine. I took a steadying breath, meeting his gaze with all the bravado I could muster.

"Well, Valaferion," I said, my tone flippant, though I felt anything but. "Here we are. All your precious allies are gone, and your troops are scattered or dead. You're standing alone, in a graveyard of your own making. Now, I'd say that's a pretty good cue to make an exit. No need to be the next to fall."

The Duke of Hell's eyes narrowed, his amusement evaporating into disdain. "Is that supposed to intimidate me?" he sneered, taking a step forward, his aura oppressive, dark as midnight. "You think I'd abandon this fight because a pair of pathetic mortals and their washed-up celestial friends managed to cull a few foot soldiers?"

"Foot soldiers?" I scoffed, gesturing to the empty space where Lioraeth and Seraphina had stood. "Your foot soldiers included an

Archangel and an archdemon. Last I checked, they're not standing here anymore." I made a show of searching the battlefield before I met his gaze, letting a grin tug at my mouth. "I'd say that's worth a little credit."

He tilted his head, his expression dismissive, as though I were a bothersome insect. "Credit?" he spat, his voice a growl that seemed to shake the air. "You mistake desperation for strength, Kalili. Those pathetic wretches were merely pawns, expendable resources. And here you stand, barely clinging to life, thinking you can negotiate with me?" His tone dripped with incredulity, as if the thought amused him.

I laughed, hoping it sounded more confident than I felt. "Negotiate? Look around you. We've cut down everything you've thrown at us, and we're still here. I'd say that's grounds for reconsidering your position." I spread my arms, giving a mocking shrug. "It's simple math, Valaferion. There's one of you and three of us. If you were smart, you'd recognize when you're outmatched."

He laughed, a hollow, mirthless sound that echoed in the desolate landscape. "Outmatched?" His voice was sharp, a blade slicing through the space between us. "You and your mortals are nothing but fools, clinging to hope in a place where hope dies. I am Valaferion, Duke of Hell! I have conquered realms beyond your imagination, crushed legions under my heel, and watched as empires turned to dust at my command. You think a handful of tired, bleeding insects poses a threat to me?"

Dakota took a step forward, her chin lifted defiantly. "Keep underestimating us, big guy. It's worked out so well for your friends."

Valaferion's gaze shifted to her, his eyes narrowing in clear disgust. "And the mortal speaks," he sneered. "Do you truly think your little toys, your bullets and your human resolve, mean anything in the face of my power? You are ants, scurrying about, pretending to matter."

McKenna took a breath, her voice cold and measured. "If we're ants, you're doing a hell of a lot of talking to us."

Valaferion's lips pulled back in a snarl, his fists clenching. "You mistake my words for weakness. I am simply amused at the depths of your delusion. Your deaths will be quick—a mercy, considering your arrogance."

"Yeah?" I countered, forcing a smirk, though I could feel the inevitability of the confrontation looming. "Seems to me you've lost count, Valaferion. You're out of soldiers, out of allies, and all you've got left is an overblown ego."

He advanced a step, his presence like a storm gathering. "Such confidence from someone whose blood will stain this ground." He spread his hands, dark energy coiling around them, crackling with barely contained fury. "Your bravado is admirable, Kalili, but it won't save you. Nothing will."

I willed myself to keep my expression steady, to keep up the act, buying seconds, buying one more breath, one more moment. "Funny," I said, tilting my head in mock curiosity, "but I've heard that line before. Doesn't usually end well for whoever's saying it." I raised the sanctified blade, holding it level to his heart, meeting his gaze without flinching. "Last chance, Valaferion. Walk away while you can."

He let out a low, humorless chuckle, his eyes glinting. "Oh, I'll walk away. I'll walk away from the ashes of your remains."

Before I could respond, Dakota stepped in front of me, her stance firm, defiance etched across her face. "Then you'll have to walk over us first."

McKenna took her place next to Dakota, her eyes fixed on Valaferion. "You'll need more than ego to get through us," she said, her voice steady. "I think you're all bluster."

I felt a surge of pride—and maybe even a little fear. They weren't backing down. And neither was I. I took a steadying breath, summoning every scrap of energy I had left, feeling the weight of Thakumis's Blade in my right hand and the sanctified blade in my left. One was imbued with the darkest energy Hell could offer, a fragment of pure demonic power; the other radiated Heaven's light, forged to pierce the most wicked souls. Together, they should've been enough.

I burst between my friends and lunged forward, driving both weapons toward Valaferion. He met me head-on, his expression twisted into an amused sneer.

The first strike was solid. Thakumis's Blade cut across his side, and a dark, seething line burned through his armor. He let out a snarl, twisting back just in time for the sanctified blade to cut across his chest, the strike flaring with holy light that seemed to sizzle against his skin.

But he didn't stagger. He barely flinched.

Instead, his gaze turned cold and murderous. With a speed that belied his size, he surged forward, grabbing me with one enormous hand and lifting me clear off the ground. Before I could react, he swung me down, smashing me against the rocky ground with a force that left stars exploding in my vision.

Pain shot through every nerve as he lifted me again, like I weighed nothing, and slammed me down once more, and then again. My weapons slipped from my grasp, falling to the ground beside me as he tossed me aside like trash. I skidded across the ground, my body a pulsing mess of bruises and cracked bones, and finally came to a halt beside Faith.

Her face was tight with pain and exhaustion, but her eyes flared with concern as she gripped my hand. *Kal, talk to me!* Her thoughts reached me in a worried rush, her precious *taaqat* flowing through our link to strengthen me, though I knew she barely had enough for herself.

Did someone catch the number of the bus that hit me? I replied, struggling to keep my breathing steady. I could barely make out the sound of erratic gunfire, punctuated by Valaferion's irritated growls.

Nothing seems to touch him. Thakumis's Blade, the sanctified weapon—it's like they annoy him.

She squeezed my hand. *Then we'll have to find another way.*

A concentrated volley of shots rang out, and we turned to see Dakota and McKenna, positioned at opposite ends of the field, firing at Valaferion with courage that was both inspiring and heart-wrenching. Each bullet struck true, peppering his armor and flesh, and though the shots barely seemed to penetrate, they made him flinch.

"Annoying little insects," Valaferion snarled, unable to decide who to focus on first.

I pulled myself up, leaning heavily on Faith as I forced myself to breathe through the pain, urgency tightening my thoughts. *They're distracting him. We have to use this—find a weakness while he's focused on them.*

Faith's eyes narrowed, her mind reaching out to mine as she took in our surroundings. *His power is immense, but if we can draw him in, catch him off guard...* She hesitated, a sliver of worry entering her thoughts. *I have an idea,* she admitted. *But I'll need every bit of* taaqat *left in us, Kal. Can you occupy him long enough for me to gather it?*

I nodded, though every nerve protested, a silent scream of agony echoing through my body. *I'll do what I have to.*

She held my gaze, her fingers tightening around mine. *You're not alone in this. Remember that.*

With one last look, I forced myself to stand, ignoring the protests of my battered body, Faith's hand holding mine. Behind us, Dakota's voice rang out, clear and defiant, as she called to McKenna, the two of them drawing Valaferion's attention in turns to keep him pivoting back and forth between them.

"Hey, big guy!" Dakota shouted, reloading her gun with a quick flick of her wrist. "Thought you were supposed to be a Duke of Hell! Doesn't seem like much if two mortals can keep you busy!"

McKenna added her own taunt, her voice cold and biting. "Is this really the best Hell has to offer? Pathetic."

Valaferion's snarl deepened, his gaze snapping between them, visibly frustrated by their constant needling. I shot Faith a quick glance, and she nodded, her focus already centering on gathering the *taaqat* we'd need for her idea. I felt it flow out of me into her.

Hold him off, she sent, her voice steady but intense. *I'll be ready soon. If it works.*

My response was cut off by a shriek from Dakota.

The air around us crackled with energy as Valaferion's gaze locked onto Dakota, his lips curling into a twisted smile. Before I could shout a warning, he extended a hand, and I watched in horror as she was lifted from the ground, her body helplessly pulled toward him through the air. Dakota fired shot after shot, screaming obscenities at him, but her bullets all went wild as she tumbled toward the Duke.

Valaferion's voice was a low growl as she came within reach. "Oh, you put up a good fight, mortal. Admirable. Futile."

With a flick of his wrist, his sword appeared in his hand, a dark, curved, wicked blade that pulsed with raw demonic power. Dakota had no time to react as he drove it through her, the blade piercing her stomach and emerging from her back. She gasped, her hand going limp, the gun falling from her grip as her body sagged on the weapon. Her eyes met mine for a brief, agonizing second before Valaferion let her slide off and drop to the ground, blood pooling beneath her.

"Dakota!" The cry tore from my throat as I started forward, but I froze, helpless, as McKenna's scream rang out, raw and furious. Her face twisted in uncontained rage, her entire body trembling with it as she leveled her gun at him. "You bastard," she spat, her voice cutting through the air like a blade.

Valaferion turned to her, unperturbed, his smile mocking. "Such anger. Mortals are such fragile, useless creatures, so bound by their attachments and their grief. Look at you... angry as a dying insect." He held out his hand, slowly curling his fingers as if gripping something unseen.

I realized what he was doing an instant too late. McKenna's body jerked, her eyes widening as an invisible force closed around her throat. She dropped her gun to claw at her neck, gasping for breath, her face contorting in agony as he squeezed, savoring every second.

"No!" I shouted, my horror giving way to desperate fury. I forced myself to run, ignoring my injuries, my body screaming in protest, and launched myself at Valaferion, hands outstretched, mind blank except for the single, driving instinct to stop him.

My impact barely registered. He turned his head as he flung me backward with a casual flick of his arm, sending me crashing into the rocks behind him. Pain jolted through my battered body, but I pushed myself up to my knees, gasping, as he returned his attention to McKenna.

I'd done it. As his hold weakened momentarily, McKenna collapsed to her knees, her eyes darting to Dakota's motionless form. She crawled to her side, reaching out with trembling fingers to clutch her wife's hand. Dakota's eyes fluttered open for a second, enough for the faintest smile to touch her lips. "Hey," she rasped, her voice barely audible. "See you on the other side, yeah?"

"Don't you dare," McKenna choked out, her hand tightening around Dakota's. But her voice broke, despair etched in every line of her face. "Stay with me a little longer."

Valaferion turned, and with a deadly calm, raised his arm, his eyes flashing with a dark promise. Before I could react, he hurled his sword straight at McKenna, the blade a deadly arc through the air.

It struck her in the back, beneath her right shoulder, driving her down beside Dakota, slamming her into the ground. She screamed, trailing off into a bloody gurgle before her breath hitched. McKenna's face contorted as she fought her way upright, the blood-slicked blade pulled from the ground crusted with dirt. Her hand still clutched Dakota's, their fingers laced even as her strength faded.

Valaferion turned toward me, his face twisted with disdain as he wiped a speck of blood from his cheek, the mockery in his gaze cutting deeper than any blade could. "Pathetic," he sneered. "You thought you could win, didn't you? Thought you could play the hero and stop me, when you're barely more than dust beneath my feet. Thirteens. I expected more from creatures of legend, but I suppose legends are always exaggerated."

I rose on trembling legs, forcing them to obey despite the burning ache that told me they'd soon give out. I was not dying on my knees. Not for this bastard. The sanctified blade and Thakumis's Blade lay out of reach, the strength in my arms long gone. I couldn't raise them if I tried. Valaferion stalked closer, his shadow seeming to swallow me as he loomed over, his eyes gleaming with sadistic satisfaction.

I braced myself, drawing a ragged breath. *Faith,* I sent through our link, a final thought of love and regret tinged with despair. *I love you. I wish I'd had more time.*

I closed my eyes, waiting for the final blow.

The air trembled, a surge of energy tearing through the battlefield, raw and wild, like unchained *kosmiskorka*. It flooded through me, a power so immense it was impossible—*kosmiskorka* was contained, it had rules, and this felt like it was tearing through every one of them. Before I could grasp what was happening, a shockwave burst through the air, knocking me backward, my body rolling as the ground trembled beneath me.

Valaferion let out a roar of rage and disbelief, his form blasted back, sprawling across the rocky ground with a heavy, undignified thud.

I forced my eyes open, disoriented, half-expecting to see some celestial army come to our aid, Avareth or Lilith in the lead. Instead,

I saw Faith, standing upright, her body healed, though her clothes hung in tatters and her face was drawn and pale.

She looked furious.

I'd never been so in love.

"Oh, fuck you, Valaferion," she spat, her voice a low, dangerous snarl that held a power I'd never heard from her before. Her hands pulsed with energy, but it wasn't the familiar silver-white light of *vashwic urja*. No, this energy was raw, blazing, and bright orange, swirling around her fists like flames barely contained.

"Faith...?" I whispered, disbelief and awe merging in my voice.

Valaferion staggered to his feet, glaring at her with murder in his eyes. "Impossible! You don't have that kind of power, even as a Thirteen," he hissed, wiping a trickle of black blood from his mouth. "What are you?"

Faith growled, "Your worst fucking nightmare." With a motion that was as fluid as it was merciless, she hurled a ball of that blinding orange energy at him.

It struck with an explosion of light and heat, the blast forcing Valaferion back several feet, his form flickering as the energy seared into him. He roared, struggling to stay upright, but Faith gave him no respite. She flung another at him, and another, and another, his composure unraveling with each blow she landed, each blast tearing through his defenses.

Faith's eyes narrowed, the fury in her gaze unwavering as she pummeled him with strike after strike of this strange power. I knew it was *kosmiskorka*, but it felt altered, untamed in a way I hadn't thought possible. As she sent another pulse crashing into Valaferion, his form wavered, his invincibility cracking like his armor.

"Get up, Kal!" Faith shouted over her shoulder, her voice as furious as the energy in her hands. "We're not done yet!"

Staggering, I forced myself up and stumbled to Faith's side. She turned, the orange energy in her hands dimming long enough for her to reach out and grasp my arm. Her touch burned, and I could feel the unchained power coiling within her, barely held back.

"Hold on, Kal," she said, her tone mixing worry and urgency. "I'm going to give you everything I've got."

The warning came a half-second too late. She released a rush of *kosmiskorka* into me, the raw, blinding current of energy searing through my veins, testing every limit of my body's ability to hold and transmute it. I gritted my teeth, focusing every ounce of my will on shifting the energy to *taaqat*, forcing the power into healing every torn muscle, sealing every raw wound. As my body healed and I felt my strength return, I desperately spindled the energy, but I couldn't contain it all—some of it spilled over into *vashwic urja*, igniting my hands in a white-hot flame as I absorbed as much as I could.

Faith's grip tightened on my arm, her eyes apologetic. "It's a lot, I know, but we need everything we can handle."

I gave a sharp nod, letting the pain wash over me, letting the *kosmiskorka* turn to fuel. When I finally managed to stand tall, every nerve alive with the combined powers, Faith released me and nodded toward Valaferion, who was slowly pushing himself off the ground, his face a mask of fury and pain.

"You'll explain later?" I managed, my voice steadier.

Faith smiled. "Later," she promised, energy swirling around her, wreathing her in a terrible beauty. "Ready?"

"Hell no. How do we want to play this?"

"Just like the catacombs."

"Wild and uncontrolled. Got it."

Together, we turned back to Valaferion, who snarled, defiance etched in every line of his face.

"You should have stayed down, Duke," I said, the words carrying the edge of every strike I was about to land.

We didn't give him a chance to answer before cutting loose. Side by side, we advanced on him, Faith channeling that new, burning energy with each strike while I pummeled him with *vashwic urja*. He fought back, his power flaring desperately, but against our united powers he didn't stand a chance. Each blow we landed tore through his defenses until he was left reeling, panting, his body flickering between its form and shadows.

Finally, when he staggered and dropped to his knees, defeated but not yet dead, we stopped. Faith stepped forward, her expression calm as she met his gaze.

"It's over, Valaferion," she said, her voice steely. "Stand down. Accept justice—Lilith's justice. You know it's coming, and you're out of options."

Valaferion glared up at her, his eyes still blazing with defiance. "I'd rather be obliterated," he spat, his voice ragged but full of venom. "I will never bow to you."

Faith's mouth twisted into a wry, almost pitying smile. "As you wish." Her tone was nearly casual as she raised her hand, energy gathering in her palm. She didn't hesitate, didn't give him time to consider anything else; in one swift motion, she released the power straight into him, her strike absolute.

Valaferion's form shattered, the shadows dissipating, leaving nothing behind. The rebellious Duke of Hell was no more.

Faith cut her connection to the *kosmiskorka* before it overwhelmed us, and we dropped to our knees, arms wrapped around each other. It was over.

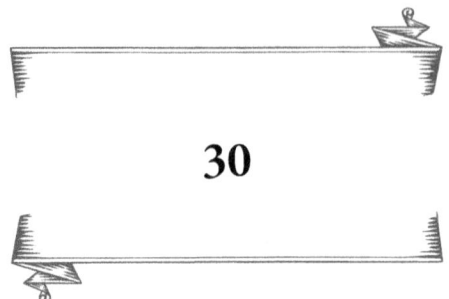

30

A groan reminded me of our friends.

"McKenna!" I shouted, scrabbling to my feet and sprinting for their fallen forms. McKenna was still impaled on the late Duke's sword, but, oh eternity, she was awake and trying to free herself. "Stop moving!"

"Have to help... Dakota," she husked, her voice thin and strained, a haunting rasp that barely sounded like her own. Her hand trembled as she reached for the hilt, but I caught it, forcing her to still. Her skin was deathly pale, and her breaths shallow.

"Not like this," I said, forcing the words through the knot in my throat. "I'm not done with you, McKenna."

This was a problem. I couldn't draw it back through her, but I couldn't leave it here. "Hold on." I didn't know what I was going to try, but...

"Faith! I need water!" *If* her majik worked here. *If* there was time.

A deluge caught us both, sluicing over us, cleaning the crust of dirt from the blade.

I braced her with one arm, taking all her weight, and lifted. The sword emerged from the ground, and I called to Faith, "Again!" Again we were soaked, but I was prepared, and pulled the sword as gently as I could. When it was out, I tossed it aside and lowered her, letting her settle to the ground with a groan.

"D-dammit, Kal, I would've sh-showered later," she said, shivering.

Her gaze drifted over to Dakota, who lay sprawled a few feet away, gasping as her body shut down, her blood darkening the ground beneath her. Despite the pain clear in her every breath, Dakota managed a weak smile as her eyes found McKenna's. "So much for getting old and cranky together, huh?" she murmured, each word a struggle.

McKenna gave a ragged chuckle, her gaze fond, even through the pain. "Could've told you I wasn't cut out for rocking chairs and slippers."

A flicker of humor passed over Dakota's face, trying to find some comfort against the rough ground. "Think I would've managed. Besides, we were supposed to do at least one more heist, remember?" Her voice faded, a glimmer of nostalgia lacing her words. "One last job."

McKenna's hand twitched, her fingers curling as she remembered, too. "Yeah... we've pulled off some good ones." She coughed, her face contorting in pain, but she forced herself to keep speaking. "Remember when we met? That jewel heist?" Dakota nodded, and McKenna continued. "I never told you, but from the moment I walked into the SVG and saw you sitting there, I knew..."

"Yeah," Dakota breathed, a spark of life igniting in her eyes as she replayed the memories. "Same. It was you."

McKenna's smile was as fragile as the life slipping from her. "Wouldn't change a damn thing," she whispered, her fingers straining toward Dakota's hand. "Well, maybe this part." She winced, managing another weak laugh. "Dying sucks."

That last laugh triggered something fierce and desperate in me. *No*, I thought. *There has to be a way to stop this, a way to pull them back from the edge.*

"Faith? Can your majik...?"

Faith's hand gripped my arm, her face full of sorrow. "I'm sorry, no. Not in the majik I know."

The *kosmiskorka* twitched in me, and I automatically converted it to *taaqat*. A rush of thoughts jumbled through me, and Faith picked up the thread. "Kal, it won't work. They're human. They don't have the connection to *kosmiskorka* we do. Their bodies aren't compatible with it."

"No, I know, we can't tap the *kosmiskorka*. It would burn them up in a heartbeat. But what if..." I swallowed, the weight of it pressing down on me, but I couldn't let it go. I met Faith's gaze, my eyes pleading. "They use *taaqat*, like we do!"

She shook her head again. "Not like us. Similar, but not the same."

"So what?" I hissed, desperate to save them. Their murmured remembrances faded in and out of my hearing. "What do we have to lose by trying? They're dying, Faith! We still have our connection, we can tap the *kosmiskorka* for what we need. If you help me—if you help me channel it and direct it—maybe it'll work."

Faith hesitated, the doubt plain in her eyes, but there was something else there, too. She understood. She'd seen the years I'd spent with these two, the bond that had grown beyond acquaintances, beyond friendship. Slowly she nodded, squeezing my arm.

"All right," she said softly, her voice filled with borrowed hope. "I'll guide it. Using *taaqat* for healing is instinctual for me. But it will take every ounce of focus you have, Kal. Every. Ounce."

I nodded, steeling myself as I moved closer to McKenna and Dakota, my heart hammering. I reached for McKenna's hand first, taking it gently in mine. Her skin was so cold.

"We're going to try something," I said, my voice rough as I twisted my lips into a smile. "Just hold on. Don't let go."

McKenna's gaze shifted to me, confusion and hope mingling as she nodded weakly. Beside her, Dakota coughed. "Whatever you're doing, make it fast, Kal. You know I don't have the patience for mystical healing mumbo jumbo."

I grinned more naturally. Faith placed her hands on my shoulders, her familiar presence calming my nerves, her power guiding mine. I closed my eyes, reaching deep within myself, drawing on the *kosmiskorka*. The energy surged, bright and fierce, but I tamped it down into *taaqat*, forcing it into McKenna. Her body resisted at first, the Immortal energy battling her human power, but then I felt it shift. Her life flickered, then strengthened.

I couldn't pay attention to the details, my mind engaged in the careful dance we were performing. Faith held back the raw power that would overwhelm her body, allowing a trickle into me. I channeled it carefully, transmuting it into *taaqat*. With her body no longer resisting my efforts, I let it flow like water to each wound, each fractured bone, every failing organ. When I felt her heartbeat steady, her breaths deepening, I released her hand and moved to Dakota.

"Your turn," I said, giving her hand a firm squeeze.

The *taaqat* met with the same resistance in Dakota, her human essence different, but I anticipated it now. Of course, hers was more stubborn, just like Dakota, but soon enough I felt her body respond. She clung to me, her unquenchable spirit adding to the energy that Faith and I poured into her. I closed my eyes against the pain from the *taaqats* clashing. I couldn't stop, no when we had a chance.

When her body had taken all it could, I opened my eyes. Dakota's chest rose and fell in a steady rhythm. A glance to the side confirmed that McKenna's color had returned, her breathing strong.

I let out a shuddering breath, looking to Faith, who nodded, her eyes filled with relief.

"It worked," she said, awed. "It actually worked."

I watched Dakota and McKenna take turns grasping each other's hands, laughing in sheer joy, before turning to Faith. I couldn't put off the question gnawing at me any longer.

"Faith, that was *kosmiskorka*." It wasn't a question, but she nodded anyway. "How did you manage to crack through Valaferion's barrier?" I asked quietly, hoping the others wouldn't hear.

She brushed her hair back and settled down beside me, clearly as exhausted as I felt. "It took some figuring out. At first, I thought it was the place—something about the emptiness here that was blocking us. After a few rounds with the angels and demons, I saw the pattern."

"Pattern?" I asked, feeling the pieces click together in her mind. "You think Valaferion was the one doing it?"

"Exactly. He was using his energy to block us, Kal, not some environmental spell or a natural force. Every time he lost an ally, I felt a shift in the *kosmiskorka*—the barrier weakened, and I was closer and closer to reaching the source. It wasn't much at first, a chink in the armor, but it was there."

I stared at her, a stunned realization settling in. "And you figured this out *while* we were in the middle of that fight?"

Faith gave a half-shrug, one that showed her weary pride. "I couldn't be certain, but I poked at it. Each time we took down one of his allies, I'd test the barrier, pushing my *taaqat* against it. That's why I was so low; every time I pushed, I lost more *taaqat*. I realized he was drawing power from each of them to fuel the shield, which explained why the barrier was getting weaker."

"Because he had fewer allies to pull from," I finished. "You were risking... Faith, if you'd failed, you would have died. Without *taaqat*..." I let the thought trail off, too appalled to say it out loud. She would've been gone forever.

"But I didn't fail," she replied. "Once it was just Valaferion, the shield was as weak as it was going to get. That's why I needed your *taaqat*; not to heal, but to smash through. I took a gamble, poured everything I had into breaking it—and it worked." She squeezed my hand. "It was all or nothing, and I wasn't going to let him take us down without a fight."

My heart twisted as I looked at her. "What was the power you used against him? It wasn't *vashwic urja*. It felt different."

Faith's expression shifted. "I've been studying the scrolls again. The ones Avy acquired from Lucifer's archives. There's another power mentioned, a counterpart to *vashwic urja*, but one designed to damage demons." She paused, the corrected herself. "Well, not demons, but the opposing Thirteen. I can do it, but since you were created on the opposite side, you might not be able to tap it. There's probably an equivalent for you, though."

I shook my head, trying to catch up. "Wait, you've been studying? And you didn't tell me?"

She had the decency to blush. "I wanted to surprise you."

"Oh, you surprised me." I stuffed the hint of irritation away to examine later. "Okay. A new power. Do you have a name for it?"

She tilted her head, remembering. "*Mitrwic urja*. It has the same root as *vashwic*, but it draws from a deeper, sharper source, one that's tuned specifically to demon eradication."

"*Mitrwic urja*," I repeated, letting the syllables settle. The sound carried weight, power, and an edge that resonated with something deep inside me. Something else to look at later. I arched an eyebrow at her. "And you decided to try it on a whim?"

Faith grinned, a flash of rebellion flickering to life. "What better time than in a fight for survival?" She met my gaze, her smile soft. "Besides, I was ready. I knew you'd pull us through if it came to it."

I couldn't help a low laugh. "You're reckless," I muttered, shaking my head.

She leaned in closer, eyes glinting. "Maybe. But we're here, aren't we? I'd say it was worth the risk."

"I agree."

We sat in silence for a piece. I shapeshifted some new clothes into existence, unwilling to wear my ruined clothes, and Faith followed suit. My mind rested then, enjoying the moment's respite, the contact with Faith, and the relief that it was over.

We were interrupted by movement. Dakota and McKenna stood, brushing off dust and bloodstains, wincing at the evidence of their wounds before making their way over to Faith and me. We rose to greet them, taking stock. They were a mess, but alive, which was more than we'd dared hope a few minutes ago. Dakota's usual mischief was dimmed with exhaustion, but she managed a half-smile.

"Is it really over?" she asked, casting a wary glance around at the empty landscape, as if something else might come crawling up out of the ground to take a swing at us.

"Yes," I confirmed, "it's over. Valaferion's gone, and with him, the last of his alliance."

McKenna narrowed her eyes, glancing at Faith. "What exactly happened to him? You did something—something big."

Faith flashed a satisfied smile. "Valaferion refused to surrender, even with nothing left to fight for. I made a choice." Her eyes gleamed, and I had a memory of Rome and the wall. "Celestial justice, as interpreted by me. He's been obliterated, and there's no coming back from this one."

Dakota let out a low whistle. "Damn. You ended him?"

Faith nodded, her gaze steady. "There was no other option."

"Hold up," McKenna interrupted. "Coming back is an option?"

"Not for him, and it's not important right now. I can explain when we're home," I said, eager to divert her attention.

It worked. McKenna rubbed her arms, wincing slightly at the motion, and then looked at us curiously. "And us? How did we make it? One minute, I was pretty sure we were both goners, and the next..." She gestured to herself and Dakota, both miraculously whole, if battered.

Faith gave me a sidelong glance. "That was Kal. She channeled her *taaqat*—our lifeforce, celestial energy—to heal you both, even though it took a leap of faith."

Dakota's eyebrows shot up, clearly impressed. "Guess we owe you one, then, Kal."

I shrugged, brushing it off with a small smile. "I think, after all these years, we can stop keeping score."

McKenna looked at us, then at the rags they were wearing. "Any chance you could conjure up some clothes for us, too? Dry ones? That impromptu shower worked, but it was cold and I'm soggy."

"Ah," I said, raising a hand with a sheepish chuckle. "This? It's an old trick, but it's a little limited. We can conjure clothes for ourselves, sure, but they're temporary. If I try to give them away, they'll disappear. As soon as they leave my body—poof. Nothing but air."

Dakota and McKenna both groaned, but Dakota's mouth twisted into a grin. "Of course. Nothing's ever easy."

Faith let out a sigh, casting a weary but amused glance my way. "Well, as much as I'd love to stick around and trade clothing secrets, I think it's time to get home."

I reached out to Dakota, who looked at my extended hand like it was a lifeline. Her hand trembled slightly as she slipped hers into mine, and I saw McKenna's grip tighten reflexively around Faith's.

"We're trying this again?" McKenna asked, glancing between us with a touch of skepticism. "Visualizing your penthouse? You're sure we'll get there?"

"I am," Faith said with a reassuring smile, taking my free hand in hers. "Just focus on what home feels like, sounds like, even smells like. Every detail you can remember."

Dakota gave a shaky laugh. "No offense, but after all this, my brain's a little scattered. You're sure this won't drop us somewhere worse?"

I squeezed her hand, meeting her gaze with all the confidence I could muster. "Valaferion is the one who intercepted us in the between, and he's not doing that again. Tell you what, you keep your minds clear, and we'll do the rest. We've got you, both of you. Trust us, okay?"

McKenna closed the circle with Dakota's hand, took a deep breath, and nodded slowly, willing herself to relax. "Alright. Home, Jeeves." She allowed herself a slight smile at her joke before closing her eyes, her features settling into concentration. Dakota followed suit, her fingers holding tight to mine as if that alone might guide her back.

Faith's voice slipped into my mind, grounding and steady, *This time, no distractions, no detours. Let's bring them home, Kal.*

I closed my eyes, letting the penthouse fill my mind: the warm glow from the living room lamps, the distant hum of the city, and the faint scent of coffee that always seemed to linger from our mornings together. That image grew stronger, enveloping us like a shield as the wasteland around us blurred, fading like a half-forgotten memory.

Then, with a final pulse of energy, the silence of that barren world was replaced by the comforting familiarity of home as we reemerged, heartbeats racing, in the center of our Manhattan penthouse.

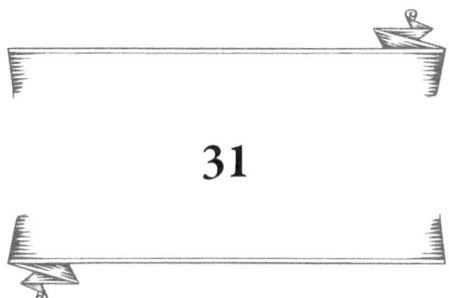

31

The warm, familiar light of the penthouse welcomed us, but before I could take in the comfort of home, I heard a voice.

"Where *were* you? And, gods, what happened to you?"

Avareth was there, waiting, her normally calm expression tight with worry, and, surprisingly, Bandit nestled in her arms like a miniature sentry. At the sight of us, she let out a breath, her shoulders sagging in relief. "Do you have any idea how close I was to jumping after you? You vanished without a trace! I thought..."

Faith held up her hand gently, gesturing for calm. "Avy, we're alright. It was complicated."

"Complicated?" Avareth's voice pitched higher, incredulous. Bandit decided she was tired of the noise and jumped down, stalking away with her tail high. "Do you know what it's like not being able to sense *anything*? I've been sitting here for hours, waiting—"

"I know, Avy. It was Valaferion's demesne." Faith met her gaze squarely, her voice soft. "The whole place was locked down through his will. There were no connections in or out."

"We didn't exactly have an invitation," I added, my tone dry as I took a seat and gestured for Dakota and McKenna to join us. They glanced at their ruined, bloody clothes, and I laughed. "It's a couch, guys. I can replace it if you're worried about the blood. Or the water."

As Avareth listened, Faith and I traded glances, deciding who would speak first.

Do you want to tell her?

Why can't we just share the memories?

And let her off the hook? No way.

I broke the silence. "Well, let's start with the ambush. The Duke of Hell made it abundantly clear he didn't plan on letting us leave." I shot Faith a look and she picked up where I left off.

"Valaferion had some friends," she continued, shaking her head. "An Archangel, a Principality, and an Archdemon. Everyone you named and then some, Avy. Guess they were even better at sneaking around than you thought."

Avareth's jaw dropped. "All at once?"

"Yep," Dakota cut in, her voice weary. "And if it weren't for our *stellar* sharpshooting skills, these two would've had an even tougher time out there." She smiled at McKenna, who nodded.

McKenna folded her arms, adding, "If we hadn't been there *someone* would be having a very different conversation right now." She shot me a wry smile. "We got our licks in."

I nodded. "Full credit, your help was invaluable."

Faith leaned forward, rubbing her neck. "It was more than any of us expected, Avy. We lost *kosmiskorka* access. It was a brutal, bare-knuckled fight to survive." I continued the tale.

"We took them down one by one. It came close, and the *kosmiskorka* barrier nearly held, but Faith figured out how to break through. That's when we took down Valaferion." I paused. "You know, that talisman might've come in handy—"

"No!" Faith and Avareth chorused and I raised my hands in surrender.

"Fine, fine, whatever. You're right, it's best left buried and forgotten. Anyway, Faith broke the barrier and from there, it was mopping up."

Avareth shook her head slowly, her eyes wide, her mouth slightly open. "You defeated Valaferion. The four of you. I mean, you've taken out Archangels, and even ambushed Lucifer, but that was with your full powers. You said you didn't have access to *kosmiskorka,* and you had two mortals to protect..."

She stopped, head still shaking in disbelief, but no more words emerged.

I raised an eyebrow, hugely amused. "Faith? I think we've finally broken Avareth; I've never known her to be at a loss for words."

That snapped her out of her daze, and she laughed. "I'll admit—*this* isn't something I see every day."

Faith chuckled, leaning back with a sigh. "You're jealous you didn't get to join in."

"Oh, yes," Avareth shot back, sarcasm thick. "Because fighting a Duke of Hell and his entourage is my idea of a *relaxing* day."

"Next time, we'll bring you along," I teased. "Might give you some excitement, a break in that routine of yours."

Avareth rolled her eyes, but her smile widened, and there was a warmth there that matched our relief. It was over. We were home. For the first time in what felt like an eternity, we could breathe.

McKenna was the first to break the silence, her voice cautious. "What's been going on here? Is it safe?"

"Safe? Well, more or less. As safe as it ever will be," Avareth replied, inclining her head. "I'll say this for the Empire: when something threatens their finances, they move quickly. They saw which way the tide was turning, and they're far too invested in maintaining their image as a neutral financial hub to risk more chaos spilling into their territory. They've closed the borders to the United States forces and are holding both sides at bay."

Dakota raised an eyebrow, skeptical. "We're supposed to believe they're all about peace now?"

Avareth chuckled. "Peace is a strong word. Let's say they're about preserving order—their order. The last thing they want is the world to perceive them as allied with anyone, especially after seeing the impact of their quiet support for the United States. The City lost billions, and if there's one thing the Empire cares about more than anything else, it's its pockets."

Dakota tilted her head thoughtfully. "They figured out they were losing more Cuomos than they were gaining, huh?"

Avareth nodded, her smile widening. "Exactly. Merchants and bankers alike were creative with their sources of income during the tensions—using the divide to make money off both sides. But now, with Empire troops at the borders of the New England Collective *and* the United States, they've managed to rein in the chaos, restoring a semblance of normalcy to the City."

Dakota's skepticism faded as hope replaced it. "We can go home?"

I nodded, watching their faces. "Of course you can. But you're welcome to stay here for the night, clean up, borrow whatever you need. We've got room, and it might not be a bad idea to take some time after everything we've been through."

Dakota looked down at her torn clothes, and a grimace crept onto her lips. "Not that I don't appreciate the battle-worn look, but I wouldn't mind feeling a little more like a human and a little less like I just crawled out of a war zone."

McKenna laughed, her eyes crinkling as she glanced over at Dakota. "Hear, hear. Clothes that don't look like we went three rounds with a Duke of Hell would be nice, too."

Faith stepped forward with a reassuring smile. "That's settled, then. I'll need to go with you tomorrow, to take the defenses off your building." Dakota nodded. "Oh! Before you clean up, I'd like to finish the healing so neither of you has to keep those scars." She looked between the two of them, her gaze warm. "It's the least we can do."

A touch of humility replaced Dakota's usual bravado. "I don't mind the scars that I've earned, but these are a bit much. Thanks."

Faith moved to the couch, standing in front of McKenna and resting hands on her shoulders. She closed her eyes, her energy radiating out softly, a gentle glow surrounding her hands as she began healing McKenna's scars.

Nice light show, I thought.

I wanted to make them feel like... Her brow furrowed, and a flicker of surprise crossed her face as she took in what she sensed.

What?

Hold on.

Avareth's eyes narrowed, picking up on the shift in Faith's expression. "What is it?"

Faith's gaze darted to me, then back to McKenna, who looked down at her hands, confused but unafraid. "I'm not sure. When we healed them before, we may have done more than we realized."

"What? How can you tell?" I asked.

"No resistance. I-I don't think their *taaqat* is human any longer."

"Impossible!" I blurted. "We can't change *taaqat*!"

McKenna looked at her, eyes widening. "Wait, what does that mean?"

Avareth crossed her arms with a thoughtful expression. I felt her shift into her second sight. "I see what you mean. Kal? Check their auras."

I did and gasped. Before, their auras were green, at the base—human. Oh, they had the usual imperfections that a lifetime did to an aura, but they were human. Now? Their auras were a color I'd never seen before, a rich blue, unstained and pure.

"What the hell, Avy? What does that mean?"

Avy, pleased as always to provide information, said, "I think it means they're no longer entirely human. I've heard of this happening before, but it's usually when an angel interferes in a human's life somehow. I think that your jump, the connection between you that was forged in the between, primed your *taaqat* for this change, made it more susceptible to altering. When Faith and Kalili healed you, using their celestial *taaqat,* yours transformed. It turned you into something beyond mortal—quasi-immortals."

Dakota blinked, absorbing the implication. "Quasi-immortal? Like... we can't die?"

Avareth chuckled. "Not quite. You're still mortal in the sense that you can be killed, but your bodies will heal faster, stay strong and healthy, and you won't die of disease, or old age. You won't age like mortals, but you're also not going to grow younger."

"Holy shit," I whispered. Avy shot me a look but continued.

"Think of it as getting a permanent pass to be your best selves, physically. No sickness, no aging. And your bodies will maintain the vitality you had in your twenties."

Dakota and McKenna looked at each other, absorbing their new reality.

"No more arthritis?" Dakota asked. Avy shook her head.

"No more wrinkles?" said McKenna. Avy shook her head again.

"Wait. Are we going to have our periods again? Maybe I don't—"

Avy laughed. "No, or at least, I don't think so."

"I guess we'll find out," McKenna said. Dakota, with a quiet chuckle, muttered, "Not exactly what I signed up for when we took on that first heist..."

McKenna grinned. "No, but I can't say I'm complaining."

Avareth laughed, and I felt her joy for me through our bond. "Funny how things work out, isn't it?"

They looked confused but pleased. I jumped to my feet and hugged them both. "What Avy's saying is—I swore I would give you as much time as this world would allow you. Guess it worked, if not the way I planned."

Their arms around me felt good, grounding, like family. When Avy and Faith joined us, I knew. We *were* family, bound by love. I'd had lovers, and I had my loves, but I'd never had family.

Now I did. Now *we* did.

It felt good.

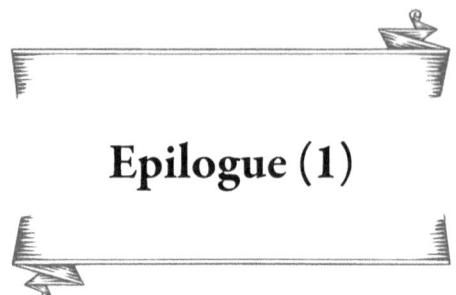

Epilogue (1)

April 15, 2112

"I'm not interested in selling," I said when the pitch ended.

The face on the other side of the videoconference frowned. I was pretty sure it was AI-generated, but I didn't care about that. I hadn't cared about how the humans pretended to conceal themselves for years. Why would I? I wasn't in the business of judgment.

"I realize you're reluctant, Ms. Keoka. After all, your group has held onto OutLook for six decades, but I'm certain you'll find our offer—"

"I don't care what your offer is, Mr. Smith." Smith. How creative. "I'm not interested in selling."

Faith, sitting across the desk and out of sight, nodded emphatically.

"OutLook has been a valuable, you might say crucial, asset in my portfolio. I'd be foolish to part with it for a few million credits."

I gazed out the window and took in the Manhattan skyline. I never tired of the view, even after a century and a half.

"Not a few millions, Ms. Keoka. The trustees of the Harriman Trust are prepared to offer you considerably more."

I knew the value of OutLook, and what he was suggesting didn't make any sense. It piqued my curiosity. "Go on."

I heard tapping, and the ping of an incoming message. "I have sent you our opening offer. I'm sure you'll find it most equitable."

"A moment." I muted the mic and shut down the camera before opening the message. "Holy shit. Faith, come here." She rose and made her way around. "Do you see what I see?"

Her eyes went wide. "If you're seeing two hundred million Sonoran credits? Yes."

"That's insane."

"I know we don't need the money—"

That was an understatement. One of the advantages of being an Immortal in the human world was we didn't have to worry about our investments outliving us. With seven thousand years of experience with humans, I could spot trends fairly reliably and figure out which industry would benefit most. And, frankly, the intelligence industry was suffering.

Oh, there was always a market for information. Always had been, always would be. But the circumstances that led me to buy OutLook sixty years earlier had changed. Then, I'd been involved in the human world, but detached. I hadn't dived headfirst into it, since I knew we could leave it any time we needed.

After Valaferion and his minions? Suddenly, the connections we'd made were more real than ever before. That Dakota and McKenna wouldn't simply vanish from our lives in what to us was an eyeblink changed everything. The immortality that was forced upon them meant they'd be in our lives until they chose not to be, not at the whim of fate or genetics.

Suddenly, my perspective on the people around us shifted. When I told Dakota we needed their humanity, I didn't realize how true my words were. With their help, we learned from OutLook, studied their methods, and duplicated their abilities in an independent network we controlled, one that didn't depend on clients and revenue.

So maybe it was time to let the company go.

"Faith? What do you think? Should we take it?"

Her answer was immediate. "Counteroffer for double that. See if they're serious."

"Four hundred?"

She nodded. "What's that human phrase? Put the money where the mouth is?"

I chuckled. "Something like that. Okay." I unmuted and restored the feed. "Four hundred million."

"Done."

I blinked, semi-stunned at the response, but recovered. "Send over the documents and we'll finish this today."

"Thank you. The trustee will be most pleased with your decision."

I caught the difference that time. "Trustee? Not the Trust?"

"No. The Harriman Trust isn't directly involved in the purchase, though it will be providing the funds. I will have the documents to you presently." Without another word, his end of the connection closed.

"Well, babe, we're going to have to depend on Dakota and McKenna's skills even more," Faith said, settling into my lap and dropping a kiss on my forehead.

"I guess so. Good thing they understand us." I returned the kiss with interest.

A moment later, another notification came in. Faith slid off me so I could open it. "It's the contract." I scanned it, looking for loopholes and finding none. "I'm going to send it to Avy, just to be sure there aren't any traps," I said, tapping out a quick message and dispatching it.

"I'm curious," Faith said, peering over my shoulder. "Does it list the buyer?"

I scrolled through until I found the relevant paragraph and read it aloud. "Derek Delos James. Wonder who that is?"

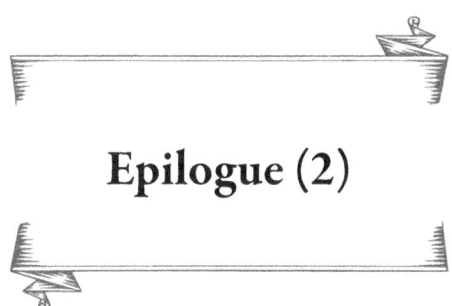

Epilogue (2)

Stardate 33811.25

"Are you sure you want to do this?"

McKenna squeezed Dakota's hand. "Have Kalili and Faith ever steered us wrong?"

"Besides the time they dragged us to Hell?"

"Hey, that wasn't their fault, and we did end up with some awfully nice perks out of it." She laid a kiss on her wife's temple and stroked the black hair, liberally streaked with white. "Besides, I think it's time for a new challenge. As much as I appreciate outliving the various statutes of limitations, sooner or later someone's going to be smarter than us."

"Well..."

Whatever Dakota was going to say was lost when the hatch to the inner office slid open. A light voice said, "Come in, please."

They stepped through and found a young-looking woman with long, brown hair tucked into a ponytail. She wore a blue uniform and rose from behind a desk. "Thank you for coming. It's quite unusual for Ms. Cassidy to take new crew members aboard directly, so I'd like to get to know you better." She gestured to the chairs. "Please, make yourself comfortable."

Dakota scanned the room with a practiced eye. Even though they were aboard a starship, it was smart to figure out alternative exits. One was apparent, a hatch to the left of the desk, but...

The emergency hatch ought to be beside that couch, McKenna thought, and Dakota gave her a tiny nod.

Then that's where we sit. Any bugs?

I haven't gotten an alert, but I can't exactly do an active scan until we have some cover.

They settled on the couch, giving every appearance of being relaxed, while the brunette moved to one of the visitor chairs and turned it to face them. She settled in with a half-smile.

"I should have known that anyone she brought in would have unique mannerisms," she said. "I am Minerva Cassidy, captain of the TSS *Dreamer*."

"Dakota Chase, and this is my wife, McKenna Cross. Cassidy. Any relation to Kendra? Daughter, maybe? I know that the *Dreamer* is a private vessel."

Minerva chuckled. "No, Kendra and Aiyana are my wives, though I haven't been married to them their entire partnership." The smile faded and she turned serious. "A question about your records. I saw that you have been married since 2031; is that an error in our file? Should it be 2331?"

"No," McKenna said. "It's correct."

A single eyebrow raised in question.

"It's a long story."

"One I'm eager to hear," came another voice, as the other hatch slid aside. "Minna, it's not polite to grill our new crew before they've had a chance to settle in."

The speaker was a tall woman with pixie-cut blonde hair in an anachronistic white uniform. She commanded the room effortlessly, obviously accustomed to being obeyed.

"I am simply trying to clear up some questions in their records, Kendra."

"Do the questions change what we plan to do with them?" the blonde asked.

"No," Minerva admitted.

"Then we'll leave it for now. They came to me highly recommended by women I trust implicitly." She focused on Dakota and McKenna. "I believe you know them. Kalili Keoka and Faith Burroughs?"

At the sound of their friends' names, McKenna was instantly alert.

What does she know about Kalili? Do you think…?

I don't know. Bluff it out. Tell the truth if we have to.

"We know them," Dakota admitted. "How do you know them?"

"Converging interests. Come on, let's take this to my quarters. I have the feeling we're going to need some drinks to lubricate the gears of trust, and I need you two to trust me." Kendra turned for the exit hatch, stopping at the threshold. "Well?"

Should we?

She's a damn hero and the founder of the Terran Federation. I don't think she's going to try to pin any century-old crimes on us up here.

It's not the century-old ones I worry about.

Dakota!

"Coming. We're not as young as we used to be," Dakota said, hoping the excuse didn't sound as lame as she felt it was.

"No, you aren't. Frankly, that was the biggest factor in my decision to bring you aboard." Noting their confusion, Kendra continued. "By the records you supplied, you're both over three hundred years old. As my wife Aiyana would say, it's highly improbable, especially since the life-extending nanotech we've developed didn't make its appearance until the Twenty-one teens."

Oh, shit.

What do we say?

Nothing for now. Dakota said, "We'd rather discuss these details in private, if you don't mind." She gestured to the corridor and the other people passing through.

"Naturally." The walk down the corridor was filled with a mix of small talk and veiled assessments. Dakota's eyes darted around, noting exits and intersections, while McKenna's gaze followed each crew member who passed, memorizing faces and uniforms.

McKenna's thought brushed against Dakota's mind. *She's looking for something. Some angle.*

That makes two of us. Dakota kept her tone light as she said, "So, this ship—*Dreamer*, right? Not exactly the sort of place you'd find two, ah, antique thieves aboard."

Kendra let out a soft laugh, glancing back at them with a curious smile. "Antique, huh? Is that how you think of yourselves?"

Dakota shrugged. "Seems a fair term. Not a lot of folks our age around."

Careful, D. McKenna's mental nudge was gentle. *She's not buying it.*

Kinda figured as much, Dakota replied silently. *Just testing the waters.*

They reached a door labeled *Admiral's Quarters,* and Kendra led them in. The suite was spacious but simply decorated—utilitarian, like everything else they'd seen on the ship, with a few personal touches that hinted at its owner's life. A small bar was tucked into one corner, stocked with several bottles of liquor that likely came from planets they'd never even heard of.

Kendra walked over to the bar, picked up a bottle and gave them a sidelong glance. "You two look like bourbon drinkers." Without waiting for a response, she poured two glasses and handed one to each of them.

Dakota sniffed the glass appreciatively. "Now that's a hell of a vintage," she said, lifting it in a silent toast.

Kendra's smile widened as she raised her glass. "To new ventures—and old friends."

They drank, the liquor a warm burn that settled the tension in Dakota's shoulders, if only for a moment. Kendra set her glass down and leaned against the bar, crossing her arms as she studied them.

"So, three hundred years," she said casually, as if she were commenting on the weather. "Quite a run. You must have seen some changes."

Dakota chuckled, deflecting. "Three hundred and sixty, to be accurate, and yeah. A few. Hard to keep up with it all, though."

McKenna's mind reached out to Dakota's, her thought a pulse of worry. *She knows too much. We need to figure out her angle.*

Dakota nodded imperceptibly, setting her glass down with a soft clink. "Look, we're not looking to cause any trouble," she said, leaning forward slightly. "Whatever questions you have, we'll answer them. Understand, some of this isn't exactly public knowledge."

Kendra tilted her head, her eyes narrowing slightly. "I gathered that. But, Dakota, McKenna—you're here because someone I trust vouched for you. Kalili and Faith don't give their trust lightly. Consider this a chance to level with me, and we'll see where we stand."

This might be our best shot, McKenna's thought came, more certain now. *But she's testing us. Let's not give her everything.*

Dakota took a breath, glancing at McKenna before meeting Kendra's gaze head-on. "Alright," she said finally. "Here's the short version: we've got some unique qualities. Things happened to us a long time ago that keep us from aging the way others do."

Kendra nodded, her expression unreadable as she listened. "Go on."

"Kalili and Faith were part of it," Dakota continued, "but we were there by choice. Whatever you've got in your files, it's not going to tell you the whole story."

Kendra's eyes softened slightly. "You're saying this isn't some fluke of science, then?"

"No," McKenna said quietly. "Not science. Not exactly."

"You mean it has something to do with our friends being, what did they call themselves? Thirteens?"

How the hell does she know that? McKenna kept the shock off her face, but not out of her mental voice.

"That's right. It might be simpler if you tell us what you know?" Dakota suggested.

"Fair. Kalili Keoka and Faith Burroughs are the last examples of a kind of Immortal being called a Thirteen. They have some serious powers, but try not to get involved in large-scale meddling with human affairs. I've known them for almost two hundred years, and this is the first time they've ever suggested I add someone to my crew, which tells me you're something special. You two have been friends with them since forever ago, and somehow became immortal along the way. Oh, and you're both criminals, even if you haven't been caught out in centuries." A grin blossomed on Kendra's face. "I can appreciate your talents. I haven't always walked on the side of law and order."

McKenna chuckled. "I read your autobiography."

Kendra groaned. "That thing. Don't remind me."

"It was good," McKenna insisted. "Really humanized you. Showed you flaws and all."

"Wonderful. I thought it had been forgotten." She took another sip of her drink before continuing. "Something Kalili told me I found interesting is that you're telepathic? With each other, I mean."

Dakota studiously avoided eye contact with McKenna before admitting, "We are."

"Good!"

Surprise at Kendra's reaction flared on Dakota's face. "Good?"

"Yeah. I mean, I'm functionally telepathic, but that's because of the implant and nanobots." She tapped the side of her jaw. "Technology fails."

"Ohhh..."

"Exactly. There are possibilities, but we'll explore them on the mission."

Dakota said, "Mission?"

Kendra nodded.

"I thought this was a private vessel, not part of Starfleet?"

"She's not, but that doesn't mean I'm not still involved in special projects. This next one is gonna take two or three years to implement, most of it in deep space." Kendra's tone had shifted from conversational to businesslike. "Shit goes sideways in space, and having people who can communicate without tech might save our asses. But it's a big commitment. I understand if you want to reconsider."

Are we in?

Are you kidding? McKenna couldn't conceal her astonishment. *Hell yes!*

"We're in. We don't want our abilities to be public, though."

Kendra studied them both, her expression thoughtful. Finally, she nodded slowly. "I can live with that. My wives have to know; I don't keep secrets from them." Dakota and McKenna both nodded. "The rest, well, we'll burn that bridge when we get there."

"Don't you mean cross that bridge?" asked McKenna.

"I said what I said." Kendra took another sip. "Besides, you won't be the only ones without nanobots."

They waited for more information, but it seemed that was all Kendra was willing to say.

"Okay. Welcome to the crew. Tia?"

An alto voice rose from hidden speakers. "Kendra."

"Who's that?" Dakota asked. *Did you pick up on a mic?*

No, at least nothing active!

"That's Tia, Brigantia, she's the ship AI and our right-hand woman."

That explains it, McKenna thought. *Passive monitoring. Probably cued to her name.*

Kendra was continuing. "She'll walk you through the rest of the on-boarding, including your quarters, pay, uniforms, and all that. Any pets?"

Dakota shook her head. "No. Our last cat died a few months ago." She shared a glance with McKenna, then added, "It was what spurred us to take Kal's advice. She's been pushing us for years to join you, but she never said why."

"Want one?" Kendra chuckled at their obvious surprise. "We've had cats since Cass was first officer aboard the old *Enterprise,* and somehow we keep ending up with kittens."

"Didn't anyone ever tell you about the birds and the bees, youngster?" Dakota teased, and Kendra laughed, a deep, hearty laugh.

"I see how it's going to be," she said, recovering. "Tia will take care of the details. She can reach me any time you have a question. Despite Minerva's best efforts, we're not particularly formal aboard *Dreamer.*"

They recognized a dismissal when they heard one and stood. "Thank you for meeting us, Kendra, and thank you for keeping our past to yourself."

"Of course, Dakota. I understand you're unusual assets, and I have no intention of prying any deeper—unless, of course, I need to."

Dakota gave her a wry smile. "Fair enough. And if you do, well, I'm sure we'll have more interesting stories to share."

Kendra laughed again, dissipating the last tension between them. "Something tells me you two are going to fit in just fine."

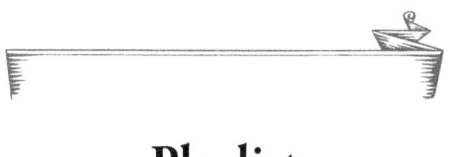
Playlist

Edge of Seventeen	Stevie Nicks
Highway to Hell	AC/DC
Bad Reputation	Joan Jett
Wicked Game	Chris Isaak
I Can't Drive 55	Sammy Hagar
Sweet Dreams (Are Made of This)	Eurythmics
Welcome to the Jungle	Guns N' Roses
Fight Song	Rachel Platten
Patience	Guns N' Roses
Locked Out of Heaven	Bruno Mars
Smooth Criminal	Michael Jackson
Take the Money and Run	Steve Miller Band
Heroes	David Bowie
Put Your Records On	Corinne Bailey Rae
Sympathy for the Devil	The Rolling Stones
Human	Rag'n'Bone Man
Life in the Fast Lane	Eagles
Changes in Latitudes, Changes in Attitudes	Jimmy Buffett
Dust in the Wind	Kansas
Valerie	Amy Winehouse
Time After Time	Cyndi Lauper
Running Up That Hill	Kate Bush
No One Knows	Queens of the Stone Age
Under Pressure	Queen & David Bowie
Fortunate Son	Creedence Clearwater Revival
Bitter Sweet Symphony	The Verve
Paint It, Black	The Rolling Stones

Immigrant Song	Led Zeppelin
Thunderstruck	AC/DC
Bring Me to Life	Evanescence
In the End	Linkin Park
Rise	Katy Perry
A Change Would Do You Good	Sheryl Crowe
A Pirate Looks at Forty	Jimmy Buffett
Space Oddity	David Bowie
The Launch	James Horner
Unstoppable	Sia

If you want to listen to the playlist, you can download it by scanning this QR code:

Author's Afterward

Hello, and welcome to the after-action report, brought to you by yours truly, the author!

Unlike some of my books, this one has a very specific origin. When I wrote the first line of "The Vault & The Vixen," I knew I was in trouble.

See, while I'd touched on the idea of Cass and Ken having some long-ago ties to the fae (see "Magic for Skeptics" and "Kendra and the Fae," also "A Christmas Kiss"), their novels were *science fiction*. Not science fantasy, not contemporary, not – well, you get the idea.

Now, I'll admit, I left the door open for science fantasy with those stories. After all, it's one of the greatest SF authors who said, "Any sufficiently advanced technology is indistinguishable from magic."[1] And I've certainly pushed the edges of that with the Tantor books. An entire planet disappearing? That takes some serious tech, amirite?

And then I went and wrote the "Godsfall" books, introducing an entire fantasy world that is fully integrated with our own reality. Octavianus was a real person, and his family was exactly as I described them. I also layered in enough exposition about the various Immortals trying to conceal their existence from humans so our ignorance of all the events in the books is perfectly understandable.

Then came V&V.

"Don't worry; my plans hardly ever fuck up." – Kalili Keoka, V&V opening line.

Once Kalili showed up in 21st century Brooklyn, it was game over. I've said over and over that Kendra's universe is connected to ours, with events and culture from *now* affecting her growing up and the choices she makes as an adult. So, if V&V is in our recent past, and our timeline is connected to Kendra's, then Kalili and Faith *must* exist in Kendra's universe.

How to tie it all together? Well, you have that in your hands now, but I'll take you through the process.

Note: Spoilers for Vault & Vixen ahead, so if you haven't read it, you may want to check it out now.

V&V leaves you knowing that Dakota and McKenna are together, and Kalili and Faith are part of their lives. That's all fine and good, but it doesn't connect them to Kendra's world. I had to take an event that's canon for the Cassidyverse and drop them into it.

Enter the Glorious Revolution of 2053.

It's canon; established in the introduction to the very first Cassidyverse book, the novella "Run Like Hell," it's one of the wars that shattered the United States through the 21st Century.[2] There's not much more about it, but that was what I needed, an event that hadn't already been explored. Not only that, but it was close enough in time to V&V that Dakota and McKenna could reasonably be expected to be alive. And, since it was a conflict between the US and the New England Collective, it made sense to have troops moving through the Empire of New York and threatening their safety.

Having Kalili want her own intelligence service was logical, and so... OutLook.

Boom.

And, if you've read this far, you know the other ties I establish in the Epilogues. One leads you *directly* into "The Cassidy Chronicles;" the other points you to a novel I haven't yet finished (as of writing this in late 2024).

Whew.

I hope you've enjoyed this. Now that this universe is officially a single universe, you can expect more characters popping up unexpectedly, though Kal and Faith aren't going to be quite so liberal in using their powers. They're still trying to blend into human society, not upend it!

There is a bit more after this – for people new to my Godsfall characters, I've listed the powers that Thirteens possess. At least, powers I know about so far. I'm sure it will grow. I also included a list of the angels and demons opposing them. I didn't use all the names in the book, but you can try to match up names to the anonymous Immortals.

Anyway, on to my acknowledgments. This time, it's pretty quick, because I've been leaning heavily on my wife, Michaela, to get this done. Maybe it's the other way around. See, she wants a book with dragons, and I've promised to get her one, just as soon as I clear out my backlog. This was one of them. She's also my smartest critic and best sounding board, as I use her ears to fine tune the story. It wouldn't be nearly as entertaining if she didn't give her feedback.

Oh, one last thing. There are a few alternate takes on chapters that I thought were good enough to preserve. If you want to read them, they're HERE[1]. If you're reading this in print, scan the QR code below.

Until next time.

Adam Gaffen, Trinidad, CO

PS Sign up for my biweekly newsletter at www.cassidychronicles.com[2] so you stay in the loop about new books, sales, and goodies from other authors!

"Writing is antisocial. It's as solitary as masturbation. Disturb a writer when he is in the throes of creation and he is likely to turn and bite right to the bone... and not even know that he's doing it. As

---

1. https://BookHip.com/XKRGKVH
2. http://www.cassidychronicles.com

writers' wives and husbands often learn to their horror...There is no way that writers can be tamed and rendered civilized. Or even cured. In a household with more than one person, of which one is a writer, the only solution known to science is to provide the patient with an isolation room, where he can endure the acute stages in private, and where food can be poked in to him with a stick. Because, if you disturb the patient at such times, he may break into tears or become violent. Or he may not hear you at all... and, if you shake him at this stage, he bites..."

– Robert A. Heinlein

Alternate scenes QR code:

Powers of Thirteens

Taaqat – not a power, precisely, but an inherent celestial energy that provides the basis for their majikal abilities, including healing, shapeshifting, invisibility, insubstantiality, and storing their wings away when not in use. Can be depleted. Replenishes naturally over time, or can be taken from another celestial. A *taaqat* pull is a celestial form of sex.

Kosmiskorka – the celestial power that the gods pull upon. Thirteens can draw on this and either store it within their bodies (spindle it), transmute it (into *taaqat*), or use it immediately.

Vashwic urja – the primary offensive weapon of a Thirteen, this consists of concentrated blasts of *kosmiskorka*, usually projected through the palms, usually white or blue-white. An angel or demon hit squarely by a blast of *vashwic urja* is dead, even if their body hasn't stopped moving. They can survive a glancing blow.

Kaalijaya – time freeze. The target stops moving in time, caught between one heartbeat and the next, for as long as the Thirteen holds concentration.

Dhakshan – a shield or barrier against celestial threats. Not useful against mortal attacks, but any Immortal who encounters it at its full power is stopped. The more powerful the Immortal, the more likely it is they can force their way through it, and if the *dhakshan* isn't fully realized, lesser Immortals can penetrate it, too.

Mitrwic urja – a power related to *vashwic urja* that usually manifests as a vivid orange glow around the Thirteen's hands and corresponding orange bolts. While *vashwic urja* is useful against a variety of opponents, *mitrwic urja* is more tuned to damage demons and other denizens of Hell. It can be used against Heavenly celestials, but with less effect.

Vashqar disaat – not strictly a power of a Thirteen, it's the angelic equivalent of *vashwic urja* with an explosive twist. Thirteens, when they choose to use it, can tap into *kosmiskorka* and increase the destructive power. Very noisy and obvious, especially in the effects.

Angels and Demons

1. **Duke of Hell**: **Valaferion** (Male)
    - A powerful and ancient demon, Valaferion commands legions and holds significant influence over the infernal hierarchy. Known for his cunning and strategic mind, he is both feared and respected in the demonic realm.
2. **Archdemons**:
    - **Azariel** (Nonbinary)
        - Azariel is a formidable archdemon, known for their mastery of dark majik and manipulation. They are a key player in the supernatural politics of the underworld, often acting as an advisor to higher-ranking demons.
    - **Lioraeth** (Female)
        - Lioraeth is a fearsome archdemoness, renowned for her ruthlessness and combat prowess. She is often sent on the most dangerous and critical missions, earning her a reputation as one of the deadliest demons in Hell.
3. **Regular Demons**:
    - **Kyrion** (Male)
    - **Zephyria** (Female)

- **Nixaris** (Nonbinary)
- Valefar, Male
- Vespera, Female
- Rhythis, Non-Binary
- Xalgath, Male
- Astarra, Female
- Zarthor, Male
- Lilithia, Female
- Drakkan, Non-Binary
- Morzanna, Female
- Zyphir, Non-Binary
- Sapphira, Female
- Malphas, Male
- Bralgar, Male

1. **Archangel**: **Seraphina** (Female)
    - Seraphina is a powerful archangel known for her unwavering dedication to justice and her radiant, awe-inspiring presence. She commands respect and is often called upon in times of great need.
2. **Principality**: **Zadkiel** (Nonbinary)
    - Zadkiel is a principality known for their wisdom and guidance. They are often tasked with overseeing the spiritual growth and protection of entire nations or groups of people.
3. **Regular Angels**:
    - **Eliara** (Female)
    - **Cassiel** (Male)
    - **Amariel** (Nonbinary)
    - **Liora** (Female)
    - **Theron** (Male)
    - **Neriah** (Nonbinary)

- Seraphiel, Male
- Amarael, Female
- Caelora, Non-Binary
- Raziel, Male
- Solara, Female
- Nyriel, Female
- Thalorin, Male
- Elyssian, Non-Binary
- Valora, Female
- Azariel, Male
- Lysandra, Female
- Aerian, Non-Binary
- Arathiel, Male

---

[1] Arthur C. Clarke

[2] This is a direct inspiration from Robert Heinlein. He had a timeline of his future history, and in the early 90s I decided to do my own and create my own fragmented country. That list and map were repurposed for the Cassidyverse, which, in a strange way, makes "The Cassidy Chronicles" officially the book that took longest to write: circa 1992 to 2020.

Don't miss out!

Visit the website below and you can sign up to receive emails whenever Adam Gaffen publishes a new book. There's no charge and no obligation.

https://books2read.com/r/B-A-PBTN-QQZGF

BOOKS 2 READ

Connecting independent readers to independent writers.

Did you love *Embers of Eternity*? Then you should read *The Vault & The Vixen*[1] by Adam Gaffen!

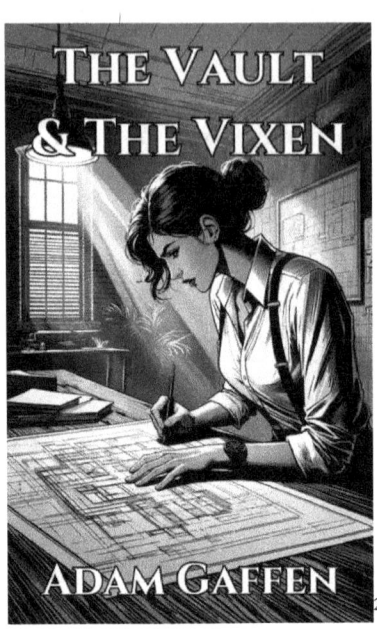

Is the heist of a lifetime worth her heart?

Dive into the heart-pounding world of The Vault & the Vixen, where heist thriller meets romantic suspense in a gripping tale of crime, love, and redemption. Set against the gritty, neon-lit backdrop of Brooklyn, this novel weaves a complex web of high-stakes heists, intricate plots, and unyielding loyalty.

Meet Dakota Chase, a master planner and the fearless leader of a crew that specializes in pulling off the impossible. With her long dark hair and iconic leather coat, Dakota is the epitome of cool, collected, and cunning. She's spent years navigating the treacherous waters of organized crime, always staying one step ahead of both the law

---

1. https://books2read.com/u/4Ed92Y

2. https://books2read.com/u/4Ed92Y

and her rivals. But as she gears up for the heist of a lifetime, the stakes have never been higher.

Dakota's meticulous plans are put to the test as unforeseen complications arise, and betrayal lurks around every corner. Her crew, a tight-knit group of skilled misfits, stands by her side, each member bringing their unique talents to the table. New to the crew is McKenna, a tough-as-nails tech expert with short blonde hair and a penchant for plaid shirts. Their relationship is fraught with tension and unspoken feelings, and could throw a monkey wrench into Dakota's plan.

As Dakota and her team delve deeper into the underbelly of urban crime, they must confront powerful enemies, navigate dangerous alliances, and uncover secrets that threaten to tear them apart. The city of Brooklyn itself becomes a character in the story, its streets and shadows providing the perfect setting for the unfolding drama.

Will Dakota succeed in pulling off the ultimate heist, or will she find herself ensnared in a deadly game of cat and mouse? Can she trust her crew—and her heart—as she navigates the perilous world of organized crime? The Vault & the Vixen is a thrilling ride, packed with twists and turns, that will keep you on the edge of your seat until the very last page.

Tropes: Heist Thriller, Romantic Suspense, Crime Fiction, Urban Fiction, LGBTQ+ Fiction, Mastermind, Loyal Crew, Heist Gone Wrong, Enemies to Lovers, Forbidden Love, Gritty Urban Setting, Complex Characters, Plot Twists, High Stakes, Emotional Depth, Tension and Betrayal.

Join Dakota Chase on her electrifying journey through danger, deceit, and desire in The Vault & the Vixen. If you're a fan of edge-of-your-seat action, intricate plots, and deeply human stories, this is the book you've been waiting for!

Read more at www.cassidychronicles.com.

About the Author

"You know me. Jump first, knit a parachute on the way down." Kendra Cassidy, A Quiet Revolution (Cassidy 4)

Adam Gaffen is the author of the near-future, hopepunk science fiction universe that began with The Cassidy Chronicles. The Cassidyverse includes the epic saga of The Artemis War (which starts with The Road to the Stars), as well as The Ghosts of Tantor (the first book in the follow-up series) and two collections of stories. He's active on the convention circuit and loves talking to fans.

He's a member of the Colorado Authors League, Science Fiction Writers of America, and the Heinlein Society. He lives in Southern Colorado with his wife, five dogs, five cats, and wonders where all the time goes.

Read more at www.cassidychronicles.com.

www.ingramcontent.com/pod-product-compliance
Lightning Source LLC
LaVergne TN
LVHW011946060526
838201LV00061B/4233